I0669409

An
UpLyfting
Love

*Maybe a detour is exactly
what they need.*

NOELLE DAVENPORT

Copyright © 2023 Noelle Davenport

All rights reserved. No part of this book may be reproduced in any form or by any electronic or mechanical means, including information storage and retrieval systems, without permission in writing from the publisher, except by reviewers, who may quote brief passages in a review.

This is a work of fiction. Unless otherwise indicated, all the names, characters, businesses, places, events and incidents in this book are either the product of the author's imagination or used in a fictitious manner. Any resemblance to actual persons, living or dead, or actual events is purely coincidental.

ISBN 979-8-9864298-0-9 (Paperback)
ISBN 979-8-9864298-1-6 (E-Book)

Publisher's Cataloging-in-Publication Data provided by Five Rainbows Cataloging Services

Names: Davenport, Noelle, author.
Title: An Uplyfting Love / Noelle Davenport.
Description: Spearfish, SD : Noelle Davenport Books, 2023.
Identifiers: LCCN 2022917037 (print) | ISBN 979-8-9864298-0-9 (paperback) | ISBN 979-8-9864298-1-6 (ebook)
Subjects: LCSH: Celebrities--Fiction. | Voyages and travels--Fiction. | Man-woman relationships--Fiction. | Romance fiction. | BISAC: FICTION / Romance / Contemporary. | FICTION / Romance / Clean & Wholesome. | GSAFD: Love stories.
Classification: LCC PS3604.A94 U65 2023 (print) | LCC PS3604.A94 (ebook) | DDC 813/.6--dc23.
Library of Congress Control Number: 2022917037

Edited by: Charmaine Tan
Proofread by: Kara Mugleston
Cover Design & Typography by: Tazia Schoenfeld

Published in the United States of America

Email: NoelleDAuthor@gmail.com
Visit: NoelleDavenportBooks.com

For Travis

Thank you for your belief in me when I struggle to believe in myself.

And for giving me both roots to grow and wings to fly.

Chapter 1

Salt Lake City Airport: Present day

Delaney Campbell watched as Jack Frost skated across her windshield in the December morning air, leaving patterns of ice that the newly risen sun would erase in a matter of minutes. Her breath formed a fog around her as she sighed impatiently in the Lyft pickup line. The Christmas rush of tourists should pick up any day now, but the month was off to an uncharacteristically slow start. The holidays usually meant busy days spent driving skiers through the snowy canyons of Northern Utah, and that the money would be good. But the past week had been slower than usual, and bills were almost due. She was grateful for the assignment this morning that would almost pay for her mortgage, so she jumped at the chance to take the long trek out of state.

The radio played Christmas music on low volume, and she hummed along as she waited. Glancing nervously out the windshield at the taxi drivers corralled nearby, she checked the clock on the dash again. They seemed more agitated at her this morning as they leaned against the hoods of their bright yellow taxis, their foggy breath filtering the glares they were throwing her. They hated competing with Lyft drivers like her, and they began to circle like wolves.

A big, brazen guy pulled up in his cab and parked with the other ones, waiting. He slammed the driver's door shut and sized up his competition. He lumbered toward her, shoving his keys in his pocket with one hand, and carrying a large soda cup in the other. The bellows of his comrades cheered him on from the sidelines as he peacocked in front of them. She rolled her eyes in exasperation and groaned as the hairy cab driver neared, puffing up his chest like a gorilla at the zoo.

Laney's small frame would never get her labeled as a tough girl, but her upbringing out in the country with five brothers made her a force to be reckoned with. She didn't look like much, but under her petite exterior was a warrior that fought her way through a sister-less childhood. The issue was that she dealt with men like this every day and liked to pick her battles wisely.

Brazen Man stretched his neck before taking a sip from his large soda and sneered through her windshield at his easy target.

She opened the driver's door slowly and rolled her shoulders back as she stood. Straightening up her five-foot-five frame as much as she could, Delaney got ready to stand her ground.

"Hey, Lyft!" he snarled, setting his drink on her hood. "You're in my spot!" He continued stomping toward her until he encroached on her personal space.

"My name is not 'Lyft,' and I have every right to be here too," Delaney replied boldly, staring him down. "Last I heard, your name wasn't painted on the pavement like some fancy CEO in a high-rise. This is anyone's spot, and I'm waiting for a passenger. Don't you have anything better to do than pick on a woman half your size?"

He smiled under his thick, dark mustache, amused at his obvious advantage over her. As she reached for the door handle, he grabbed her arm and spun her around. With a condescending hand, he touched her cheek, gripping her wrist with the other hand.

"Listen, Princess. You can't hack it with the big boys. We were here first, so take your pretty little face back to the kitchen," he seethed.

Her blood boiled, and pressure crowded her ears, making her pulse pound in her temples. At that moment, she knew she needed to make an example of him in front of his buddies, or she would fight this battle every day following this one. So, she mustered every ounce of courage she could find and let it swell within her chest. If they wouldn't give her respect, she'd take it from them.

Delaney took hold of his thick arm with her free hand, and with a calculated twist of his wrist, he was on his knees at her feet. The cabbie's eyes grew to the size of golf balls, and a groan left his slackened mouth. Looking down into his wincing face, she said as low and intimidating as she could, "I'm just doing my job, so leave me alone. I can't afford to have my passenger catch me beating up a cab driver when they arrive, can I? It's bad for business, and I have a five-star rating to uphold." Then, Delaney tilted her head, smiled sweetly and added through clenched teeth, "So back off, okay?" She twisted his arm harder just for emphasis before she let him go. "Who's the princess now?" She folded her arms across her chest. The laughter of the other cabbies filled the air behind him as he scrambled back to his feet. He rubbed the wrist she'd almost pushed to its breaking point and spat on the frozen ground.

"You ever assault me again, Princess, and I'll slash your tires," he growled. He grabbed his soda from the hood of her car and splashed it all over her windshield. He glared over his shoulder at her as he skulked away toward a laughing crowd.

She blew him a kiss. "See you around!" she wiggled her fingers in a wave at him and turned to do damage control before her passenger arrived. "Great, this is definitely not what I need," she muttered under her breath.

She pulled her long, blonde waves into a loose ponytail and raced to clean up the mess, but she was too late.

A hush fell among the bustle of the airport before the din of the crowds rose again like the wave at a ballgame.

"Hey," came a voice from behind her. "Thanks for waiting. My flight got rerouted because of storms up north. I appreciate you agreeing to the long trip. I'm not used to driving in the snow anymore," the stranger said as he adjusted the backpack he had slung over one shoulder.

"You bet!" Delaney said as she turned around. When she saw who her passenger was, her jaw dropped, practically hitting the snow. Standing behind her was Blake Logan—one of Hollywood's A-list movie stars. Planes roared overhead, and cars buzzed in and out of the parking garage, but all that slowed to a halt as she processed what she was seeing. His recent superhero film smashed records at the box office, and his face plastered magazines on every newsstand. Yet, there he was with a suitcase in his hand, ready to get into her car. She stood there dumbfounded, so to save face, she hit the trunk button on her key fob and motioned for him to follow her. She knew she had about five-seconds to turn her awkward steps into a calm and casual stride, but her internal fangirl was screaming too loudly to make anything look cool.

Her voice lowered in pitch with each word as she squeaked, "You can put your bags in here." She cleared her throat to reset her vocal cords. "Thanks." He ran a hand through his tousled dark hair and grinned. "You know, I'm glad you're my driver and not that hairy cabbie who looks as if he smells like a day-old sandwich and too much aftershave." Blake tipped his chin toward the angry cabbie. "Why is he glaring at you so hard?"

"Ah, you know. Ride-share and cabbie rivalry, I'm guessing." She waved off the comment and shifted on her feet as she glanced over her shoulder toward the cabs. "Sorry, I've forgotten my manners. I'm Delaney… Delaney Campbell," she muttered, stiffly sticking out her hand, "but my friends call me Laney."

"Cool. I'm sure you already know who I am." He flashed a cocky smile and shook her hand. Then, he clipped his aviator glasses on the collar of his plain white T-shirt and shoved his hand into the pocket of his dark wash designer jeans.

If Laney had to describe the appearance of her dream guy, Blake would fit the bill. Tall, athletic, with dimples deep enough to swim in. It's no wonder he was America's Golden Boy.

An involuntary wave of elation rose above her and crashed over her head, causing her breaths to quicken. She tried to quiet her excitement as she attempted to lean casually against the rear fender of the car. But she misjudged the distance and crashed into it instead, leaving her with a grimace and a potential bruise she'd have to check out later.

Blake hefted his expensive suitcase into the trunk, and she watched, suddenly aware of the fact that she wore yesterday's wrinkled shirt in her rush to get dressed.

Leather can sure take a beating! Laney giggled inside as she watched his arms bulge underneath his jacket. *No, Laney. Stay focused,* she chided. *Don't let a handsome face and a chiseled pair of arms throw you off your game.* Despite that, she discreetly pulled her ponytail holder out and combed her fingers through her hair. She clenched her jaw tight to keep it from dropping and pinched herself on the arm to ensure she wasn't dreaming. Then, she cleared her dry throat to make room for words—any words—to come out.

One step at a time, Lane. You've got to get everything under control, her brain begged. *He's a ridiculously handsome guy with a fancy job. That's it. Not to mention the women who line up around the block to throw themselves at him. To him, you are a mere peasant. So be cool, please be cool!*

"So, where's your entourage? Don't movie stars usually travel with, like, twenty people?" she fumbled as she tucked her hair behind her ears. She always thought that she'd act completely normal if she ever met a celebrity like Blake, but her pitchy voice and sweaty palms proved her wrong. Any minute now, he'd hear her freaking out in her mind, and he'd run for the Hollywood hills.

"Most of the time, I do. But it's just me today. My manager had a last-minute thing come up, so he stayed back in Los Angeles. And the rest of my 'entourage,' as you say, have the time off to spend with their families," he replied. He looked over his shoulder at the crowd forming with cell phones poised in front of their faces. He paused, his bright blue eyes sparkling with mischief and unzipped his suitcase. He pulled out an identical white shirt like the one he had on and tore his jacket off. He removed the coffee-stained shirt he was wearing and screams erupted from the crowd. He grabbed a permanent marker from his backpack and removed the lid with his teeth.

"What are you—" Laney hissed, raising a hand to her eyes to block her view of his bare chest, "—it's thirty degrees out here!"

Grinning through the lid between his teeth, he scribbled his autograph on the shirt. "Giving the fans what they want. Don't be bashful. It's not like you haven't seen this before," he teased her.

Laney whipped around, trying to avoid the sculpted torso causing all the women to squeal. Despite the cold biting at her cheeks, her face was on fire. He tossed the shirt into the crowd, and watched the women fight for it like a bouquet at a wedding. Immediately, Laney's defenses flew back up.

She could take on one cab driver, but probably not a whole group of crazed Blake Logan fans.

"Looks like it's about time to get out of here, Romeo," she said over her shoulder, and made a beeline for the driver's seat. Blake slammed the trunk and jogged to the passenger side of the car.

She took another deep breath and fanned her face as Blake opened the front passenger side door.

He pulled on the clean shirt as he dropped into the passenger seat and said, "I hope you don't mind if I sit up here with you. I hate sitting in the back when being driven alone. It feels so… impersonal."

And with that, Blake Logan was sitting two feet away from her in her SUV.

"That's fine," she muttered, trying to redirect her thoughts away from his ripped abs. "I'll even let you play DJ. But if you have horrible taste in music, I'll hit the seat ejector button and leave you with the cougars," she teased, handing him her phone. "You sure know how to draw a crowd. Looks like we're getting out just in time."

She glanced at her blind spot and waited for an opening in the traffic. "But before we hit the road, we have to visit the car wash. I had a sticky situation with Mr. Too Much Aftershave." She nodded toward her windshield at the clumps of frozen soda as she pulled away from the curb.

"Sounds like we've both had a rough morning. Do the cab drivers always give you a hard time?" he asked, checking himself out in the side mirror. "Yeah, they hate competing with drivers like me," she said. "But you should see the other guy…" She grinned from ear to ear.

"Mmmm-hmmm," he muttered with a nod as he sent a text on his phone and glanced up without any more response.

The air hung thick in the car, and Laney fought to find something—anything—to say to him. Not that she had daydreamed about a moment like this often, but she had hoped if the opportunity like this ever arose, she would at least be able to keep the conversation flowing. She swallowed hard and tried again.

"So, you've had a rough morning, too?" she asked.

"Yeah," he replied and nodded, staring out the windshield as a gas station came into view. "Woke up late, almost missed my flight, and spilled hot coffee all over myself on the plane. Then, I was having a hard time finding my way up north after my flight got rerouted. I guess the storm is pretty bad up there today, and it's been too long since I've driven in the snow. I expected Salt Lake City would have more elite car services considering the Sundance Film Festival comes every year, but none of them were willing to ditch their bookings for me. I know it's a long drive, but you were my last hope." He grinned over at her.

Her heart pounded, yet she couldn't see through the haze of full-of-himself energy he exuded.

"Well, I'm glad I could help," she said without making eye contact. She pulled through the open bay of the automatic car wash and stopped the car inside. "This should only take a few minutes, and then we will get on the road."

"Perfect," he responded, sliding his sunglasses over his eyes and angled his seat back. "I might even catch a few z's if you don't mind."

"Of course not," she muttered, forcing a smile to hide her disappointment.

Chapter 2

The miles stretched on as Laney drove, quietly listening to her favorite road trip playlist as Blake slept. She stole glances at him every once in a while, and he looked like a completely different guy in his sleep—vulnerable and approachable. The cocky grin was gone, and for a moment there, he was an ordinary, albeit gorgeous, guy. He was definitely more attractive without all the pretenses, even if he did snore a bit.

Suddenly, Blake stirred. "No, I don't want another kitten in my lap," he insisted in his dream. Laney laughed louder than she meant to, startling him awake.

"Sorry, I didn't mean to wake you." She stifled another chuckle. "Not a cat person?"

"Huh? How long was I out?" Blake asked as he wiped the sleep from his eyes and adjusted upright in his seat.

"You've been sleeping for about an hour," she replied, "but don't worry, you only told me a few secrets. And I pride myself in keeping a secret. What happens in my car stays in my car."

Blake smiled, and it wasn't the cocky grin he had before, but what she could only assume was a real, genuine smile.

"Well, I'm glad I at least kept you entertained." He dipped his head, imitating a bow. "People usually pay good money for that, and here I am, giving it away in my sleep." He laughed and ran a hand through his thick, dark hair to fix the slept-on side.

"Ah, don't feel bad," she said, waving a hand in dismissal. "I've had way more entertaining drunk guys that rank higher in my hall of shame."

Blake laughed, and there was that glimpse of authenticity again. Her heart stirred and flipped, but she pushed it away, turning her eyes back to the endless road ahead.

"How'd you sleep?" she asked.

He stretched and replied, "Better than I have in months, actually. You'd think that for what I paid for my mattress at home, I'd at least get some good sleep, right?"

"You'd think …" she trailed off.

"So," he cleared his throat and started, "were you born in Salt Lake City?"

"Um, yeah. Raised in a tiny town near the banks of the Great Salt Lake."

"That's cool. I swam in it once as a kid. Got saltwater in both my eyes and nose at the same time. I wasn't sure which part of my face burned worse," he said with a laugh as he adjusted in his seat for the hundredth time.

Laney laughed. "That'll get the tourists every time. It's definitely not the friendliest lake to swim in, but being able to float in it like that is pretty cool," she added with a shrug.

"True. I did like that part." His eyes drifted out the passenger window at the snow-covered pastures blurring past. The Rocky Mountains were long gone, and what mountains he could see were way off in the distance. "Where are we?"

"We are a few hours north of Salt Lake. Do you need a pit stop?"

"Nah," he replied. "Just wondering."

Conversation slowed from a snail's pace to a halt. Laney was used to chatting it up with her riders, and she had a full repertoire of topics to make the ride go faster. But with Blake, things dragged, making everything exchanged between them feel forced.

With a subtle nod, she cleared her throat and tried again. "So, why is a fancy-pants guy like you going all the way up to Idaho? It's a completely different world than Hollywood, that's for sure."

"It sure is." Blake laughed again, a sound she was unwittingly enjoying. "I grew up in Idaho, in a little town sandwiched between Boise and the mountains. It's called Juniper Hills. My mom and sister still live up there, and my sister is doing some graphic artwork for my book. I'm going up to see the final designs before it's sent to the printer."

"But why do you need to fly in for something that could be done over email?" Her words slipped out before her brain filter turned on. "Wait, I'm sorry, it's none of my business." Her face flushed with heat. *You are a mere peasant*, she mentally reminded herself.

"No, it's okay," he reassured her. He fidgeted in his seat and smoothed out the creases on his jeans. "It's just time to go home, that's all," he lied, although, a part of him wanted to be honest. *Why on earth do you want to tell this girl the truth, Blake?* he thought to himself. *Get your head on straight, man. She's a complete stranger, and you have no idea if you can trust her*. He glanced over at her, humming to herself as she drove. *But then again, she was the only one willing to drive you hours and hours up north. The least you could do is give her authentic conversation, not this surface-y stuff you're tossing her way. She deserves that much, and you know it. You have two choices here. Dive in with both feet, or stand on the edge like a hydrophobic coward. What's it going to be?* His mind raced as he decided, and he rubbed his neck red. *You want authenticity, Delaney? Well, here you go.* He took a big breath before continuing, "Actually, it's more than that," he sighed. "I haven't been back home since my dad's funeral. I've avoided it at all costs, actually. But my sister insists I come home, and she's right. It's time I quit running; you know?"

His admission took her by surprise, but she was going to take whatever crumbs he gave her. "What exactly are you running from?"

He shrugged and clipped his sunglasses back onto his collar. "I'm not even sure. The way life back home will feel without my dad, most likely. I spend most of my time in L.A., where it's easier to ignore the elephant in the room. It's a corner of my world that he hadn't touched, you know?" His throat tightened around his words, as he strained to say them. "I haven't faced that giant yet, and I'm afraid it will crush me."

His face changed as he spoke. His eyes grew softer with an undertone of sorrow, uncharacteristic of the arrogant ladies-man she'd seen so far. And she believed what he said—every word of it.

"I've never admitted that to anyone, not even myself," he mumbled and sighed. "I'm sorry, I totally killed the vibe."

"Actually, it's finally taking off," she said, looking over at him. As her honey-colored eyes met his, she saw for the first time the man behind the star. Any reservation she had about having a movie star in her presence faded away. And left in its place was a palpable reality between two regular people trying to get through life. She smiled sympathetically.

"I'm sorry I pried if you weren't ready. I tend to speak before my brain gives my mouth permission. So, if I cross a line you're not comfortable with, call me out on it. I won't take offense, I promise." She crossed a hand over her heart.

"Deal. I'm not very good with opening up anymore, so the fact that it happened at all says a lot about you." His eyes darted back toward the windshield.

Sensing his discomfort, she sugar-coated her words and said, "Honestly, sometimes it's easier to talk to a stranger. Especially in the car, where eye contact is sporadic. I'm like a bartender. Strangers spill their secrets to me all the time, especially the drunk ones. I take my driver-passenger privilege very seriously. Your secrets are safe with me." A smile spread across her face, and her warmth poured over him like hot fudge on a sundae. Then, she added, "So, you mentioned you're writing a book? What is it about?"

"Well," he began with boyish pride. "It's always been a dream of mine to publish a cookbook with the recipes my mom and I created together. My manager and I planned to go up this weekend and approve the final designs. But after he got tied up in something else, I figured it was a sign that it was time for me to do this one alone. My family can't be that tough on me, right?" He smiled. "Then, if everything goes well, I'm hoping to stay up there with them for Christmas. Heaven knows I owe it to them to be present..." he said, trailing off.

"I'll bet they're thrilled to have you come back home. I can't imagine spending years away from my family. I couldn't avoid them if I tried. Sharing a small town with my parents and five brothers, we tend to run into each other everywhere. And now that they've all gotten married and started families, we're taking over the whole town."

"Five brothers?" he gaped in astonishment. "Holidays at your house must be crazy! In my family, it's just me, my sister and her family, and my mom. And here I thought that was wild." He laughed. "I have always wondered what a Christmas where the whole house is bursting at the seams with people would feel like!"

"It's more than I could ever ask for," Laney agreed, feeling grateful for her loud, rambunctious family. "I mean, I sometimes have to climb out on the roof to get a few minutes of solitude, but they're the best."

"You sit on your roof in the snow, in the middle of winter, in Utah?"

"Well, it's been my thing as long as I can remember, no matter what time of year it is." Her defenses were dying a slow, torturous death at the hands of her candidness. But the more he shared, the more she wanted to as well. She smiled as all the memories of her sitting out there on her rooftop perch under a blanket of stars flooded in. "There are times when nothing in the world makes sense until I slow down and look up. Then the answer is as clear as the moon shining in all its phases. It reminds me that life constantly changes, just like the moon. And that it's okay to feel full one day and a sliver of ourselves the next. We're simply going through another temporary phase in life. My rooftop spot has gotten me through a lot of tough times…" Before she spilled anymore, Laney stopped herself. *Let's not completely throw open the floodgates, Laney*, her thoughts warned. Feeling like she completely overshared, she added, "Plus, I shovel the snow away from where I sit, and I don't stay out there forever if it's cold, so it's not that bad!"

Great, now he thinks I'm crazy. She shook her head, embarrassed for her verbal vomit. *We still have hours ahead of us, and already he's breaking through my security clearances.*

He chuckled at her obvious discomfort. Her vulnerability was charming, and watching her squirm a little made him feel less weird about his own emotional upheaval.

Yep, he thinks I'm a huge dork, her inner voice groaned. She wanted so badly to climb under her seat and hide. Being open with him was hard, but only because it was way too easy.

"My escape was a treehouse I had as a kid," he said shyly. "My dad and I built it together. I used to spend hours up there, contemplating the universe, or playing on my Game Boy. Whichever the mood called for." Blake smiled.

"Naturally," Laney responded, laughing.

"It's where I had my first kiss, my first heartbreak, and my first inspiration about what I wanted out of this life. My parents thought it was just my hangout spot. They never knew how much I needed that place," he said, his blue eyes sparkling with fond memories.

"Is it still there?" Laney couldn't help but relate to his words, and the excitement in her voice made him laugh.

"Well, yeah. But since my sister bought my parents' house, it belongs to my nephew now. He uses it to get away from his twin sisters."

Blake's chest felt strange and tight with excitement, yet he was scared to death all at the same time. He wanted to throw caution to the wind and completely be himself with her. But he wasn't even sure he knew how to do that anymore. He watched as she cautiously peeled away a tiny piece of herself at a time, revealing beautiful new depths to her story. He loved how she lit up when she talked about home and how well she listened to him ramble on about his life, home, and family. And when she smiled, her whole face followed suit, from her sexy mouth to her brown eyes that shined like a shot of whiskey in the sun. He'd only had a sip of her, yet he was already feeling intoxicated. And he couldn't help but want more. To know more, to see more. He ached to cast aside everything about his celebrity world to get a better glimpse into hers.

"When my dad passed away—" Blake's voice snagged on his words, and he slowed down his speech. "—I wished more than ever to be a kid back in that treehouse again. But I was stuck on location, mourning the loss of my hero alone. I was able to sneak away long enough to attend the funeral, but I couldn't stay much longer than that. While I was there, I cried and cried in the treehouse—hidden away from everyone else. I saved my brave face for my mom and sister because they needed me. And then I couldn't be there, not like I should've been. My mom got overwhelmed with maintaining the house and the land. My dad was like Superman, and he took care of everything, but it was too much for my mom alone. So my sister and her husband bought the house from her. They built a little mother-in-law cottage for her in the back, and she opened a diner in town to stay busy. That made all the difference, and she did a lot better after she had her diner to focus on."

Blake's heart grew that old familiar twinge inside when he spoke about his dad. His father passed away years ago, but some days, the sting of grief was as potent as the day it happened. Needing to change the subject, he turned the topic of conversation to his mom.

"My mom is the one who taught me to cook. She makes the best meals I've ever tasted," he said proudly. "I've been to restaurants all over the world, and her meals are still my favorite."

Laney laughed. "That's awesome. I'm not that great in the kitchen, but I can make a mean piece of toast."

The awkwardness they fought at the beginning faded away, and words flowed between them with little effort. Laney was real. No façades, no pretenses, no filters. Just real. It was the most refreshing thing he had experienced in a long time. As she shared her depths, he swam into them willingly, allowing himself to sink deeper and deeper as they drove.

Suddenly, a loud pop interrupted the flow of conversation, and the steering wheel began to wobble in Laney's hands. She veered over on the lonely stretch of highway and got out to assess the damage. One rear tire hissed and fizzled out, sending its last exhale into the cold winter air. Laney sighed, pulling up her long wavy hair into a ponytail so she could get to work.

Blake got out of the passenger seat and came around to her side.

"Tire's flat," she said nonchalantly, and opened the back hatch. She moved his luggage aside to access the spare and added, "I've got a jack and a spare in here."

She tossed the jack onto the frozen ground and discovered that the spare was as lifeless as the flat tire on the car. *Great,* she thought, *this is exactly what I need right now.* She grabbed her phone out of the front seat and dialed roadside assistance.

Beep beep beeeeep! No service.

They were in the middle of nowhere, and her cell service was letting her down, big time! Blake grabbed his phone, frowned, and shook his head before putting it back into his pocket.

Laney sighed and grabbed the keys from the ignition and slung her purse over her shoulder.

"Well, the road sign that we passed a half-mile back showed that there's a town up ahead," she said, nodding northward. "I can walk there and see if there's a shop that can fix it. It might be a while, though. I'm sorry."

Blake laughed, "Am I supposed to sit here, let you do all the work, and wait for you to come back and rescue me? I'm the one who saves the day, remember? I'm coming with you," Blake said as he grabbed his jacket from the trunk and caught up to her.

"Ooh, I've never had a superhero in my midst before!" she mocked, throwing her hand up in front of her forehead like a dramatic damsel in distress. "How have I gotten along in this life without you?"

"I saw the way you handled that cab driver back at the airport," he teased. "So I know you don't need me to swoop in and save the day. But I'd much rather take the long walk with you than sit at the side of the road and wait like a chump."

She felt her face turn eighty shades of red and hotter than the noonday sun in summer. She wasn't ashamed to be a strong, independent woman, but professionally, that wasn't her best move.

"So … you saw the whole run-in, huh?" She avoided his gaze and brushed away a stray hair blown into her face. "Well, that's not a great first impression," she chuckled.

The encounter at the airport flooded into Blake's thoughts. He had rushed through the parking lot to help her until he saw her force the cabbie down to his knees. At that moment, he slowed his step to see how she'd handle it, and pride filled his chest for a woman he'd never even met. She was strong despite her stature. And her long, beachy curls framed her determined face as she commanded respect in a man's world. He remembered the way her whiskey-brown eyes narrowed as she spoke to the blockhead in front of her. She was fierce, fiery, and intriguing, and she pulled Blake in like a riptide. She was not a victim but a force of nature, and it was the most refreshing thing he'd seen in a long time.

"Are you kidding? It was awesome! I wanted to come and help you, but you definitely had it all under control without me ruining your smackdown. You were so fearless." His eyes lit up as he spoke. "You're not the kind of woman I'd like to meet in a dark alley, that's for sure, but I don't mind a driver who can kick butt like that!" he teased, nudging her side. "You'd make a pretty good sidekick."

"Well, I'm more of a Wonder Woman than a Robin."

"I don't doubt that one bit." He glanced over at her.

She laughed nervously, grateful that instead of wanting to run for the hills, he was actually drawn to the real her. Laney forced herself to make eye contact with him. The grin that covered his face made her feel proud to be who she was. She was not a Hollywood starlet who wore fancy heels and carried an expensive purse. She didn't command a room and make men stare with slacked jaws. But with a comfortable pair of shoes and her hair in a ponytail, she could do just about anything. And that was enough for her.

"There's the exit up ahead," she said, squinting. "Let's hope the town of Redmont has an auto shop. Then maybe I can redeem myself."

"What do you mean, 'redeem yourself?'"

"Well, since this morning, I've beaten up a cab driver, stuck my nose in your personal life, and gotten us stranded in the middle of nowhere. I've got a lot of making up to do to keep my five-star rating intact," she explained with a laugh and kicked a chunk of ice.

"Well, in that case, I'll raise my expectations for the rest of this drive," he teased. A frigid wind blew at them, and with a shiver, Blake zipped up his jacket all the way.

"Is that what I think it is?" Laney pointed down the main street at the end of the exit ramp. The weathered and cracked road stood as a huge contrast to the blue sky above. "Yes! Redemption is mine." She picked up her pace as she hurried toward the auto shop.

The old garage was devoid of the normal mechanical chatter that a typical auto shop has, especially for 11 am on a Friday. All the industrial-sized doors were closed, and no traffic was going in or out. An oil-stained, hand-written sign hung on the locked door that said, "Back in 30."

"Well, looks like we've got some time to waste," she said, nodding toward the diner across the street. "Wanna get an early lunch?"

"I'd love to. I'm starving!"

The smell of maple syrup and pancakes met them at the door as they stepped inside the tiny cafe, and they sat down at a red vinyl booth. The breakfast rush had died down, but a handful of tables were still occupied by old men drinking coffee behind their newspapers and a group of ladies who hadn't taken their curlers out of their wiry, gray hair yet.

"Oh man, I haven't had real pancakes in so long," Blake gushed as he opened the menu. "The stuff my trainer makes me eat tastes like sadness and cardboard. 'Gotta keep that sculpted physique, Blake. No one wants to pay to see a fat Sentinel,'" he imitated. "Just once, I want to eat a whole stack of pancakes and not worry about how many burpees I'll have to do to burn them off."

"Then do it. Order the biggest stack on the menu," she dared. "I won't tell on you, I promise," she said over her menu with a wink.

"You mean like a 'cheat meal?'" A mischievous smile crept across his face.

"I say throw caution to the wind and have a whole 'cheat weekend.'"

"You rebel. I like the way you think. If I get back to L.A. and my trainer even smells carbs on me, I'll be a dead man," he said with a laugh. She grinned. "You'll only ever regret the pancakes you didn't eat. Come on, Captain. Live on the edge."

The waitress approached with a pad of paper and a coffee pot. "Good afternoon, what can I get you two?" she asked without looking up as she filled their mugs with coffee. But as Blake spoke, her chin shot up abruptly, and her jaw dropped. A puddle of coffee formed under Blake's cup before she grabbed hold of her senses and stopped pouring.

Blake raised a finger to his lips, begging silently for her discretion, and she winked above her reading glasses.

"You know what? Let's do this," Blake beamed. "I'll take your lumberjack stack."

"Atta boy," Laney cheered him on from across the table. "I'll have the same."

The waitress pulled a pen from her gray bun and scribbled the orders down. As she turned to leave, her eyes stayed on Blake until the kitchen door swung closed behind her.

"So, tell me about being a Lyft driver. I'm sure you have some crazy stories to tell," Blake said.

"Well, I've been proposed to six times by some really nice, really drunk guys. I've delivered a baby in my back seat. And this one time, I took this pretty fancy celebrity on a wild road trip. You could say I'm a pretty big deal now," she dusted her shoulder with style.

"Ooh. That sounds like the drive of a lifetime." He showed off his perfect dimples and made her heart race. "But seriously, you delivered a baby?"

"Yeah, my nursing degree came in real handy that day." She grinned over her coffee mug.

"Wait, nursing degree? I thought being a Lyft driver was your job."

"It is right now, but I worked for several years as a nurse before I took a break." The sparkle in her eyes dimmed, and she changed the subject. "So, fancy celebrity, what's a day in the life of the incredible Blake Logan like?"

He sighed. "Not as glamorous as you think. It's a lot of memorizing, exercising, and pretending I'm someone I'm not. Don't get me wrong, I love making movies. But it gets exhausting to keep up pretenses sometimes. That's the side-effect of being a celebrity, I guess. I have to create a person that people will love. Then I have to be that person in public for the rest of my career.

"I had no idea," Laney said quietly. "That must be tough."

"Yeah, but unfortunately, you get used to it."

When the pancakes were devoured and the coffee ran dry, Laney began stacking plates and moving them to the edge of the table. Blake laughed when she started arranging the salt and pepper shakers back to their spot below the window.

"Don't laugh!" she said defensively, giggling as she lined up the creamers and syrup. "I worked at a restaurant in college, and I know how it feels to work for peanuts. The least I can do is clean up my mess!"

He flashed his winning movie star smile, but by now, it didn't look how it did in the magazines. It looked real. Genuine. Flawed, even. But the best part was that it felt warm and familiar, like home. Laney noticed for the first time little flecks of green in his eyes that most don't get to be close enough to see, and a tiny scar hidden in his eyebrow. It was only when the waitress came and dropped off the bill that Laney realized she had been staring too long.

Blake snagged the check, paid the cashier, and returned to the table to leave a giant tip. He paused outside the window to watch as the waitress clutched the money to her chest and wiped away a tear as she picked up the stack of plates.

"I know how it feels to work for peanuts, too," he said warmly as they crossed the street. "The least I can do is to pay it forward. One of my favorite things about money is the good I can do with it. I will never understand why people put so much energy into pushing others down. Being kind takes the cake every time!"

He had a joy on his face that no makeup artist could create. This man, *this* Blake Logan, was the real deal.

The door chimed as Laney and Blake entered the garage, drawing the attention of the greased-up mechanic. He slid out from under an old rusted truck and clambered to his feet, wiping his hands on an old shop rag as he walked toward the lobby. A worn-out patch with the name "Cal" sewn onto it sat above his left pocket, partially covered by an oil stain. He scratched his thin gray hair on top of his head, making it stand up on end. When he spoke, the small gap between his front teeth caused a slight whistle to his "S" sound.

"What can I help you fine folks with today?" Cal asked.

"Well, I blew a tire down the highway, and the spare is flat too," Laney replied. "Do you have tires in stock for a 2017 Subaru Outback?"

"Let me have a look at my inventory," Cal said, stepping behind the dusty computer on the counter.

After a few minutes of typing, he looked up and said, "I'm out of tires that size here in the shop. But by the time we tow your car in, I can have one brought in from our warehouse on the other side of town." He pulled the rag out of his back pocket again and wiped down the mess he left on the keyboard. "My tow truck driver is on a call right now, but he should be back in about an hour. Then we can go and get your car. Where'd you say you left it?"

"It's a gray Subaru Outback about a mile south of here. How long will it take to get a new tire?" Laney asked.

"Once I get it here in the shop, about twenty minutes. But you'll have to wait a bit for my driver to get back. If you'd rather explore than wait here, there's a Christmas festival going on in town," he said, pointing out the dusty garage window. "I can call you on your cell when I'm done."

Laney checked her phone to find two bars of service. "That'll work," she told Cal. Turning to Blake, Laney apologized, "I'm sorry for more delays. It sounds like fun to me if you're game!" Her eyes searched his face to gauge his reaction. "Wanna go?"

"I'd love to!" Blake replied, heading for the door.

She wrote her number on a post-it note at the counter and turned to leave. "Thanks again!" she called over her shoulder to Cal as she disappeared through the doorway.

Blake took this opportunity to sneak back into the garage.

"Hey, before she realizes I'm not right behind her, I noticed her other tires needed changing too. Please replace all four, but don't tell her. It's on me." Blake said, shaking Cal's hand and passing him some cash. "Oh, and please take your time," he added as he stepped toward the door.

"Sure thing, Mr. Logan. Your secret's safe with me," Cal nodded as Blake left the shop.

The quaint main street of Redmont stretched out a few hundred yards past the garage. Laney and Blake could hear live music echoing off the weathered brick buildings that lined Main Street. The happy sounds of celebration grew louder as they neared, and the smell of chestnuts roasting was the first thing to meet them in the street. Crowds gathered outside the windows of storefronts, trying to get a glimpse of the intricate Christmas scenes inside. Each display showed a different verse of *'Twas the Night Before Christmas,* and the crowd shuffled from window to window to see the story unfold.

Evergreen boughs and giant red ornaments dangled from the lampposts that lined the old-fashioned town. Icicles that hung from the Christmas lights canopy overhead glistened in the afternoon sun.

"I'll bet this whole town transforms when these lights go on, giving Tinseltown a run for its money," Laney said, looking upward.

Blake's eyes moved from the lights strung above to Laney's face. He couldn't help but picture what she would look like in the romantic glow of Christmas lights. For a moment, he allowed his mind to run away with the idea of Christmases with Laney. The low hum of an old Christmas record playing in the background. Having hot chocolate after a long day of shopping, the tree giving off the only light in the room. He imagined rosy cheeks, thick socks, and snowed-in days, snuggling under blankets watching "White Christmas" together. The reality of his daydream felt so real that he could almost reach out and brush the snowflakes from her freckled nose. It was only when his pulse raced off to join his thoughts that he shook his head, reigning it all back in.

"Let's get lost!" Laney said spontaneously, looking back over her shoulder at him as she disappeared through the crowd.

Blake weaved through the pop-up tents until he caught up to her. Displays of handmade crafts and goodies lined the main street, and the low hum of the crowd buzzed with laughter. The aroma of cinnamon almonds and hot cocoa floated like snowflakes through the air, filling the streets with smells of Christmas. If Hallmark had a city, this would be it. And if Hallmark had the perfect subject for a story, it would be her.

Blake broke the silence between them with a satisfied sigh. "I forgot what it was like to walk through the streets without having to dodge screaming fans and paparazzi. I mean, sure, people have been whispering and grinning at me as we pass by. But not one person has interrupted us to ask for a photo or an autograph today. It's kind of refreshing."

Laney slowed her pace and turned to read his expression. "It must be so stressful to be recognized everywhere you go."

"It is. And don't get me wrong, I love my job, and I love my fans. But people get so caught up in the whole 'movie star' thing that I almost don't feel like a real person sometimes. Like I have to live up to their idea of who I am instead of actually getting to be who I am." His smile faded, and a storm clouded over his eyes. "There are so many people in my life who only stick around when things are good. When the highs are high, and when there is something in it for them. I see who my true friends are when the lows come—that's for sure. My list of people who are in it for the long haul is pretty short." Blake sighed.

"I can't imagine living my life wondering if the people in it are sincere or not," Laney said, looking over at him. "And honestly, it's great that you're so successful, but that's not what matters most. I'd rather see the deeper parts of a person, you know? The love people give is what resonates to me. It's the person you are when no one is watching. When you do kind things for others because it brings joy, not publicity or acknowledgment." Blake slowed to a stop as he listened. "I try to look here," Laney added, putting her hand on his chest, over his heart. "That's where true beauty lies."

Blake held her gaze as the lightning from her touch coursed through his veins. He wasn't sure whether to cover her hand with his own, or let the moment float away like a softly falling snow. His heart pounded in his rib cage beneath her fingertips, and his stomach fluttered like butterflies in a jar. Time slowed, and the hum of the crowd faded as a change in the air swirled around them. Her magnetism pulling on him was strong. But it was nothing compared to how electrified he felt when she touched him. Her fingertips held powerful energy, and in one small brush, something sparked inside him. It was as if his broken heart had been shocked back to life, ripping his soul from a lonely, dark world to one filled with sunshine and joy. Laney Campbell was unlike any woman he'd ever met. Like a breath of fresh air to a drowning man, and he knew he was in trouble.

Realizing that her hand was still on his chest, Laney abruptly pulled her hand back, and shoved her hands into her coat pockets. She shied away and shuffled her feet back in motion.

Suddenly, a loud siren blast shattered the thick air between them like a snowball through a window. Blake's attention shot to something down the street, and Laney followed his lit-up gaze. At the end of the block, a fire station stood with the garage doors flung open and an old fire truck parked in the driveway. A banner flapped in the breeze above the garage, that said, "Help us buy a new rig. Donate today!" The crew walked through the crowd holding upturned helmets as the townspeople filled them with donations.

"My dad was a fireman!" Blake said with boyish enthusiasm. "I used to hang out at the station with him all the time when I was younger. If the actor thing didn't pan out, I planned to be fire chief like him. Or a chef like my mom.

"Come on!" Blake instinctively grabbed Laney's hand and pulled her down the street to the station. He removed his wallet from his back pocket, slid some money in one fireman's beat-up yellow helmet and smiled at the fireman. He thanked him for serving the community before disappearing with Laney back into the crowd.

"Your dad was a fireman, huh?" she questioned, thrilled to receive another piece of his puzzle.

"Yeah, he worked for thirty years at the station where I grew up. Our community admired him so much for the behind-the-scenes things he did. One time, during a terrible storm, our neighbor's hundred-year-old tree fell on their house in the middle of the night. He wasn't even on duty at the time, but he went over there and helped clear the damage so our neighbors could get out. I may play a superhero on screen, but he was one in real life." Blake beamed while he spoke.

"He sounded like an amazing guy."

"Oh, he was. I don't think I could ever fill his shoes."

She smiled as he met her eyes. "Well, from what I know of you so far, the apple doesn't seem to fall far from the tree."

"That means more than you'll ever know. Thank you." His voice cracked with emotion.

"I'm only speaking the truth," she replied as she brushed a hair from her face. Laney's eyes wandered toward the street and stalled on a booth filled with handmade ornaments. She stepped under the tent to touch a delicate glass bulb. "These are gorgeous!" she said with joy radiating from her face. "I have a whole collection of ornaments at home. When I moved out on my own, I decided my tree needed a story, so I started buying a special ornament to sum up my entire year. Sometimes it's funny, sometimes it's a souvenir from a vacation, and sometimes it's meaningful. Decorating my Christmas tree soon became my favorite tradition because it was like taking a walk down memory lane. Almost every ornament on my tree now has meaning."

"That's awesome. I love that idea!" Blake's eyes shined with interest. "What ornament have you gotten to sum up this year?"

"I haven't found one yet," she replied. "This year has been a bit of a roller coaster for me, so I'm not sure what I want to remember most about it."

"Really? How come?" he asked.

"Well, I lost a close friend to cancer this year," Laney said softly, her voice straining. "It still bothers me that Bridget never understood how deep of an impact she had on my life, you know? I lived in survival mode on the surface of life for so many years. The thing I regret most was not telling her how much she meant to me. I never dove deep into the good parts with her, not even with all the time we spent together toward the end. And every day since then, I have wished that I had. After her death, I promised myself that I wouldn't live another day without telling the people I loved how I felt. I got this starfish tattoo in honor of her and to remind me to give life and love everything I've got. To really make a difference in this world." She exposed her left wrist to reveal a tiny, purple starfish.

"How does the starfish symbolize making a difference?"

"There's an old story I read somewhere about a little boy. He was throwing stranded starfish back into the ocean after the tide went out. There were hundreds all over the beach, and they were dying without water. A man walked up to the boy and said, 'You'll never make a difference. There's too many starfish to save.' But the boy continued rescuing them. He replied, 'I just made a difference to that one.' So this little starfish reminds me that even if I can't make a difference to everyone, I can make a difference to someone."

The softness of her voice as she spoke captivated Blake, immersing him in her story. The way her lip quivered when she tried to steady her emotion said more than her words ever could. And the sparkle in her eyes when they brimmed with tears made them shine like raw honey. Blake hung on her every word, drowning in their depths. It had been a long time since he felt anything real, and it rejuvenated a part of him that he thought was lost forever.

Blake's gaze lingered on her soft features as she spoke, studying everything that hid between the lines. *Don't fall for her, man. Don't fall for her...* his mind raced. But more than anything else, he wanted to ignore the voice inside him that kept him cautious and alone. When she turned to look up at him, he smiled shyly.

She cleared her throat. "Boy, I sure—what did you say earlier—'killed the vibe?'" she shifted uncomfortably. "Sorry about that."

"It's finally taking off," he repeated her response in the car.

"I have an idea, let's play a game," she said, walking to another rack of handmade ornaments. "I will buy you an ornament that I think is symbolic of what I know of you so far, and you do the same for me. Then we'll exchange when I drop you off. That can be our 'ornament for this year' and you can start your own collection!"

"Sounds like fun. Have you seen anything that stood out to you yet?" he asked.

"You'll have to wait and see," she teased before wandering off.

Blake perused through the booths, turning his back to her so she couldn't see what he was doing. Although shelves and crowds put distance between them, they grew closer through stealing glances and unspoken conversation. Her eyes were soft and intense when she looked at him, and his face was warm despite the cold air nipping at his cheeks. She hid from him behind a tall shelf that disguised the fact that she was grinning like a fool, but her smiling eyes gave her away. She was a poker player holding all her cards facing outward, but didn't seem to care that he could see her hand. She held her gaze on him, making his heart race. And when the clang of the shelf she ran into ripped her from her trance, she realized she had been staring a bit too long. Blake's laughter rang out across the crowd as he pointed to the sign: "You break it; you buy it!"

She shook her head in shame but couldn't help laughing along. Her face flushed red, and she had to let her embarrassment fade before she could lock eyes with him again.

Blake crept to the register to pay for his treasure, glancing over his shoulder to make sure she wasn't looking. Excitement bubbled up inside him, and he realized it had been so long since he felt real joy that it was almost foreign to him. He sighed and rode the wave as long as he could, not knowing whether another would come again.

Outside the booth, he leaned against a brick building and waited patiently for her to pick an ornament for him. She chewed on her bottom lip as she glanced between an object in each hand, and it warmed him from the inside-out that she took so much time choosing the perfect ornament. A loose strand of hair fell across her face, and she brushed it away softly before making eye contact with him. She was the most beautiful woman he had ever met, and it was not because she was perfect, but because she wasn't. His heart ached for a time that a woman like her would be willing to step into his world full of spotlights and flashbulbs and not be completely swallowed up by its current.

After making her purchase, she skipped toward him, a brown bag in her hand and a huge grin covering her face. "I can't wait to see your face when you open this."

"Well, I found the perfect one for you, so you've got some stiff competition," he teased.

"Game on, Captain." She nudged him playfully, and his hand fell instinctively to the small of her back, staying there. Touching her was natural for him, and his hand lingered as long as possible before he finally slid it away.

A ringing tone from her pocket cut the moment in half, and she begrudgingly pulled out her phone.

"It's the mechanic. He got the tire fixed," she told him with a frown, a bit disappointed that their little jaunt into town was over.

Blake's feet grew heavier as they trudged back to the garage.

"I have to admit," he moped, "Even though it's freezing cold out here, I kinda hoped he'd take all day. This has been really nice. I enjoyed spending time here with real people, with you…" He stopped walking and turned to face her. Their eyes met, and he stepped closer.

At that moment, the world faded into the background. Although they were standing on a busy sidewalk in the middle of town, they were the only two people on earth. The crowds swirled around, and music rang loud in their ears, but everything within the space between them slowed and quieted.

"I know exactly what you mean," she admitted as his fingertips grazed hers at her side. She laced her fingers into his, and a wave of chills rushed up his arms. His gaze moved from her eyes to her lips as he leaned in closer. Laney tipped her chin upward slightly and closed her eyes. He could almost taste her kiss when a tap on his shoulder shot the moment dead where it stood.

"Mr. Logan, I'm sorry to bother you, but would you mind signing my helmet and taking a picture for the station's 'Wall of Fame?'" asked the fireman he'd donated to earlier.

"Of course." He dropped Laney's hand, and she took the man's cell phone. "Will you take one with your phone, too Laney? I left mine in the car," Blake said to her, sounding as distant as he could possibly be while standing three feet away.

Once people noticed Blake taking photos and giving autographs, they swarmed. And as fast as a crowd descended upon him, Blake morphed back into the shell he portrayed for his fans. The poses, the smile, the shaking of hands, the signing of autographs—it all felt so false now that Laney knew what he looked like behind his mask. She snapped the photos with a forced smile, blinking back tears as Blake paraded for his fans.

After the crowd dispersed, they turned and headed back to the garage. She didn't touch him again, and they walked without saying a word. But the silence blared in Blake's ears like a foghorn. The fear of looking at her overwhelmed him, and when he finally mustered up the courage to turn her way, she looked far away. The magic they shared had faded, and Blake hated himself for letting her slip through his hands.

Inside, he ached for the hours he had with her that were genuine. Where he was Blake Logan without his walls up and pretenses high. He wanted back the moments when he felt safe to share secret parts of himself that few people knew. He wanted back that feeling that made his heart race at the thought of finding love again. But most of all, he yearned for the possibility of being loved for the man was. But her movements were stiff and her guard was back up. And he wondered if he had blown his chances for good.

Back at the garage, Laney stuffed her debit card and receipt into her oversized purse, and Cal handed her the keys.

"Thank you for your help today. We had a blast at the festival," she called over her shoulder as she pulled open the driver's door.

"Come see us again in the summer. We have live concerts every Saturday night in the park," he replied, waving.

Blake hung behind and whispered to Cal, "Did what I gave you earlier cover everything?"

"Sure did. In fact, I owe you some change," Cal replied, popping open the register.

"Keep it," Blake insisted, "and thank you for the festival suggestion. It was a lot of fun."

Laney started the engine as Blake slid into the passenger seat. A heavy tone hung in the air like a minor chord from an out-of-tune organ, and Blake's discomfort settled on his shoulders.

He sat stiffly in his seat and to ease the tension, he grabbed his bottle of water and gulped it down.

Laney took a deep breath and released it slowly.

"I just want to clear something up," she said boldly. "What happened back at the festival, I'm not sure if it was real or not to you, but it was to me. And I know you can basically have any woman you want, so I understand if I've misinterpreted what happened. But you should know that I'm not really a 'fling' type of girl."

"Is that really what you think of me? After everything we've talked about, you still think I'm some player?" he asked with hurt in his eyes.

"Well, I'm sort of confused. One minute, you're a completely different person, ripping your shirt off for fans. Then the next minute, you're this amazing guy who is relatable and fun to talk to. I feel like I'm looking at 'Tabloid Blake' again, not who I've spent the last few hours getting to know today. It just threw me off, I guess. I've got two differing opinions of you now, and I'm not sure which one is more you."

"Understandable," he said with a nod. "But hear me out. What if I have been—with the exception of my time with the fans—and will continue to be completely myself with you this whole drive? No act, no show. Just me. Then, when this drive is over, you be the one to decide if the tabloids are right. Can you do that?"

"Depends. I'd be lying if I said I'm not at all skeptical."

He laughed. "I believe it. I don't expect you'll be easy on me, but I'd at least like the chance to try."

"Why? Why do you care what my opinion is of you? There are a million women out there who think you hung the moon. Why does my opinion matter?"

"I care because, since the moment I sat down in your passenger seat, you've made me feel seen. And I mean *really* seen. It's been a long time since I felt like that," he said, letting out a sigh. "I'm tired of being someone they want me to be. I can't recall the last time I looked in the mirror and saw *me*. And at this point, I almost don't even know if I remember who that is. Back there, I morphed easily into who they wanted. It's getting harder to rid myself of that act, and I don't want to get so far away from who I am that I lose myself." His eyes were soft and pleading. "I'd like to start over. Can we? Because honestly, you know as much about the real me as I know about you. Can we wipe the slate clean and try again?"

Her clammy hands gripped the steering wheel. Her heart raced, and it became harder to breathe. *Why are you even considering this? Laney, you know how this will end. You will leave him in your taillights in a few hours, and he will fly off into the sunset without even giving you a second thought. And you'll go home to nurse your broken heart, even though you knew from the start that this would happen. 'Mere peasant, remember?* Her logical inner monologue argued. But the hopeless romantic in her sabotaged her thought process, and before she knew what she was doing, she heard herself agree.

"Fine," her voice forced through a dry throat. "I'll give you another shot."

"Awesome." He pumped his fist and smiled. "But there's one more thing."

"And what's that?" she asked, raising her eyebrow.

"You have to be unapologetically authentic with me too, Laney."

She shook her head. "I can't believe I agreed to this, but okay. And by the end of this drive, we'll know whether the tabloids were right about you or way off-base. I'll be the judge of that," she dared, pointing her finger at him. "But I'll have you know, it's going to take more than knee-weakening charm, sparkly blue eyes, and a perfect smile to convince me."

"Challenge accepted," he said with a grin, making her stupid brain turn to mush. "And I'll have *you* know, Laney Campbell, it's gonna take more than smiling brown eyes, hair that smells like fruit, and pretty awesome butt-kicking to decide what I think of you too," he added with a flirty tone in his buttery-smooth voice.

She turned away and focused hard out the windshield, a smile forcing its way across her face that she was unable to hide from him. *He noticed how my hair smelled.*

Laney shifted in her seat. "So, we've still got a few hours before we get up to Juniper Hills, and I promised you could play DJ," she said, handing her phone over to him. "I hope you've got good taste in music."

Blake smiled as he scrolled through her playlists.

"This is quite the variety. You're a very well-rounded person to have both Louis Armstrong and Aerosmith together in one playlist."

"Hey, they have more in common than you think," she insisted.

"Like what?"

"Well, both Steven Tyler and Ol' Satchmo are extremely talented, distinct in their sound, and…they have huge mouths."

A laugh burst out of Blake and spread from him to her like a contagious yawn. It felt good to laugh a little and ease the nerves she had.

"You're right about that." He caught his breath. "Okay, here's a good one to start us off," he said, hitting play.

Laney laughed as a familiar intro played.

"I wouldn't have pegged you for a girl-power hits kind of guy," she nudged his arm as "Since You've Been Gone" started pumping through the speakers.

"Hey, I can have a unique taste of music too." He looked over at her. "Honestly, I listen to a playlist with a lot of sing-at-the-top-of-your-lungs music like this before big fight scenes," he admitted. "There's nothing like belting out a Kelly Clarkson song to get me in the mood to beat up some bad guys."

"Are you laying it on thick with me right now, or is this for real?" Laney asked, doubt seeping into her voice.

"One-hundred percent real. Just like I promised."

His eyes darted toward the windshield, and he ran a hand through his hair, messing it up slightly. His perfect, magazine-ready appearance faded into realistic and human—approachable even.

Oh, great. His imperfections make him cuter. Swell. Her inner voice groaned.

"Although, confessing things like my love for girl-power ballads to someone I barely know isn't something I normally do," he said, rubbing the back of his neck red.

A grin spread across Laney's face. "Well, if it's any consolation, I'm sure more people than not will belt it out alongside you. You can't help it. It's Kelly's fault; she makes us all sing at the top of our lungs. And she's not sorry for it."

Blake laughed and relaxed into the calm acceptance Laney offered. She didn't miss a beat, jumping right into a commonality they shared without making him ashamed. The pressure to be perfect in his life was constant. But with Laney, it was like he had shrugged off all the expectations of fame and left them behind like lost baggage. She sucker-punched holes in the wall he built to protect himself and the image he sold. Being authentic made him feel like a tourist in his own head. But instead of being afraid of it, he wandered around and looked in awe at the man he hid for so long.

"Yep. I definitely blame Kelly. I'm under her spell."

As the chorus started, he smiled wide, turned up the volume, and raised his voice to match. Laney joined in, going toe-to-toe with him as he held out his imaginary microphone for her to share.

The way he threw caution to the wind was contagious. And despite her efforts in the past to protect herself, she considered letting him past her first line of defense. After Blake opened up a small piece of himself, she found it increasingly harder to fight the urge to join him on the ledge.

Soon, the song faded into silence, leaving empty air between them. As the next song started, he lowered the volume.

"So, I have been wondering something since lunch." He cleared his throat and turned in his seat to face her. "You have a nursing degree? Where did you work, and what made you quit to be a Lyft driver?"

"I worked in pediatric oncology for a few years at a children's hospital in Salt Lake City," Laney replied, glancing toward him. "It was the hardest yet most rewarding job I have ever had. It took my whole heart every day, and it was devastating when I'd lose a patient to their disease. Then, when Bridget was diagnosed with cancer in March, I quit my job to help take care of her. That's when I became a Lyft driver. The schedule was more flexible, so I could take her to chemo treatments. She didn't have any family nearby, so I stepped in."

Laney's throat tightened at the memories of her sweet innocent patients and warrior friend who lost the battle.

Blake's voice was soft and slow when he spoke, "You worry she didn't know how much she meant to you, yet you quit your job to support her during the biggest fight of her life. I'm pretty sure she knew." He smiled gently as he watched tears fill her eyes. "Will you ever go back to nursing again?"

She took a ragged breath and blinked her tears away. "Yeah, someday. I just needed some time to heal. I'm not sure I'll ever go back to the children's hospital, though. I loved it so much, but working there was hard on my heart, you know?"

"Well, I'll bet those kids loved you," he reassured her. "My nephew had Leukemia when he was three, and the nurses and doctors were paramount in keeping us positive. I can't imagine having to experience that, day in and day out. I can see why it would be taxing on your heart. You are someone who gives everything to those around you, so I can't even imagine the toll it takes."

Tears swelled and stung her eyes. She blinked them away as best as she could, but one escaped down her face. Without hesitation, he reached up and wiped it away with his thumb, letting his hand linger on her face.

"You are so beautiful," he whispered without thinking. He raised a fist to his mouth, then froze as a look of sheer panic enveloped his face. "Wait, I said that out loud! I'm sorry. It kinda slipped out." He ran his hand roughly through his hair and laughed uncomfortably. "Not that I didn't mean it, of course, but I, uh…" he trailed off.

He fidgeted in his seat and avoided eye contact while Laney stifled a laugh. Blake was even cuter when he was flustered, and she couldn't help but poke fun at his discomfort. She jabbed his arm playfully.

"Well, you certainly know how to lighten the mood," she teased as a burst of nerves exploded in her rib cage. "I'd be lying if I said I wasn't flattered. I mean, I'll ride this ego boost for a decade."

As her words permeated his eardrums, he massaged his temples, squeezing his eyes shut.

"And just so you know, you're pretty cute when you squirm, Captain," she added.

"Sure, go ahead. Exploit my humiliation. I can take it," he replied, resting his elbows on his knees. "I'm only having seventh-grade flashbacks of rejection right now. It's fine. Totally fine."

Her tears of sorrow from reminiscing changed to tears of laughter. And the harder she tried to stop, the harder she laughed.

He shook his head, his expression showing the discomfort of a person falling down the stairs. Yet under all his embarrassment was an adorable sincerity. He looked mortified, but sure all at the same time, and it completely won her over.

Blake Logan thinks I'm beautiful, she mused with a huge grin, her heart swelling at the thought.

"Oh man, this moment could end at any time now, and I'd be totally cool with it," he joked desperately.

Like an electronic Superman swooping in to save his dignity, Laney's phone buzzed. A message notification came in and he let out a loud sigh of relief.

"Will you see who that's from?" she asked, handing him her phone and wiping her tears of laughter away.

"It's from Angela," he said.

"Oh, she's my best friend-turned-sister-in-law. She married my older brother last year, and I was so glad to officially make her family. Can you read her message since I'm driving?"

"That's cool," he replied as he opened the message. "She says, 'I haven't heard from you in hours! Where are you? Are you okay?'"

Laney laughed. "We talk like, three times a day. I guess I lost track of time and forgot about our daily chat. Will you reply to her message and say I'm on a drive up to Idaho and that I won't be home until later tonight?"

"Sure. Should I tell her with who?" The mischievous look from the diner returned to his face.

"I'm game if you are!" Laney giggled thinking about how Angela will react "But she will want pictures, or it didn't happen."

Blake leaned in closer to her and took a selfie. Laney immediately noticed how good he smelled. Like the perfect blend of masculinity and a hint of nice aftershave or cologne.

After he snapped the photo, he attached it to the message and sent the reply, reluctantly moving back into his own space.

"Hey, while I'm texting with your phone, is it okay if I send myself that photo you took of the fireman and me today?"

"Of course!" she replied, secretly grateful that she'd now have his phone number, and he'd have hers. *That was smooth.*

Angela's response chimed in with her message in ALL CAPS. Blake burst out laughing but refused to read it aloud to Laney.

"Come on!" she begged. "You know I can't read it while I'm driving!"

"Nope, it's embarrassing to read stuff like that about myself. You can read it later," he said sheepishly, putting her phone away.

"Oh, you're killing me," she whimpered. "You say you're not what the tabloids say you are, but I never would've pegged you as shy. Is that why your manager makes you be someone you're not? Because you're bashful?" she teased.

"Well, how many successful actors do you know out there that are terrified of their audience?" He laughed and shook his head. "Not many. Joe, my manager, was afraid my fans would be disappointed if they met me in person and I wasn't who they thought I was."

"That's ridiculous. I've thoroughly enjoyed your company without the whole 'playboy act.' You're so much more than a chiseled, flawless face. The real you is even sexier *without* your Sentinel uniform."

Laney gasped as her hand slapped over her mouth, but she was too late. The words had already slipped out. It hurt to have the tables turned on her, and she could feel his eyes burrowing into her silhouette. But she couldn't bring herself to look at him. His snicker broke the silence, and she took a big bite of the humble pie placed before her.

"Okay, fine. Laugh it up now that I'm the one who wants to crawl in a hole and die. I deserve it," she muttered, the flush still washing over her cheeks in waves. "But let's be honest here. We both know you're good-looking, so let's get that out of the way. But even more so, you have the substance to back it up. You are an incredible human being, Blake Logan. There, I said it. And I regret nothing." She reached over and lowered the temperature of the heater to cool her face of fire. "It's suddenly very warm in here."

He raised an eyebrow and leaned onto the console between them. "You think I'm sexy?" His tone was playful and giddy.

She fanned her face. "Well, duh, doesn't everyone? Including the fine folks at 'People Magazine 'with their 'Sexiest Man Alive' campaign. Now stop adding to it with that eyebrow thing. I'm dying here."

Blake laughed and poked her ribs, leaving tiny hot spots wherever he touched. "You're certainly taking this whole 'Tell the people in your life how you feel' thing seriously enough, eh?"

"Well, at least I won't live with regret. Maybe skin-melting humiliation, but not regret." She pulled her curls off of her burning neck and readjusted the vents.

Smiling warmly, Blake chuckled and said, "You're the most real person I have ever met. And you're pretty amazing yourself, Laney Campbell."

A smile crept across her face that didn't stop until it hit her eyes, and he returned her glance with the same foolish grin.

"Today is good," she marveled. "So good."

Up ahead, dark storm clouds collected, traveling fast toward the highway. Without warning, the traffic came to a screeching halt, stalling everyone in the northbound lanes to a standstill.

"Yes, it is," Blake replied, as more time with Laney clicked onto the clock.

Chapter

5

Red brake lights glowed as far as the eye could see, twisting and turning for miles. The sky darkened as the sun set behind the approaching storm. And what was supposed to be a five-hour drive had ended up taking eight hours at this point. Although Laney was grateful for the extra time with Blake, the nagging feeling that he was so delayed sat in the backseat like an extra passenger. Little did she know, he was breathing a sigh of relief that he didn't have to watch her drive away quite yet.

"Oh boy. I hope you didn't have plans for this evening. I'm not sure how much longer this is going to be. I'm sorry." She tapped the steering wheel nervously.

"Don't worry at all! I'll just send a quick message to my mom and sister, telling them that traffic is worse than we thought. Besides, I can think of worse ways to spend the time," he said, glancing her way with a smile that made her heart flutter.

An alert from her GPS interrupted them as it reported, "There is a large snowstorm four miles ahead moving southward. And a five-car pile-up blocking both northbound lanes. Delays are estimated at two hours."

"Well, I'm glad we have emergency snacks," she said, reaching into the backseat. "I have junk food, trail mix, and water. Plus, the cookies we got from the festival. Pick your poison." Blake started for the trail mix, then went for a licorice rope instead.

"You won't tell anyone about this either, will you?" he pleaded, giving her the saddest, most pitiful puppy dog eyes he could.

"Not with a look like that! Who can resist a good set of sad puppy eyes?" she surrendered, biting into her own licorice. "All your secrets are safe with me, remember?" She zipped her lips closed, locked them shut, and threw the pretend key. "So, you're a closet foodie, huh? Tell me more about cooking with your mom."

He grinned and bit into his licorice again, chewing thoughtfully before starting. "My mom is the most incredible cook you will ever meet. She can take the most random ingredients and make a meal for an army, and it always tastes incredible. Nights when the firemen were out late on calls, she'd sneak over to the station and make the best meals for them. Sometimes, she'd even let me come and help. The guys loved my mom and her cooking. I hear they come into her diner on occasion and ask for an old 'firehouse favorite.' She has a secret menu only for them." He swelled with pride as he spoke of his mom. "When I was younger, she insisted I learn how to cook because 'a man should know how to make a nice meal,'" he imitated her. "What she didn't realize is how much I'd grow to love it. I treasure those times in the kitchen with her so much, but it's been years since we got to cook together."

"Well, it sounds to me like you've got some catching up to do while you're in town," Laney said with a smile. "Your mom sounds wonderful."

"She really is," he gushed. "You should come and eat at the diner before you head back home. You'll never have a better meal in your life."

The whole thought of meeting his mom made Laney's stomach flip. The idea that he even wanted to share that part of his life with her felt pretty awesome.

"That sounds nice. I'd like that," she replied. "Man, this traffic hasn't moved in ten minutes. Now we know why your plane couldn't land up here. Look at those clouds!"

"Wow," he said in awe as he watched their angry display. "Hey, I have an idea," Blake suddenly piped up, glancing at the freeway parking lot out the windshield. "As long as we're at a standstill, we might as well play a road trip game. I'll pick a random song from iTunes, and if you can guess it within three-seconds, you get one point. Then you can do it for me. Whoever gets to five points first wins. What do you say?"

"Oh, absolutely!" Laney exclaimed, putting the car in park. "This will be fun!"

Blake scrolled through the lists of songs in her music app and hit shuffle. Laney got three notes into the riff before shouting, "'Sweet Child of Mine'—Guns N Roses. Come on, that was too easy. Everyone knows that guitar solo. Okay, my turn to pick one."

Music started to play, and Blake sat for a second, focusing hard on the notes being played. Right as the five-second mark came, he yelled, "'To Love You Again'—Austin Grant!"

"No way! I thought you'd miss that one! He's not super well-known yet."

"I love Austin! He is one of my closest friends in L.A., so I'd better know his music," replied Blake.

"Wait, you're actually friends with him?" Laney squealed in excitement.

"Yeah, one of his songs was the main track on the soundtrack of a movie I did a few years ago. He came to the premiere, and I met him there. He's such an amazing guy. Super positive, which is infectious and rare in our circles. So we bonded a bit, and we also play basketball together a couple of times a month."

"Oh man, I love his music!" Laney told Blake. "I got to meet him at a concert once. I can't imagine being his friend. That's crazy!"

"Yeah, he's pretty cool." Blake replied and took the phone back to play another song for her. The song he picked was definitely one Laney recognized.

"'Don't Worry Baby'—The Beach Boys," Laney said confidently. "This one is impossible to miss because it's in the ending of one of my favorite rom-coms. The handsome teacher comes running out of the baseball stands to kiss her on the pitcher's mound, and this song plays. It's swoon-worthy! I love a good happily ever after!"

Then, Laney took the phone from Blake and picked another song for him. The moment the first few chords on a guitar strummed, Blake practically shouted, "Oh I know this one! I know it, the name is on the tip of my tongue! Shoot!" The time ticked away and he lost his point.

"The answer you were looking for was, 'Blackbird' by The Beatles.

"That's right! I can't believe I missed this one, I even learned this song on the guitar in junior high!"

"So you play guitar, huh?" Laney asked curiously.

"Yeah, a little. I play the piano too, but I'm a bit rusty because I don't have one in my house in L.A."

"Interesting. The layers continue to unfold," Laney said smiling at him. "You definitely should get one. A guy who can play an instrument is a total chick magnet—not like you need any help with that, but, you know."

"Well, maybe I will." Blake said bashfully as he switched to one last song. He stared down at her phone in search of the hardest song he could think of.

"Okay, this is it. If you can get this one, you win. There's no way I'll be able to catch up to you after that last fumble. But if not, I get a double-or-nothing chance to take home the random-song-guesser trophy."

"Oh, is that a thing?" Laney joked. "Sounds totally legit."

"Oh, it's a thing, and it's super prestigious," he replied, trying to look serious by holding back a smirk. "So don't blow it. No pressure."

The song Blake selected began to play. It was a simple melody with piano, bass, and drum, but Laney knew it immediately, especially after ol' Satchmo began to sing along. "A Kiss to Build a Dream On—Louis Armstrong!" she shouted excitedly. "Oh, this is my most favorite song ever!"

"You win the make-believe trophy! Although, I have to admit I'm kinda surprised."

"At what? That I beat you senseless at your own game?"

"Definitely not that part," he said with a laugh. "I guess I never would've guessed that this would be your number one song."

"I didn't listen to Jazz music at all until Angela and I went on a college trip to New Orleans," Laney began. Her eyes drifted far away in reflection as she spoke. "We were walking down the beautiful old streets in the French Quarter, admiring the architecture. Then a musician began playing this song on his trumpet in the middle of Jackson Square. I was so captivated by it that I stopped dead in my tracks and listened. This old couple, who looked like they had been married for 50 years, stopped, put down their groceries from the market, and started dancing. The cute old man sang along to her the whole time, and she laughed like she was twenty years old again. I wept like a child while I watched them. It was at that moment that I knew what kind of love I wanted, and I wouldn't settle for anything less. Sometimes, on a rough day, I put that song on." She closed her eyes, a look of contentment and peace filling her face. "And I'm right back in New Orleans again, hearing the trumpeter play. I can almost feel the humid air filled with the scent of beignets as I watch that cute couple dance. It makes my heart happy and gives me faith in love again. It's not just a favorite song to me anymore. It's an anthem of hope that true, long-lasting love exists for me, somewhere."

Laney opened her eyes and looked over at Blake. A glint of hope flashed in his eyes, and the magnetism of the emotion in the air pulled her in. She couldn't look away from him even if she tried to.

"You look at life in the most beautiful way," he whispered. "I don't think I've slowed down and breathed in life the way you do in a very long time. You see the good in everything and live so deeply. How do you do it?"

"I didn't use to be this way," Laney confessed. "But one day, I realized how much I was missing out on because I was in such a hurry. I never allowed myself to feel much of anything because it meant letting the bad in along with the good. But with that came the fact that nothing brought me joy; nothing made me feel hopeful. So I told myself that I would try to see only the good in a situation at least once a day. As I practiced that, I began to do it more and more often. And it slowly turned into a life I never imagined. Gratitude made me see opportunities I never thought possible, kinda like this one. This one is pretty great."

Traffic began to move again, so they crept a few feet then stopped.

"Well, that's a good sign. At least we're kind of moving now," she said, nodding toward the cars in front of them. "I thought we were going to have to dig into my emergency overnight bag in the trunk!"

"Wait, not only do you have snacks and drinks in the back seat, but you have an emergency overnight bag too? Is it full of foreign money and fake passports in case you have to flee the country? Are you a secret agent? Do you work for the CIA?" He side-eyed her suspiciously.

"Don't go blowing my cover now, or you'll have to make the rest of this trip hog-tied in the trunk."

"You don't have to convince me of that. After what you did to that cab driver, I believe it," he replied with a laugh. "But seriously. If you work for the CIA, blink twice. I know your car is probably bugged."

Laney belly-laughed. "I don't have a double life...that I'm aware of, but it's not a crime to be a little over-prepared for things, you know."

"A little?" he echoed.

"There's a legitimate reason for the mania, I promise."

"I sure hope so. Otherwise, you've got some explaining to do."

"Well, one time, Angela and I were up snowboarding at a resort near Salt Lake City. It was snowing perfect powder all day, and it was the best snow we'd had in a long time. But what we didn't plan for was that the perfect powder we played in all day was also falling all over the steep canyon roads. They closed the canyon because it became too dangerous to drive on. So we spent the night up in the ski lodge with a hundred other unlucky strangers until the roads were cleared. Ever since then, I've made sure I had a bag with a change of clothes and a few other things with me at all times. You know, just in case," she said.

"That actually makes sense, though I'm a bit bummed that you're not James Bond," Blake said, dejected.

"Well, he's a dude, so that doesn't work out anyway."

"Jane Bond then," he said, laughing.

"Well, maybe I am after all. I just don't want to have to kill you after I tell you," she told him in a mysterious voice. "I'm kinda enjoying your company and would hate to off you now."

Chuckling, he looked at her and said, "I appreciate the courtesy."

"Okay, now that I've made an over-prepared dork out of myself, it's your turn to share an idiosyncrasy. Spill."

Blake thought for a moment, then grinned. "I like to use the names of the characters from Golden Girls when I book reservations and hotel rooms. Other celebrities use cartoon characters, I like the Golden Girls. They're old-school funny, and no one ever catches on that it's me. Also, I love socks. Weird dress socks are my favorite—the goofier, the better! I wear them to all my interviews and junkets. Wardrobe can make me look however they want. But if I sneak on some silly socks under my fancy suits, then a small piece of who I am isn't lost."

Laney couldn't hide her smile as she pictured Blake wearing weird socks. "That is awesome! Do you have a favorite pair? Or a lucky pair? Please tell me you wash them, though, or it's a deal breaker for me."

"Well, I'll have you know that I do, in fact, wash them. And my lucky pair are ones with cats all over them that my sister gave me for Christmas a few years ago. I wear them when I start to miss home. It helps me take a little bit of her and my mom with me, wherever I am. That way, I don't feel so alone."

"I love it! Now I'm going to have to scour the internet looking for photos of you wearing weird socks!"

"You don't have to search too hard. I'm wearing some right now," he told her as he pulled his pant legs up and put his feet on the dashboard.

They were the ugliest socks she had ever seen in her life. They were chocolate brown and red argyle with Santa Clauses all over them. And they went halfway up his calf with the words 'Naughty' and 'Nice' along the cuff at the top. They were hideous in every sense of the word yet adorable because they worked so well on him. A cute guy who loves his mom and sister, as well as a great chef with a knockout smile, a heart of gold, and quirky socks. He couldn't get any more lovable unless he turned into a puppy. She allowed her thoughts of him to fill her with warmth, then her smile faded. *Mere peasant, Laney,* her obnoxious logic reminded her, slamming her back down to earth. Every time she felt herself starting to have feelings for him, her know-it-all reasoning stopped her right in her tracks.

"Penny for your thoughts?" Blake spoke softly, pulling his feet back down to the floor mat. "My socks aren't that hideous, are they?"

"No." Laney forced a smile. "They're awesome." *It's not like he's yours anyway. You are his driver, and you had a fun day together. That's it. In the real world, he's a gorgeous movie star with everything going for him. He could choose any girl in the world, and she would be happy to love him. Odds are definitely not in your favor, Laney.* Yet, there was an electricity between them that she couldn't ignore—no matter how hard she tried.

"Boy, the air sure got sucked out of the room." He exhaled on the window and drew a face in the fog. "Did I say something wrong?"

"No, no. Nothing like that. I'm just trying to get out of my own head, you know?"

"More than you realize," he replied sympathetically. "It's like a civil war in here," he added, pointing to his head. "Sometimes, I'm amazed that I can remember my own name, much less trying to figure out who I can and can't trust."

"Have you thought about moving away from L.A., even if it's just a second home to go to when you need an escape?"

"Yeah, I have," he replied, "but I haven't found another place to call home. Well, besides my sister's place in Idaho. But I don't want the crazy to infiltrate their lives too, so that's another reason I don't visit as often as I should."

"Makes sense," Laney replied, nodding her head. "I hope you find genuine love, friends, and a peaceful place to put down roots. Everyone deserves that, including you." Then, she hesitated for a few beats before the next sentence came out of her mouth. "H-have you ever been in love? For real?"

Blake shook his head and looked down at his wringing hands. "I'm not sure. There's always the underlying question of whether she loves me for who I *am*, or for *who* I am. I haven't gotten past that part yet."

All of a sudden, the glitz and glamour that came with a life of fame was not all it seemed to be. And a star like Blake was still a man who just wanted to be loved for who he was inside.

"Well, now that I've thrown a bucket of cold water on the fun, let's lighten the mood," he said, trying his best to change the subject. "Favorite movie, and why."

"Okay," Laney agreed. "But you go first. I have to think about it for a minute."

"It's a tough one for me," he replied while deep in thought. "I'd have to break it down into genres."

"Okay, break it down for me then."

"Drama: 'Life Is Beautiful.' His love for his family and the positivity he has during such a horrible time are so moving! I bawled like a baby more than once!" Blake admitted.

"A man who's not ashamed to cry—I like that."

"Well, I think you'd have to be a heartless robot to not cry in a movie that touching. Now, for Comedy, I choose both 'Dumb and Dumber' and 'Tommy Boy.' 'I have to include them both because who can decide between two things that make them belly laugh?'"

"Of course," Laney agreed. "Your game, your rules. What about suspense?"

"Suspense? I'm an old-school guy with those. Alfred Hitchcock is brilliant, so a lot of his movies make the cut. Although, 'Rear Window' is one of my favorites because I-I love Jimmy Stewart," he said in his best Jimmy Stewart impression.

Laney laughed because it was just like his socks—awful and adorable all at the same time.

"Action: I'm a James Bond, Jason Bourne kind of guy. I love spy movies; the fight choreography is so calculated and cool. It's on my bucket list to do a spy movie someday. Now it's your turn," he said, nodding toward her.

"Hang on!" she protested. "You forgot one very important category!"

"Oh yeah? Which one?"

"Romance, of course!" She laughed. "You can't forget romance!"

"Yeah, I think I'll skip that one. I don't know if I'm ready to admit that favorite out loud quite yet. Especially after I've already let my love for Kelly Clarkson slip."

"Oh, come on! There are no judgments from this girl, remember? Plus, I've seen your socks. You have no dignity left," she teased.

"Ouch, that cuts me deep. I bore my soul when I told you about my socks. And you threw it back in my face," he gasped dramatically.

"I'll only tell you mine if you tell me yours. Please?" she begged, turning the tables and giving him her best puppy dog eyes with a pout on her lips for extra punctuation.

He smiled his million-dollar smile, leaned into her space on the middle console, and looked straight into her eyes.

"Fine. It's 'Sweet Home Alabama.' But if you tell a soul—even Angela—I'll tell your whole family about your rooftop sanctuary."

"You wouldn't!" she exclaimed. "But your secret is safe with me, you know that by now. Besides, that's one of my favorites too."

Then she said young Melanie's famous line in her best southern accent: "Why would you want to marry me for, anyhow?" And without hesitation, Blake replied like young Jake in the film: "So I can kiss you anytime I want."

In that instant, lightning struck, starting a wildfire between them, awakening a hunger she'd starved for years. A fire raged in his hungry eyes, and she became a defenseless moth, knowing she'd never survive the burn but unable to resist her searing fate. His lure persisted, beckoning her to come closer. And knowing she didn't want to fight it, she lowered her shield and welcomed the flames that could both lighten and ruin her, all at once.

He leaned in slowly, shrinking the space between them. At that moment, she was faced with a choice—dive in and risk getting hurt, or stand strong in her skepticism and live with the regret. Her blazing heart pounded in her chest, scorching her all throughout with every pulse. With a split decision she threw caution to the wind and met him halfway.

Just before his lips touched hers, a smile crossed his perfect lips—delaying the gratification a little longer—before giving in. When his warm lips pressed against hers, she melted into him like she had been kissing him for a hundred years. His hand traveled softly up to her jawline from her chin into her hair. He combed his fingers along the nape of her neck, leaving shivers in their wake and a plume of fruity scents lingering behind. A charge flowed between them, electrifying every cell, every neuron, and every beat of her racing heart.

Laney ignited. And she floated like ash over a bonfire, completely defenseless over where the rising heat sent her. She buried herself within the moment—his lips so soft yet eager, his touch warm and familiar. Intense, yet gentle. And it was good. Like the kind of kiss that causes a cartoon-character-to-have-hearts-shoot-from-their-eyes good. It was the kind of kiss that she'd giggle with Angela about later. The kind of kiss she would never, ever forget. *Ever.*

But just like a bucket of water poured onto glowing embers, a soul-crushing, dream-shattering horn honked behind them. Completely dousing the moment into a fizzled ending. They crashed back to Earth as the car behind them impatiently flashed its headlights to signal them to crawl along. Laney peeled away from him, leaving her fingertips on his face a few seconds longer.

"I guess traffic is moving again," she could barely squeak out as she caught her breath.

"Yeah," he whispered, his voice hoarse. "That's a shame." Blake frowned as the car behind them honked again.

If I ever met the person in the car behind us in real life, Laney thought, *I'm going to give them the bossy-cab-driver-treatment. Total buzzkill.* She thought.

"Fine! I'm going! I'm going!" Laney groaned in frustration at the car behind her as she put her car into drive. They crept along at a snail's pace toward the exit ahead.

"So…" Blake cleared his throat, waiting for the smoke to clear. "I gave you my list. What's yours?" He leaned back into his own space in the car.

"Well, it's very sophisticated. Are you sure you can handle it?" she questioned with a smirk.

"Oh really?" He folded his arms. "I can't wait for this!"

"Drama would probably be 'Casablanca' or 'Dances With Wolves,' but I'm not much for drama movies. I like them, but a lot of the time, when I watch a movie, I need a fun escape, a good laugh, or a light-hearted rom-com. Dramas are too heavy. But I love the music in 'Dances With Wolves,' though. It has a brilliant soundtrack."

"True. It's so relaxing!"

"With comedy, I'm with you on 'Dumb and Dumber.' It's hard to beat the belly laughs that come from watching that movie. It's so stupid, yet so funny! So it would be that, or 'Pitch Perfect.'"

"I knew you had good taste! What about suspense?"

"Either 'Wait Until Dark' or 'What Lies Beneath.' I like the thriller types, not the gory horror movies. I can't even imagine what it would be like to be Audrey Hepburn in 'Wait Until Dark!' The whole idea of a blind woman having criminals lurking around in her house was so suspenseful that my muscles were sore the next day. Honestly, I even had a hard time being alone in my house for a few weeks after that one—and I can see!" she giggled.

"I won't even admit how long it took me to shower after watching 'Psycho,'" Blake confessed.

"And that is why I refuse to watch 'Psycho.'"

"Ah, but you must. It's a rite of passage, you know," Blake insisted.

"I'll keep that in mind the next time I feel the urge to be scared into never showering again," she replied. "Scary movies are fun, but action movies, are hands-down a favorite genre for me. I love them."

"I can see that," he said, giving her a playful side-eye. "You've learned your skills from somewhere. If it's not from the CIA, then…"

Laney looked away and tucked her hair behind her ear. "I took a few self-defense classes in college—my dad and brothers insisted on it. Plus, growing up with five brothers, you learn quickly how to hold your own."

"They sound like smart guys. It's nice to see that they love you that much. Your whole family sounds great."

"They are. I couldn't ask for a better crowd in my corner," she said softly, her face beaming.

"Well, if action movies are your go-to, then which is your favorite?"

"It's hard to pick a favorite but my most-watched one would have to be 'The Italian Job.' I love the genius plots. I love the chemistry between the characters. And I love the fact that the thieves get to be the 'good guys' for once and how the villains are *really* bad guys. It has such a unique dynamic than what we're used to seeing in movies. And it's kind of fun to root for the thieves for once because we don't normally do that."

Blake nodded and smiled. "Honestly, I've never seen it. Sounds like I'm going to have to add it to my must watch list."

Her jaw dropped. "Oh, that has to be remedied right away! How is this possible? It's so great!"

"It's too bad you have to turn right back around and go home after this," he murmured. "I think I need to watch it with its biggest fan sharing my popcorn to get the full effect."

The thought of snuggling up on a couch with Blake, sharing a bowl of popcorn, and watching her favorite movie was Laney's idea of a perfect night in. She'd give anything to experience that—just once.

The reminder that their time together had a fast-approaching expiration date hit them both like a ton of bricks. And the change in mood hung heavy in the air. She could sit in traffic with Blake and talk forever. He was amazing in every way—quite possibly the man of her dreams—and yet he would likely stay that way. He was too out of reach for a girl like Laney, and she knew it. Her heart sunk like an anchor to the ocean floor. She didn't want this car ride to be over. Because the moment she left him in her rear-view mirror, it would very likely be the last time she would ever see him. There's no way a movie star like Blake would choose a girl like her for long-term love. Even if they did have good chemistry, their lives were polar opposites. They'd never fit in each other's worlds.

She glanced over at him in the passenger seat, and he seemed to be having the same train of thought. The sparkle in his eyes clouded over, and he stared out the windshield into the distance.

"Hey, wait," he said as he jerked his head to face her, breaking the silence and heavy mood. "You skipped your favorite romance movie! If I have to confess mine, you have to confess yours too!"

His diversion back to movies was the perfect distraction, and she was grateful to send the thoughts of impending doom to the back of her mind. Their time together may be short, but it wasn't over yet. She needed to soak up every bit of it for all it was worth.

"Right," she replied. "But mine is split between two because they're both too good to leave out. It's a tie between 'Roman Holiday' and 'The Princess Bride.' I love the fire between Buttercup and Westley. And when he whispers 'As you wish' to her, I get full-body chills. They have this explosive, deep, death-defying…fireworks love." Blake grinned. "And what exactly is 'fireworks love?'"

"You know, the type of love that makes you look at it in awe with mouth slacked open, breath held, eyes fixed, watching it shine and sparkle. So amazing that you wonder how it can possibly be real. The kind you live and die for. The kind where two people's eyes can meet from across a crowded room, and connect with an energy that no one else understands. A love where eye contact alone says more than words ever could. It burns inside their chests, and it consumes and melds them together, forming a bond that can't be broken, even by death. It's more than a feeling; it's a hunger. Like the very air that you can't survive without. Does that make sense?" She bit her lip shyly and looked over at Blake.

His expression softened as he gazed back at her. "It's starting to," he whispered. "Do you think it's real? That kind of love, I mean. Or do you think it's just good acting?" he wondered.

"I sure hope it's real. If not, what's all this even for?" she answered, her voice barely audible. "There's nothing in this life more powerful than love."

Traffic crawled along again, and Laney broke the spell by turning her focus back to the road. The GPS broke the silence and said, "In a half-mile, exit to the right."

"Well, I'm glad she was paying attention because I would've made us miss our exit," Blake admitted with a laugh.

"There's no way you would have forgotten your way home," she joked.

"Definitely not," he responded. "But I've been a bit distracted on this ride…"

"Oh yeah? Distracted by what?"

Blake shrugged playfully. "Well, don't tell anyone, but there's this really great girl…"

Laney's face warmed, and she couldn't hide her ear-to-ear smile as they veered toward the exit and headed in the direction of the pine-filled canyon ahead.

The windshield wipers whipped back and forth, fighting hard to keep up with the ever-increasing snowfall. The closer they drove to the canyon, the harder the snow fell. Blake's brow furrowed as he looked out the windshield.

"My sister's house is in the valley on the other side of that ridge up there," he told her as he pointed out the window. "Do you think we'll make it?"

The flashing yellow lights from a snowplow lit up in front of them.

"Well, that's a good sign. We'll just stay behind him," she said as they crept along through the dark canyon.

Chapter 6

𝒯he snow fell hard on the canyon roads ahead, and although Laney followed behind a snow plow, the road slipped beneath the tires. She gripped the steering wheel with white-knuckled hands and slowed her Outback to a crawl. The snow on the road crunched under the tires, and the wipers frantically swept the windshield to keep up with the falling snow. The deep, ominous woods that loomed around them suffocated the fun, airy day, adding to the increasingly uneasy ride. Laney turned the radio down to a low hum and focused her eyes out the windshield.

The tension in the car was palpable, and Blake's heart pounded as thoughts of finally coming home became more of a reality. With each landmark he recognized, the knot in his stomach wound tighter. The realization that soon he would see Laney's tail lights driving away made it difficult to get comfortable in his seat. Every mile that passed brought them closer to goodbye, and there was still so much left to say before this was all over.

He cleared his throat, gathered some courage, and spoke before he changed his mind. "Laney," he stated, "it's not like me to dive headfirst into things like this. I have been hurt a lot in the past, and I don't trust very easily anymore. But what started out as an exciting adventure has evolved into something I never expected. I'm not sure what to do, or what to think, or how to feel, but I can't leave this unsaid, or I'll regret it forever." His throat tightened around his words, and he swallowed hard before continuing. "You made me feel things today that I've not felt before. You are amazing! You effortlessly brought out a depth in me that most people don't even know about, and I feel like I've known you forever. Like our souls are made from the same pattern. And I know this is short-lived, and you and I both have very different paths to follow. But I can't help but feel dread at the thought of having to watch you drive away soon. You breathed new life into my broken heart, and because of that, I will never again be the person I was before I climbed into your car."

Laney kept her eyes on the dangerous road ahead, but the tension in her shoulders softened and she bit back a smile. Part of him felt like an idiot for opening up to her the way he did. But she gave him the safety to be himself. She gave him a respite he needed, and now that he had it, he didn't want to let it go.

"Honestly," she confessed, "I tried not to, but I feel the exact same way. I was too afraid to admit it to myself, let alone to *you*. You could have any woman in the whole world. Why on earth would you want me?"

Blake chuckled and pulled her hand to his chest. His heart pounded like a drum through his T-shirt.

"You feel this?" he whispered as his pulse quickened even more. "This, right here, happens when I'm with you. You think I can have any woman I want, but no one else has this effect on me."

Laney's breath hitched.

"But why me? I'm nothing but a small-town girl from rural Utah."

"That's just it, Laney. You are the closest thing I've felt to home in a long time," Blake admitted.

"Yeah, well, this isn't fair at all," she voiced. "You clearly have the upper hand on me. I never had a prayer in resisting you and those silly socks."

"Oh, you think so, huh? Well, you stole my heart right out of my chest the moment you forced that cab driver to his knees. I knew I was in trouble when I got in this car with you. If there's an advantage here, it's yours."

Laney smiled until her eyes crinkled in the corners. "You're a sucker for my awesome self-defense skills. I knew it!"

"You certainly can't blame me. There's a reason why Wonder Woman is so popular, you know."

"Well, I'm no Diana Prince, but flattery definitely scores you points."

Blake lifted her hand to his mouth and kissed it. "I'm not sure what will happen next," Blake said softly, "but if it's okay with you, I'm just going to live right here in this moment and be completely present in it. Worrying about tomorrow is stealing today's joy, so I'm going to put that aside for now and just breathe."

"I like that idea," Laney replied in agreement.

Before too long, the tiny town rose into view through the storm. The darkened windows of businesses stood lonely in front of their empty, snow-covered parking lots. But glowing through the flurries, one *Open* sign stood out.

"Hey, are you hungry? We can stop at the cafe and grab some dinner," Blake suggested, hoping to prolong the inevitable. "It's the least I could do for you before you head back home. Then you can meet my mom—unless it makes you feel uncomfortable."

"I'm starving! I think the stress of that storm burned all my calories today. And I'd be delighted to meet her."

"All right, let's do it. She will love you and feed you until you burst."

"I'm game if you are!" Laney replied with a grin.

Snow settled into the words "Diane's Diner" on the sign above the door, stacking high on the flat-topped letters. Snow-filled planter boxes hung all along the front windows, waiting for spring flowers. And an old shovel stood at attention against the door frame like the Queen's Guard.

The bell chimed as they walked through the door, alerting the few people inside of their entry. "Pick a place to sit. I'll be right back," Blake whispered quietly in her ear. His fingers grazed the small of her back, feeling more and more like home there.

The customers who knew Blake well stood up to greet him with hugs and handshakes. He was the hometown hero to the village who helped raise him, and he was always greeted with enthusiasm.

Laney crossed the black and white checkered tile and took a seat at a booth near the jukebox in the corner. Blake spun each of the red vinyl bar stools at the glossy counter as he passed before disappearing through a hinged door. Laney watched through the pass-through window as his mom cupped his face and wrapped her arms around him.

The last of the crowd filed out the door, eager to get out of the storm, leaving Laney alone in the dining room. Suddenly remembering her text from Angela, Laney grabbed her cell phone from her purse. She opened up the message Angela had sent earlier, and laughed out loud as she read,

Angela: YOU ARE WITH WHO??? BLAKE LOGAN IS THE HOTTEST GUY ON THE WHOLE PLANET! SERIOUSLY!

SMOKIN' HOT! THIS CAN'T BE REAL! GIRL, I WANT EVERY DETAIL WHEN YOU GET HOME! CALL ME WHEN YOU CAN! I AM DYING TO HEAR HOW THIS ALL HAPPENED!!!

Laney giggled under her breath as she replied,

Laney: Hey, today has been wild! Sorry that I've been a bit out of touch. I was a bit preoccupied. ;) I may have to stay here in Idaho for the night because the snow is still coming down pretty hard. But I'll call you in the morning. Will you let my parents know too?

As she hit send, Blake came around the corner with his arm around his mom. Laney stood abruptly from the booth, and fidgeted uncomfortably with her hands.

"Delaney Campbell, this is my mom, Diane," Blake introduced proudly. Laney smiled and extended her hand for a handshake, but Diane enveloped her in a big hug that somehow only moms can give.

"We hug around these parts," she said with a smile. "It's so nice to meet you, Laney. Blake told me you two had quite the adventure today. You must be starvin'! Let me make you somethin' to eat."

"That would be wonderful!" Laney gushed. "We've been surviving on licorice ropes and trail mix since lunchtime."

"Blake, honey, what would you like me to make for you both?" Diane questioned, squeezing Laney's hands before releasing her.

"Well…" he replied, smiling back at his mom. "If you've got any of my favorite mashed potatoes and meatloaf left, that gets my vote!" Then, he turned to Laney and said, "Her meatloaf has won awards at the State Fair. It's amazing, but how does that sound to you?"

Blake half-expected Laney to just order a salad with a lemon wedge like the women he had dated back in Los Angeles. But to his surprise, she replied enthusiastically, "Oh, that sounds wonderful! I can't wait to try it!"

"Perfect! I'll have 'em right out," Diane replied as she re-tied her apron and turned off the *Open* sign.

Laney and Blake talked and laughed in the corner booth while they waited. Laney's face lit up with excitement as she spoke, and he hung on her every word. Blake's laugh echoed throughout the empty diner, causing Diane to smile as she approached with an armful of plates.

"All right, you two, I added some extra potatoes to fill you both up," Diane said as she placed the steaming plates in front of them. "I'll be cleanin' up in the kitchen. If you need anythin', just give me a holler." And with a knowing grin, she pivoted on her heels and crossed the dining room floor.

"Wow, you were right," Laney raved between mouthfuls. "She's a food magician."

"Wait until you have her world's best Cherry Pie."

"Cheers to that! I never turn down dessert," Laney replied, clinking her fork with his. After they finished eating, Blake and Laney stacked their plates and headed back to the kitchen.

"Oh, I don't think so!" Diane said with a laugh, reaching for the dirty dishes. "You two let me take care of these."

"I'm pretty sure doing the dishes after an amazing meal like that is customary," Laney replied, refusing to hand over her plate. "Thank you so much. It was delicious! Please let me do these. It really is the least I could do."

"Yeah, Mom, that was the best meal I've had in a long time. Thank you," he said, kissing her on the top of her head. "You've been on your feet all day. Go home and get some rest. We'll close up tonight," Blake insisted, taking Laney's side.

"Do you remember how? It's been a while," Diane quizzed.

"Of course I do!" Blake feigned insult. "Now get outta here and go put your feet up."

"Well…all right," Diane gave in as she hung up her apron and grabbed her purse. "But you two stay out of trouble, you hear? That dessert case isn't gonna last the whole day tomorrow if you get into it." She pointed an accusatory finger at them and laughed. "I'll see you at home, sweetie. Laney, it was an absolute pleasure."

Diane tossed the keys to Blake, turned the last of the dining room lights off, and left the diner. A bell chimed softly as she opened and shut the door behind her.

Blake locked the door, and watched as Diane disappeared in her car. He turned to Laney, and raised an eyebrow. "I think we're alone now. Wanna raid the desserts in the display case?" Laney squealed and said, "You know I do!"

With a mischievous grin, he dug past the cakes and brownies, reaching for the pies. "This is the world's best cherry pie, made from scratch every day by my mom." He pulled out the pie tin and grabbed two forks. "Can you get the whipped cream in the back fridge?" he asked her as he set the pan down on the counter and dished them each a slice. Laney nodded, walked through the kitchen and grabbed the can of whipped cream from the industrial-sized fridge.

Shaking the can as she came back into the room, Laney exclaimed, "Let's do this!"

Blake sat down on a barstool and slid her plate toward her, a swirl of whipped cream piled high on the pie's golden, flaky crust. Laney's eyes lit up as the first bite of pie passed her lips.

"Mmmm. 'World's best cherry pie' doesn't do this justice. I have never tasted anything like this in my entire life!" Laney raved. "It's the perfect combination of crumbly homemade crust and tart cherry filling. My mouth won't stop watering!" After devouring her pie, she used her fork to collect every last crumb. "This is sin on a plate."

"I told you," Blake said, licking his fork clean. "It really is an art form only a select few of us can pull off."

"Wait, do you know how to make this?" she gasped.

"Of course I do! I helped my mom make it all the time when I lived here at home," he said proudly. "But it's a secret recipe, so if you want it again, I'm the one who will have to bake it for you." He leaned forward and put his elbows on the counter.

"Hmmm, a handsome guy making homemade pie in my kitchen? I think I could get on board with that arrangement," Laney responded flirtatiously. "When are you available?"

Blake's thoughts flashed to what it would be like being with her long-term. Sharing a home together, cooking in the kitchen after a long day at work, and swapping stories about their day over a delicious meal. He could almost hear the music playing in the background while they danced around, singing into wooden spoons. He imagined surprising her with a weekend getaway or having her practice lines with him. And he ached inside for that beautiful life that would never be.

Before she could catch on to his wistful longing, he redirected her to the jukebox in the corner and said, "I don't know about you, but I can't clean up without music. There's a trick to this old thing," Blake said, wandering over. "There's a button on the back of it that will play music without charging you." He reached behind the jukebox to flip the switch. "The only thing is, the songs play randomly, so you never know what you're going to get."

An old fifties sock-hop song filled the room as they gathered up the rest of the dishes to wash.

Laney started to sing along while she piled the dishes into an industrial-sized sink full of hot soapy water. Blake came up behind her with a drying towel slung over one shoulder, and he rinsed and dried as she washed. Even doing the dishes with her was nice.

Blake looked over at Laney as the last light left on in the kitchen lit up her profile from behind. He stared, hypnotized, while she sang softly with her eyes closed. Her hair, which was tied back in a loose ponytail, exposed her slender neck, and his eyes traced each silky inch. She was everything he'd ever hoped for—beautiful, smart, fun, full of life, and with a golden heart brimming with love. She epitomized what was missing in his life back in L.A., and he craved her depth and joy. He imagined what it would be like if he took her back home: the flashbulbs, screaming paparazzi, and crowds everywhere he went. The lack of privacy, the scrutiny, and constant gossip could suck the life out of someone if they weren't careful, and a pit formed in his stomach. As much as he wanted her sunshine in his life, he didn't want her exposed to everything that came with fame. Her soul was too beautiful for that—yet his heart ached for a world where they could fit. He was a fish, and she was a bird. Would there ever be a way for them to exist together outside this dream? Maybe he needed to take a step back to protect her from the harsh world he lived in.

Blake sighed and it caught her attention. She looked over at him with concern on her face, moving closer. Studying his face, Laney grinned, holding steady eye contact as she leaned in. Blake gazed down into her eyes, determined to hold out against her gravitational pull. Her warmth emanated next to his body, and he felt his resolve slipping. He was powerless under her spell, and although he wanted to keep her from getting hurt, he couldn't resist her warm brown eyes. She pulled him closer by the shirt with one wet hand until he surrendered. When he was close enough, she reached down into the sink full of bubbles, scooped a big handful up, and plopped them on top of his head. Then, she burst into laughter and ran out of the kitchen, shrieking.

"Oh really?" he hollered. "Is that what we're doing now? Exploiting my weakness for you so you can put bubbles in my hair?" He grabbed a huge handful of suds and chased after her. She squealed as he caught up to her and covered her cheeks in bubbles. They laughed, tangled up in each other's arms, soap suds flying everywhere.

Holding her this close made him long for her even more. She fit perfectly into his arms like she was molded for that very purpose. He gently wiped away the suds on her button nose, his expression softening from the laughter and play. When his eyes met hers, he had no choice but to kiss her. She may be a bird, but she made him soar. And he was a fish, but he would give her a safe haven. She welcomed his lips and melted into his strong body as his arms tightened around her. Her hands ran through his sudsy hair, sending chills down his back.

The song playing on the jukebox quieted into the next, and "I Can't Help Falling in Love" began to play. Blake spun her out, then pulled her closer and wrapped his arm around the small of her back as they began to sway to the music. Elvis sang it perfectly. Were they fools for rushing into things? Probably. But what would be even more foolish is not taking a chance on something this rare.

He grinned as he brushed the remaining bubbles from her face and kissed her gently on the forehead. She nestled into him and lay her head against his chest. With a sigh, he was carried away to a place where none of the logistics about their relationship mattered. A place where love was enough, and everything else worked itself out. His heart pounded against her ear, exposing any emotion he tried to tuck deeply away. It was hard to act cool and collected with a girl like Laney because she could see through the guise. She knew the man behind the curtain by now, so there was no use in still trying to convince her that he was The Wizard of Oz.

Outside the window, the snowfall had turned into a blizzard, making her return home tonight too dangerous. He breathed a sigh of relief.

"Hey, I don't think it's a good idea for you to try and drive home tonight," he cautioned. "It's late, the snowstorm is getting bad, and I don't want you to get hurt or stranded."

"You're probably right," Laney agreed. "Is there a hotel in town I can stay at?"

Blake shook his head. "No, this town's too small for that. But my mom's cottage has a guest bedroom you can stay in, and I'll use the one in my sister's house."

"Are you sure she'll be okay with that? I'm practically a stranger to her," she pointed out.

"Oh yeah, she'll be fine with it. I'll message her and make sure it's okay if you want," Blake said. "Hey! Now we can watch 'The Italian Job' before you go!" He smiled, his heart speeding up slightly at the thought.

"It's a date," Laney said, smiling back. "But only if you'll share the popcorn."

Laney's Outback pulled into the driveway of Blake's sister's house around ten o'clock. A lonely table lamp in the corner illuminated the front window through the sheer curtains. Blake hurried around to the trunk and grabbed their bags as Laney ran through the snow and waited for him on the porch. He paused in the storm, suitcases in hand, and stared at his childhood home. Like the snow blustering around him on the outside, the emotions he had run from for so long rattled around him on the inside. Being back home with his father gone flooded his heart with the pain he had forced away for years. His emotional dam weakened, cracked, and burst, engulfing him in the pain that awaited him. His throat strained under the pressure of it all, forcing tears to well up in his eyes. His breath labored, and his lungs refused to allow their full expanses to fill. And just when he wanted to give up, lay in the snow, and succumb to the storm, a warm arm looped through his and patiently urged him on.

"Let me help you," she said gently, taking her overnight bag and leading him toward the porch.

She was a life preserver to a drowning man, pulling him safely back into her harbor. He dropped his bags on the porch and buried his face in her hair.

"You are surrounded by love here. You can face this, Blake. You're safe to feel however you need to."

He clung to her and cried for a few minutes before his arms began to loosen around her. He wiped his face and silently opened the door. He carried the weight of the storm raging inside heavily on his countenance and his eyes dimmed.

He hung his leather jacket on the stand by the door and surveyed the room. The house had changed enough that the reminders he expected were dulled or gone. He exhaled, letting some of the burdens he carried fall away.

"You okay?" Laney asked, concerned.

"I'm trying to be," he whispered back.

"Well, I'm here if you want to talk. You don't have to go through it alone."

Blake cleared his throat and swallowed hard. "I'm going to run my bags to my room real quick," he said in a low voice, almost a whisper. "Wait here. I'll be right back."

Laney looked around the room and was drawn to a gallery of photos displayed on the wall. One photo of Blake as a child with his father stood out among the others. He had on his dad's fireman helmet that hung largely on his tiny boy head, and his father held him in front of a fire truck. James stood strong and proud, with the same blue eyes as Blake. She reached up and touched it lightly, knowing the significance this photo must hold for Blake.

After a few minutes, when Blake had not returned, Laney wandered down the hallway toward a lighted doorway. Through the crack of the open door, she saw him sitting on the side of the bed, holding a picture frame in his hands.

"Blake?" she called out, knocking lightly against the door. "Can I come in?"

He wiped his eyes and set the photograph back on the nightstand. "Of course. Sorry for leaving you hanging."

"It's fine. I was just going to head out to the cottage if you needed some time to be alone. I don't want to push you."

"I'm sorry I'm not very good company tonight. I didn't expect to be hit so hard with everything all at once."

"I completely understand."

"I'll show you to your room," he said in a hushed tone as he got up, grabbed her overnight bag, and led her out to Diane's cottage.

The hinges creaked as the door to the cottage swung open. Blake brought her down the hallway and flipped on the light switch to the guest bedroom. The floral-patterned bedspread had been turned down with a mother's touch, and a stack of fresh towels sat on the dresser. He set her overnight bag down on the bench at the foot of the bed before turning to face her. Laney breathed in as she looked around and laid her purse on an overstuffed chair in the corner.

"Do you have everything you need?" Blake asked, wanting to make sure she would be comfortable. "I can grab you some extra pillows if you need them."

Laney glanced over at the bed covered in pillows and laughed. "I think I'll be fine with what's here."

"Right," Blake mumbled, laughing along nervously as he took her coat from her and hung it on a hook. "Uh, I don't think I'll be able to sleep. Do you still want to watch the movie?"

"I'd love to if you're up for it. But we can also just stay up and talk if you need a sounding board," she offered.

"I think a distraction would be good right now, and I don't want to waste what little time I have with you sulking. If you want to throw on your PJs and meet me in the family room, I'll go make the popcorn," he said, smiling weakly. "See you in a minute." And with that, he turned around and disappeared into the dark hallway.

Laney unpacked her wrinkled-up flannel pajamas and shook them out. They weren't pretty, but in an emergency, they would do. She unrolled her wool socks, still cold from the car, and put them on her feet. With a small exhale, she walked into the guest bathroom and studied her face in the mirror.

"Okay, Laney, he's just a regular guy," she said to her reflection. "No need to be all nervous and guarded. He already said he likes you, so quit freaking out."

She splashed some water on her face and combed through her hair with her fingers. She grabbed her phone and dialed Angela's number. If anyone could calm her down, it would be her best friend since first grade.

"Girl! I have been dying to hear from you!" Angela said as soon as she picked up the phone. "How on earth did you end up with Blake Logan? And why are you in Idaho? I've been keeping tabs on you on Find my Friends, and you haven't moved in hours! I need all the details!"

Laney laughed. "Hey! I have to make it quick because he's waiting for me to watch a movie with him."

"Wait, what??" Angela squealed. "You mean you're still with him? You've got a story to tell me, so spill."

"He was my Lyft passenger this morning," Laney began, telling the whole story under her breath. "I agreed to take him up here because I didn't have anything else going on today, and I also figured it would be a nice paycheck."

"So he just *strolls* on up to your car and gets in? Is he as hot in person as he is in the movies? Is he nice? Did you freak out?" Angela was firing off a hundred questions and not waiting for Laney to answer them.

"He's even cuter in person than I could have ever imagined." Laney giggled. "Yes, he's nice, he's really down to earth, and amazing, and so much more than what we get to see in the magazines and movies. I am really trying hard not to lose my senses. You have no idea—he's amazing, Ange."

"Oh my gosh, girl, I can't believe this! Your mom is going to flip. I have so many more questions! So why are you still in Idaho? I thought this was a quick trip?" Angela pressed.

"Well, we had a few delays along the way, and the weather got worse the closer we got to his sister's house. So I'm staying the night in his mom's guest bedroom. She has a cottage that's behind his sister's house. I'll be home tomorrow afternoon if the roads are better in the morning. But I've got to go. A gorgeous man is waiting for me, and I'd rather snuggle with him than talk to you." Laney teased. "I'll call you tomorrow."

"Fine," ceded Angela with a sigh. "But you owe me details when you get home. Have fun, and don't do anything I wouldn't do!" she laughed as she hung up.

When Diane was about to raise her hand to knock on the guest bedroom door, she overheard Laney's conversation with Angela. She paused in the hallway outside the door and waited. After she heard Laney hang up the phone, she knocked and called out, "Laney, honey, do you have everything you need?"

"Yes! Thank you," Laney answered from the other side of the door before opening it. "Thank you for letting me stay. This is a bit unorthodox, but I truly appreciate you opening your home to me."

"You're so welcome, sweetheart. Any girl who makes my Blake smile the way he has been smiling tonight is welcome here anytime," Diane said as she squeezed Laney's hand. "I hope you sleep well. I'll see you in the morning. Goodnight."

On the living room couch, Blake was dressed in sweats and a T-shirt, with a bowl of popcorn on his lap and the TV remote in his hand. He waited with his bare feet propped up and crossed on the ottoman in front of him, and a wave of relief smoothed over his face when Laney strolled in. The welcoming fireplace gave the room a soft, warm glow, and Blake studied the way it highlighted her soft features. As she came closer, he lifted the blanket and patted the couch next to him so she could snuggle in. He felt a tug in his chest as she sat down next to him, her body molding itself to his. Blake had been all over the world, yet he couldn't think of anywhere else he'd rather be at that very moment than on the couch next to her, sharing her warmth.

"You doing okay?" she asked quietly.

"Yeah. I'm sorry I'm in such a heavy mood, but I'm glad I don't have to face this alone. Thank you for being patient with me," he said as he rested his head against hers.

"Of course. No one should have to shoulder that kind of emotion on their own."

"I've been so used to dealing with his death by myself that I don't quite know how to talk about it."

"That's fine. I'm here if you want to talk or if you want a distraction," she told him as she laced her fingers into his and kissed the back of his hand.

"What kind of distraction?" He raised an eyebrow and smirked at her.

Laney smacked his leg playfully and laughed. "You are trouble, you know that? But I *did* walk right into that one, didn't I?"

"Yeah, you kinda did. I couldn't resist, sorry."

She giggled and shook her head.

He kissed the top of her head and chuckled. "You make me feel better," he said softly. "Thank you."

"Mission accomplished," she replied.

Turning to the TV, Blake raised the remote in his hand and pressed play. He nestled into her body, feeling each of his muscles relax in their new space.

"So, I was wondering. Is there somewhere in town I could go tomorrow morning so I could grab a few things?" Laney lifted her head and said to him as the opening credits rolled.

"What did you have in mind?" he asked.

"Well, I didn't pack any makeup or a new change of clothes in my emergency bag, so I'd like to run to the store so I can get some. Would you like to come with me?"

"I'd love to, but I have some business calls with my manager and sister to talk logistics and designs tomorrow morning. Maybe my mom can go with you." He paused, hesitating for a moment before continuing, "What do you think?"

"That's a great idea!" she replied. "If she doesn't mind…"

"She loves shopping, so I'm sure she'd be happy to. We can ask her in the morning."

Laney nodded, resting her head on Blake's shoulder. The comfort set in for them both, and they melted together like crayons in the July sun, creating a whole new color as they merged. Her warmth enveloped him and his eyes grew heavy. Before the movie ended, they had both fallen asleep.

Chapter 8

Diane woke up with the sun the next morning, and she crept into the kitchen to start a pot of coffee. It was only after the clanging of dishes and cupboards that she spotted Blake and Laney, still fast asleep on the couch. She snapped a quick photo on her cell phone and sent it to Blake. She poured a cup of coffee, sat in her favorite sunspot at the kitchen table, and turned on her tablet. The front-page story blared in large, bold letters—the very thing she had prayed for.

Canyon Road Closed!

Icy conditions caused a major accident on Juniper Hills Canyon Road. A snowplow slid off the road late last night and into a tree, causing the tree to fall on the roadway. There were no injuries to the driver; however, the large pine tree has blocked both lanes of traffic. Conditions remain dangerous and cleanup is slow. The canyon is closed until conditions are deemed safe. Mayor Hughes has asked all residents to notify expected visitors to reschedule until further notice.

"We appreciate your patience, Juniper Hills citizens. Our crews are working hard to get everything cleared. In the meantime, please stay safe and use caution on the roads," he stated early Saturday morning.

Diane sighed as she read the article and then looked over at Laney and Blake, asleep on the couch. "Thank you, James," she whispered. "I knew I could count on you to send help from heaven. Let's keep these two together a little longer."

The soft aroma of fresh coffee stirred Blake from his slumber. He nestled against Laney and he sighed with contentment against her warmth. He lay still, trying to liven up his numb limbs without rousing her at the same time.

"Good morning, sunshine," Diane greeted him as he stirred. "I assume you slept well." She giggled quietly into her coffee cup.

Blake slid out from under Laney's arm and stood up, smoothing his hair and shaking his dead arm. He laid a blanket over her shoulders and walked over to the coffee pot. He poured himself a cup in his dad's favorite mug, and sat across from Diane at the table.

"Good morning," he murmured in a sleepy voice. "And yes, you could say that." He glanced over at Laney, asleep on the couch, and smiled.

"So, what's the deal with this whole thing?" Diane probed. "You both seem pretty cozy for two people who have only known each other for such a short period of time."

"Yeah," he replied as he ran his fingers through his thick brown hair. "I'm not really sure how this all happened, Mom. We just connected on the car ride yesterday. It almost felt like fate was stepping in at every turn to give us more time together. You know me, I'm not one to rush into anything, especially relationships. And I'm not sure what will happen next. But all I know is, that amazing woman over there could very well steal my heart. And I don't think I'd ever want it back…"

"I'm happy for you, son. You've needed someone like her to fill the void in your heart. I just don't want to see you get hurt." She reached across the table and cupped her hand over his.

"See, that's the thing, Mom. She's great. But we also live very different lives. And because of that it almost seems doomed to fail from the start," Blake replied, burying his head in his hands.

"Well, you'll always fail with a perspective like that." Diane patted his arm. "Plenty of people make long-distance relationships work. The thing is, son, I haven't seen you this happy in a long time. I'd hate to see you let it go over a technicality. If it's something you both want, you'll find a way to make it work."

Laney stirred on the couch, and for a moment, she had forgotten where she was and how she got there. Her eyes flew wide open when she realized she wasn't at home in her own bed. She sat up in a panic and looked around. Seeing Blake and Diane at the kitchen table shocked her back into reality, and she turned away from them. *Am I a complete mess? Did I snore? Holy cow! That wasn't just an amazing dream!* She thought to herself. She stood up, straightening her hair and PJs and avoiding eye contact with them both.

"Morning," she mumbled to them both as she scurried down the hallway to her unused room.

"Good morning!" they both replied, smiling at her from the table as she disappeared down the hall.

Laney leaned against the sink in the bathroom and looked at herself in the mirror. *What does his mom think? Did Blake wake up filled with regret?* She ran her fingers through her messy hair, grabbed her toothbrush, and quickly brushed her teeth.

Back out in the kitchen, Diane showed the article to Blake.

"It looks like fate has stepped in yet again, sweetheart. So, the question is, what are you going to do to help it out? Are you going to miss this opportunity given to you, or are you going to take a leap of faith and see what happens?"

Laney got dressed in yesterday's clothes and went back out into the kitchen. Feeling a bit insecure as she approached the coffee pot, she kept her focus on the task at hand.

"There's sugar and cream here on the table, Laney. Why don't you come and join us?" Diane called out.

After pouring herself a cup of coffee, Laney crossed the room timidly and took a seat next to Blake.

"Blake tells me you need to do some shopping today. Would you mind if I came along with you? I'll take you to all the best boutiques in town," Diane offered gently.

"That sounds great, if you don't mind," Laney replied, looking up from her cup of coffee. "Thank you."

"Well, I'll hurry and go get ready, and we can leave in an hour. Does that work, darlin'?" she asked, squeezing Laney's hand on the table.

"That's perfect." Laney looked up and smiled.

Diane stood up from the table and took her coffee cup to her room.

"So it looks like we'll get a second chance at 'The Italian Job' tonight. The road through the canyon is closed," he told Laney, nodding toward the article. "You wanna try again? I promise not to put you to sleep this time." He chuckled nervously.

Laney studied his face to try and read his emotions. Her palms sweated, and her throat tightened as self-doubt screamed in her brain. *Is he only being nice only because I'm stuck here? What if he woke up this morning and realized what a mistake he had made? What if I'm just another conquest, and he's already bored with me? Was I a fool to let my guard down, and now he wants nothing more than to get rid of me?* She forced a smile through her inner turmoil, and the worry in his face dissipated a bit.

"I'd like that," she said, meeting his gaze. "But first, we need to talk about yesterday. I'm not sure what to think this morning or what to feel. I'm afraid I'm part of some cruel joke, and I don't know if I should stay."

"What?" Blake exclaimed, confused. "Why would you think that? I thought we had an amazing day yesterday. And I don't regret one minute of it. Do—do you?" he stuttered, rubbing the back of his neck red.

"Of course not," she replied quietly. "It was one of the best days I've ever had. But did you *really* mean everything you said in the canyon last night?"

"Everything."

"But, you're Blake Logan. The whole idea that you would want an ordinary woman like me seems silly. Any minute, things could change, and I'll be left standing here like a fool with my heart in my hands."

"The only heart you'll be holding in your hands, after all this, is mine, Laney. And it's completely up to you whether you break it or not. You know the first thing I felt when I woke up this morning? Relief. I was relieved that yesterday wasn't a dream. And when I saw that you were right next to me, I couldn't wait for you to wake up so we could pick up where we left off. I don't want this to be over." He looked directly into her eyes and put his trembling hands over hers. "Stay," he whispered. "Please stay."

She thought for a moment. "Okay." The tension in her face relaxed and she was back to the same old Laney. "But not in these clothes again. I've gotta get something else to wear."

The mood in the room shifted. By the time Diane had finished getting ready to go, Blake and Laney were filling the kitchen with laughter and the aroma of breakfast cooking.

"No. There's no way on Earth that ketchup goes on eggs!" Blake laughed and playfully stole the bottle away from Laney. She laughed and stole it back, insisting that if he could put salsa on his, she could put ketchup on hers.

"They're both tomato-based," Laney argued. "It's totally acceptable!"

"But salsa is so much better," Blake rebutted, stealing the ketchup back.

"Says who?" she scoffed, wrestling the ketchup bottle from his hands.

"All of Mexico and Texas! Just try it," he begged, offering her a forkful.

"Fine, but only if you agree to taste mine too!" she insisted, holding up a bite on her fork too.

"Okay, on the count of three. One. Two. Three," he said, and at three, they exchanged bites.

"What do you think?" he asked her.

"It's not bad!" she replied, laughing. "But mine is better."

"No way!" Blake argued, laughing along with her. "Your taste buds can't be trusted."

"Are you ready to go, Laney?" Diane asked as she walked into the kitchen.

Laney finished up the last of her eggs and placed her plate in the sink.

"Don't worry about it. I'll clean up," Blake said, scooting behind her at the sink.

"Thanks," she replied gratefully, leaning back against his chest. She stood there with his arms around her for a moment before peeling herself away and heading to her room. "Let me grab my coat, Diane. I'll be right back."

"Seems like things are better now," Diane said to Blake as he washed the dishes.

"Yeah, I think so. Thanks for your advice this morning, Mom. I don't know what I would've done if things had stayed the way they were an hour ago," he said and gave her a side-hug to avoid getting soap on her.

"Well, what are moms for?" She laughed, wrapping her arm around him. "Your happiness means the world to me. And I couldn't just stand by and watch while everything fell apart."

"I'm ready to go!" Laney called out, slinging her purse over her shoulder as she walked into the kitchen. She looked at the snow outside and zipped her coat to her chin. Diane and Laney walked out the cottage door together and into the blustery winter wind. Unable to help herself, Laney looked back over her shoulder as she closed the door. She waved subtly, mouthing the word "bye" and sneaking one more look at Blake standing at the kitchen sink. He smiled his winning smile back at her, raised a sudsy hand, and waved back. *He really is beautiful.* She thought to herself as she tucked that warm image of him away like a cashmere scarf wrapped around her heart.

Laney strung her shopping bags along her arms as she and Diane headed back to the car. The trunk popped open, and as Laney threw the bags of clothes and toiletries inside, Diane got an idea.

"Hey, Blake and Danielle's meeting with his manager is supposed to go until around two o'clock. Do you want to go grab some lunch? I don't have to be to the diner until right before the dinner rush. We might as well kill some time together."

"I'd like that." Laney smiled. "It's my treat. After all, without you, I would've come back with too many tops and gotten completely lost," Laney replied as she closed the trunk. "Thank you again for coming with me. This wouldn't have been as fun alone. I've really enjoyed myself today."

"Me too," Diane said. "I can see why my son has taken to you so quickly. You are everything he said you were."

Her words sunk into Laney's heart, planting a tiny seed of joy.

Diane drove to a quaint little cafe down the street, and they were led to a booth by the window. Laney hung her coat and purse on a hook next to her seat and sat down across the table while Diane did the same. When they were both seated, Diane's expression suddenly changed to a more serious one as she laid her hand on Laney's.

"I just wanted to thank you for bringin' my Blake back," she said. "He hasn't returned since his father passed away a few years ago, and I've missed him terribly. It has been extremely difficult for all of us to navigate life without James around, but Blake has had an especially difficult time. He looked up to his father so much, and I knew how much his heart ached at the thought of coming home without his dad here. Takin' the trip back with you seemed to make it a little bit easier on him, and I will always be grateful to you for that."

"I am so glad that I was able to help him," Laney replied, trying to hold back a sudden flow of emotions. "I can't imagine what it was like for you, after losing James—then not seeing Blake for so long. Having him that far away must be tough. But I guess I'll understand that part soon enough," she sighed.

Diane could sense the shift in Laney's mood, so she squeezed her hand a bit tighter.

"When I said, 'thank you for bringin' my Blake back,' it wasn't just because you drove him home. You brought him back to life, Laney. I had not seen such joy in his eyes or heard a genuine laugh from him since before his father passed. But seein' him with you has given me hope that his heart is finally mendin'. And that is not somethin' I can ever repay you for."

"I think I might be falling for him," Laney mindlessly blurted out before her brain caught on to what her heart was doing. "And I don't know what to do, Diane. His life is in L.A., and mine is in Salt Lake City. And we *just* met! He could walk away in five minutes and pretend I never existed. He could just move on and rip my heart out, and I would be left with a huge void. What if he hurts me, and I was foolish enough to let him?"

"Well, as his mother, I can tell you he's not that kind of man. He means what he says and keeps his promises. So if he says he cares about you, then he does," she reassured Laney.

"Even still, I don't know if we will even fit in the real world. His path is so different from mine, but I can't imagine moving forward without at least trying to see what could be. I know this whole thing is ludicrous, and I'm completely blind-sided by how fast I let my defenses down with him. But I don't know what will happen after I leave."

"Oh sweetheart, I knew from the second I saw you two in my diner that you both were developin' feelin's for each other. I've never seen him look at anyone the way he looks at you," Diane began. "And I'm not sure I have the answer for you, as far as what steps to take next. But I do know a thing or two about love—and it always finds a way. Fate has stepped in more than once already to pull you two together. Sometimes, you just have to do your part to help it along." Then, she paused for a moment before continuing, "When you love someone, it's like carryin' a canoe together. Sometimes, you feel far apart. Sometimes, you can't see the path ahead of you, and you have to trust that your partner is going the right way. Sometimes, it's like you're not even walkin' on the same trail. Sometimes, you feel like you've got your own struggles, and he's got his own, and you're both going through it alone. But at the end of the day, you're both still carryin' the same canoe. As long as you don't drop your end, you're a team, and you'll find your way."

Laney wiped a tear welling up in her eyes. "Thank you, Diane. I needed some motherly advice today," she said softly.

"Oh sweetheart, it's my pleasure. Now, let's let go of the heavy stuff and fill our bellies. I'm starvin'!"

"So, Mom tells me you brought a girl home with you," Blake's sister, Danielle, pressed while his manager was on another call.

"Well, I didn't exactly bring her home. If anything, she brought me home," he corrected with sarcasm. Danielle shoved his arm playfully. "But seriously, her name is Laney. She's a nurse and a Lyft driver, and she's pretty great." He grinned like a fool.

"Does Joe know? He hates to be the last to find out things like this."

"No, I haven't told him yet. And I'd like to stop talking about this now before he clicks back over to our call and overhears us," Blake said emphatically.

"Overhears what?" Joe asked loudly, as he clicked over from his other call.

"Oh, nothing. We were just talking logistics of Sunday dinner with the family," Blake fibbed.

"Okay, well, we don't have time to discuss dinner plans now, do we?" Joe laughed condescendingly. "The publisher is on board with the changes we've discussed, and I'll be sending proofs to you soon." Joe rattled off a long list without pausing for Blake to respond, then added, "Have a nice holiday, and I'll see you back here in the sunshine next year." Then, he abruptly hung up the phone.

Blake glared at Danielle. "That was a bit too close for comfort. You know he hates it when I take over my own personal life."

"Heaven forbid!" Danielle mocked. "You deserve parts of you that he doesn't dictate, Blake. If you like this girl, see where it leads without worrying about your career for once."

"I know, but I feel like I owe him because he helped me get my big break."

"Yeah, he did. But he doesn't own you. You need to loosen the chain he's got you on, brother, or you'll start to feel less like a man and more like a dog."

"Easier said than done. But I'm trying. Now, I was going to bring her over to meet you when she gets back. Don't be all weird and smiley, okay? You might freak her out."

"Weird and smiley? What does that even mean? I'm perfectly normal," she defended, sticking her tongue out at him.

"Yeah, right. And then your voice gets all high-pitched, and you start oversharing until you've told some story about how I ran around outside as a kid wearing nothing but a cape and a grin. You know, 'weird and smiley.'"

"I don't even know where you're getting this from," she teasingly scoffed with a mischievous sparkle in her eyes. "I won't embarrass you one bit."

"I'm not so confident about that...but I do know you'll like her. She's amazing." He beamed.

"Well, we'll see how she handles my 'weird and smiley' personality," she said, crossing her arms over her chest.

Laney and Diane pulled into the driveway just after 2 p.m. and found Blake and Danielle sitting in the kitchen, poring over something on her laptop. After sitting in the same place at the table for hours, the interruption was welcomed with open arms.

"Hey! How was shopping?" Danielle greeted them as she stood and stretched.

"We had a blast, didn't we?" Diane replied, wrapping an arm around Laney's waist.

"It was perfect," Laney replied with a shy nod.

"Glad to hear it," Blake said, his face lighting up. "I hope you found everything you needed." Then, he grabbed his sister by the shoulders and led her across the room. "Dannie, I'd like you to meet Laney. Laney, this is my favorite sister, Danielle."

"I'm your only sister, so I'm your favorite by default," Danielle said, laughing. "Laney, it's nice to meet you." As she shook Laney's hand, she slowed her movements and furrowed her brow. "Have we met before? You seem so familiar."

"I'm not sure," replied Laney, "but you seem familiar too."

"Nurse Laney!" shouted Danielle's son Noah from the hallway as he ran over to hug her.

Laney stood there in disbelief. She did know this family! But the last time she saw them, Noah was a sick little boy with no hair, and Danielle was a worried mother with dark circles under her eyes.

"Noah, you've gotten so big!" Laney exclaimed as she knelt down to hug him back. "You must be, what, ten years old now?" she teased.

"No way! I'm just five. I had my birthday at Thanksgiving time!" He pulled away and enthusiastically patted her face. "I got a dinosaur and a robot!"

"That's right!" Danielle recalled enthusiastically. "You helped take care of him when he saw the specialists in Salt Lake City. I knew I'd seen you before. What a small world this is!"

"Are you Uncle Blake's girlfriend now?" Noah asked innocently.

Laney blushed a bit and smiled up at Blake before replying, "I am Uncle Blake's good friend." She stumbled on her words, unsure of how to answer the question.

"Oh, okay!" Noah replied, smiling up at her. And as he ran off down the hallway, he shouted, "I hope you get to come and play with us lots more!"

After Noah left, Danielle turned and looked directly at Laney. "I don't think you realize how much of an impact you had on us. There were so many sleepless nights where I wasn't sure we'd get to Noah's next birthday. Thank you for being there to cheer him on from the sidelines and for the support you showed to Ryan and me. I don't know how I'll ever repay you for all you did for us. Thank you," she expressed, wiping tears from her eyes.

Instinctively, Laney reached out and wrapped Danielle in a big hug. "You have no idea how much I needed to hear those words," she replied. "Lately, I have struggled with feeling like I don't make a difference, so it's nice to hear that I have."

From down the hallway, the echoes of baby cries interrupted their conversation.

"Sounds like the twins are up from their naps," Danielle said hurriedly. "Laney, I'm so glad you've come back into our lives again."

"This was such a pleasant surprise!"

"It really was," Danielle hugged Laney tightly and whispered in her ear, "You've made my brother happy again. He has needed you more than you know."

"I've needed him too," Laney whispered back as Danielle let go and disappeared down the hallway.

Blake stood in the doorway of the guest bedroom while Laney put her shopping bags away and hung up her purse.

"Don't hang your coat just yet," Blake said.

"I've got a surprise for you. Let's go!" Blake led her to an old shop out in the backyard and covered her eyes.

"There's someone I want you to meet," he said as he opened the door and flipped on the light, illuminating an object hidden under a canvas sheet. "Okay, you can open your eyes now."

The moment Laney opened her eyes, Blake grabbed the edge of the drape and pulled, sending dust flying through the air, revealing a fully restored, cherry red, 1971 Ford Bronco.

"Laney, this is Scarlett," Blake introduced proudly.

"Wow! She's a beauty!" Laney exclaimed, walking over and running her fingers across the shiny front fender. "Did you restore her yourself?"

"Yeah, my dad and I did after I got my driver's license," Blake recalled nostalgically. "We had some of our best times out here working on her—both our hands covered in grease, hours on end talking about everything under the sun. He became my best friend after that summer. My admiration for him grew so much when I saw the amount of sacrifice he made to spend all that time with me. He turned down offers to go on fishing trips with the guys and invites to Boise State football games. He even worked overtime to help me save up for a new engine. I'm not sure I realized just how much he cared about me until we fixed her up together. Scarlett will always be something I treasure because she brought me closer to my dad."

"I love that," Laney said softly, stepping back to admire her.

"Let's take her out for a spin." He grinned. "It's been way too long."

He opened the passenger door for Laney and lifted her inside, their faces brushing together. He lingered for a moment, causing Laney's heart to race, then stepped back and closed the door. He walked around the front of the Bronco and glanced at Laney through the windshield as he wiped a smudge from the hood. Then, he climbed into the driver's seat and wrapped his fingers around the steering wheel. A boyish excitement spread across his face as he started up the car.

"She sure puts some thunder in your chest, doesn't she?" Laney said loudly over the roar of the engine.

"Yeah, she does!" Blake replied excitedly, putting it in reverse.

As the smalltown streetlights of Juniper Hills passed outside the window, Laney asked, "Where are we going?"

"Wherever Scarlett wants," Blake said glancing in Laney's direction. "Man, it feels good to sit behind the wheel again. The last time I drove her…"

he trailed off. "My dad and I were going fishing. Gosh, I'm so glad I took the time to come home. That was the last time I saw him."

Laney gently covered his hand with hers on the gear shifter.

"But we aren't focusing on the sad things today. I wallowed yesterday. Today is all about you," Blake added.

"We definitely need some music, though," Laney insisted. "You can't ride in a pretty gal like this without something blasting."

"Will you just push play on my phone, please?" he requested, handing his phone over to her.

Laney pushed play, and jazz music came on over the speakers. Blake slowed Scarlett down at a red light and climbed out.

"Where are you going?!" Laney yelled in shock as he crossed in front of the car.

He opened her door and extended his hand to her. "I can't very well let your favorite Louis Armstrong song play without dancing with you," he answered. Then he led to the front of the Bronco and pulled her in close to him, and began to sway to the music in the snowy street.

Cars drove past on the opposite side of the road and whistled at them as he spun her around. And when the light turned green, people patiently went around them as if what they were doing was a normal occurrence in Juniper Hills.

Laney rested her head on his shoulder, breathing him in deeply. Never in a million years had she imagined her life would go this way. His muscular arms wrapped around her tightly, and she swayed with his strong body. There was so much about him that made her feel like she was finally safe—that no matter what, Blake was in her corner, cheering her on. With him by her side, she could do anything. If he asked her to fly, she'd grow wings and soar. There was something to be said about a person who can give you both wings to fly and roots to grow. Whatever came next for the two of them, Laney decided she didn't want fear to keep her from trying. After all, destiny had a hand in this whole thing, and she couldn't deny it. When the song ended, Blake gave her one more tight squeeze before he helped her up into the passenger seat again.

"That was probably the most romantic thing someone has ever done for me," she gushed as they drove off down the road.

"Seriously? You dated the wrong guys then. You deserve so much more than a dance in the street, and they were idiots not to see that."

Blake pulled into a parking lot and killed the engine. "I thought we could spend our last night together—"

"At a grocery store? How romantic!" Laney teased.

Blake laughed. "No, silly, I want to cook for you. But I need some ingredients first. You're such a diva," he chaffed, taking her hand as they walked into the store

Laney giggled. "It's your fault for not seeing my high-maintenance ways before now. They flash around me like a neon sign. Now you're stuck trying to please me," she joked.

"Not stuck, just lucky." He turned to her and smiled.

Laney's face warmed. It was nice to feel important to someone, especially to a guy like Blake.

"Truth be told, I'd go anywhere with you—even the grocery store—and it would be nice because I'd be with you." She smiled, her eyes sparkling. "I'd drive through a snowstorm in heavy traffic and even get a flat tire if it meant that I got to be with you."

Blake wrapped his arm around her and kissed the top of her head. "I know exactly what you mean."

Back at Diane's cottage, they spread the ingredients out on the kitchen counter to make a gourmet meal.

"Mom is working late at the diner tonight, so we have the whole house to ourselves for the next few hours. I want to spend every minute with you until you go, and I wish we didn't have to sleep."

"I feel the same way," Laney murmured as she slid up behind him and wrapped her arms around his waist. She could feel his washboard abs through his T-shirt, which made her heart race. She rested her head against his muscular back and sighed. If she could bottle this feeling, his scent, his warmth, and this moment, she would.

Blake took one hand away from washing the vegetables and held hers. He raised it up to his lips and kissed it softly before letting it drop back down on his chest. The pounding of his heart matched hers, and she was glad to know that at least she was in good company.

"What can I do to help?" Laney offered, pulling herself back into reality.

"Will you grab me that cutting board?" he asked.

Blake began chopping vegetables and sautéing them on the stove. The kitchen filled with happy sounds and laughter mixed with pans clanking. Laney snuck a taste of the sauce simmering on the stove and closed her eyes as the flavors danced on her tongue. She tried to ditch her used spoon in the sink, but Blake turned, catching her red-handed.

"It's supposed to be a surprise!" he chided, stealing the spoon away from her.

"I couldn't help it!" Laney protested with a guilty pout. "It smells so good that it practically begged me to taste it."

"You're trouble, Campbell," Blake replied, shaking his head.

When the food was ready, Blake lit candles on the table and poured them each a glass of wine.

"So, what do you think?" Blake asked between bites.

"This tastes as good as it looks. It's delicious. Now I completely understand why people can be so obsessed with food. It's an art form when done right. Is this recipe going to be in your cookbook?" Laney inquired.

"Yes. This one holds special meaning for me because it's the first meal my mom ever cooked for my dad when they were dating. He once told me, 'Son, after I tasted that meal, I knew right then and there that I wanted to marry her. She stole my heart through my stomach!' It's only fitting to include the recipe that got me here in the first place."

"They must've been great together, huh?"

"Oh, yeah. You know those solid couples who have each other's backs no matter what? That was my mom and dad. I've always wanted a love like that. Not just true love but being married to your best friend, you know?" Blake said as he looked into her eyes. "They were the type that would dance in the kitchen and talk on the porch swing for hours. I've never wanted anything else but that."

"That's a good thing to want. Love and passion are great, but if you can lean up against your best friend through the hard times, then you've got it made, that's for sure," Laney said, returning his gaze.

With as quickly as they fell for each other, Laney wondered if they would develop a friendship over the long distance. A flame like theirs can fizzle out if it's solely based on chemistry. Only time would tell if there were more to grow in the distance.

Laney reached across the table and took Blake's hand. The thought of leaving tomorrow made her feel like she'd get sucked into a vortex of dread if she didn't hang on to something real in front of her. She tried her best to focus on this moment—as fleeting as it was. Ignoring the countdown clock ticking away in the back of her mind was proving to be more and more difficult. So after they finished eating, Laney turned her focus to cleaning up instead.

Chapter 11

Laney tossed and turned in bed with overwhelming thoughts raging inside her mind. She wasn't ready to leave in the morning and as much as she tried to push them away, they kept returning to haunt her. Laney wondered what would happen with her and Blake, and the looming dawn made her sick inside. After staring at the ceiling for hours, she decided to get up and look for some chamomile tea.

The dark hallways and rooms took on a life of their own as she paced the house. She was a ghost, aimlessly wandering around with a cup of tea that she was too distracted to drink. A light flickered on outside, and she tip-toed over to the window to get a closer look. It was high up in the yard, and it stood out like a lighthouse in the middle of a dark winter night. She grabbed her boots and coat and went outside to investigate. As she neared the light, the soft play of music became louder, and she realized it was coming from Blake's old tree house. It loomed over the yard and seemed to stretch taller when she stood at the base of it and looked up. She hesitated with her hands on the rung in front of her, weighing the pros and cons of fulfilling her curiosity, versus falling and freezing to death. Ultimately, curiosity won the battle, and she began to climb, gingerly at first but getting bolder and bolder as she neared the top. When she got to the door of the tree house, she paused to catch her breath. As she stood there, Blake flung open the door, startling her.

"I thought I heard someone walking around out there. I'm just glad it's you and not a mountain lion." He grinned.

"Wait, there are mountain lions out here?!" Laney glanced nervously around and rushed inside, pushing past him.

Blake snickered. "Not usually, but thanks for that reaction. It was exactly what I was going for."

Laney playfully smacked his arm. "Haha. Very funny."

She glanced around at the inside of the tree house; windows lined three walls, and a giant orange couch sat under the largest window across the room. She crossed the floor, pivoted, and sat down on the couch. "So, this is the tree house where Blake Logan's deepest thinking happened, huh?"

"Yeah." He smiled. "And also the most hours logged on a Gameboy ever, probably. I rescued Zelda sitting in a bean bag chair in that corner over there," he said, pointing across the room.

"Nice," she said nodding. "So, what are you doing out here in the middle of the night? I assume it's not to brush up on your mad gaming skills."

"Unfortunately not. Although that sounds like more fun than insomnia," he answered with a sigh, sitting down next to her.

"What's on your mind? Anything you want to talk about?" she asked as she turned to face him.

"I'm just not ready for this to be over," Blake replied. "I have so many more things I want to do with you before you leave. There are so many conversations we haven't had and so many things about you that I don't know yet. Like what your favorite color is, your favorite ice cream flavor, and what is it about you that I find so irresistible. And then there's the question of what happens next. Do we say goodbye and go our separate ways, or do we try and see if this can work?" Blake turned to face her with uncertainty in his eyes.

Her eyes reflected the same uncertainty as he laced his fingers into hers.

After a few beats, she said, "Purple, anything with dark chocolate and nuts, and honestly, I'm not sure what you see in me, Blake. I've been asking myself that question all weekend. I'm not like the women in L.A., and I'm okay with that. But I don't fit into a world where all the women wear fancy shoes, have perfect makeup, and carry small pets in a designer bag. Most days, I wear boots or scrubs and a ponytail, and I don't think my cat would appreciate me cramming him into my purse."

Blake laughed at the image her words painted. "I like a girl who can be spontaneous and go somewhere at the drop of a hat without needing to primp first. A girl who can rock a ponytail, change a flat tire, and hold her own against a manner-less cab driver. You, Delaney Campbell, have swept me off my feet with barely a word, and you stripped me of my defenses in less than a day. You captivate me with your zest for life. And it's kind of my favorite that your smile lights up your whole face."

Laney smiled bashfully, lowering her head to tuck her hair behind her ear.

"Yeah, just like that," he said. "And your eyes, they smile too. They turn into these cute little crescent-moons. And I love that you have like, eighteen dimples in your cheeks. You exude joy, and to someone who doesn't encounter real joy often, it's like the prettiest sunset I've ever seen." He caressed her cheek with his thumb. "It's hard not to want to be around you. I need you. I've never met anyone who can steal my heart and kick my butt all at the same time." He laughed softly. "You are one of a kind, and I don't think I'll ever find someone quite like you again—even if I lived a thousand years. I don't know how we are going to make this happen, but I'd sure like to try."

"I'm game if you are." She smiled. "The whole idea of walking away from you tomorrow has made me sick inside. I'm pretty sure I paced a trail in your mom's kitchen floor. And I don't know what else to do either, but after a rough year, I make me feel like I can finally breathe again. I don't want to go back to the way things were before I knew you."

Blake leaned in earnestly and kissed her. He had a vulnerability that she had not yet seen, and his need for her intensified his kiss, making it hard for Laney to catch her breath. Her hands wrapped around his neck and combed through his hair as he pulled her in, enveloping her in his strong arms. His body felt like home, and his kiss, like a warm summer day. This was a place where she could live forever.

Laney pulled back, resting her forehead against his. "So, there's something we need to do before I go tomorrow," Laney said, fixing the mess she made to his hair.

"Yeah? And what's that?"

"We haven't exchanged ornaments yet. Hmm, I know!" Her eyes lit up with excitement. You go get yours, I'll go get mine, and then we'll rendezvous back here in ten minutes and trade. Deal?"

Her enthusiasm made Blake laugh. "But I haven't wrapped yours yet."

"That's okay! I haven't wrapped yours either. We can just close our eyes and count to three." Laney said, jumping up from the couch and heading out the door.

"See you in a minute." She grinned and gave a tiny wave.

Blake rushed to his room and found the ornament in his suitcase. He found a pen and wrote a note as fast as he could for her to read later, then tucked it into the bag. Grabbing a blanket from his bed, he headed back toward the tree house.

Laney and Blake met at the gate to the yard and scurried back out to the tree house, giggling like kids who were going to be in trouble if they got caught. Cozying back up on the couch under Blake's blanket, they each closed their eyes in anticipation.

"Okay," Laney said. "On the count of three, I'll put my gift in your hands, and you put yours in mine. Ready?

"But wait! If we both have our eyes closed, how are we supposed to know we are hitting our target?" Blake wondered, cracking one eye open.

"Just do your best. Worst case scenario, they land in our laps," she replied. "Okay, One. Two. Three." When Blake opened his eyes, he was left with a small white box in his hand, and Laney had a brown bag from the festival dangling from her finger.

Blake laughed. "See? I almost missed!" He tapped the bag, making it swing.

"Close enough," she insisted. "I'm too excited to see you open yours. You go first."

Blake opened the box and immediately started laughing.

"This isn't an ornament!" He laughed, pulling out the ugliest purple socks he'd ever seen. "But they're awesome! The pineapples with sunglasses add the perfect touch!" he exclaimed. "I love them, and I think they're taking first place as my new favorite pair. Danielle will just have to understand." He continued as he slipped them on.

"I found them while shopping with your mom. Aren't they fun?"

"They're perfect! Thank you," he said, sticking his feet out to admire them.

"There's more," Laney said, nodding toward the box.

At the bottom of the box was a tree house ornament made out of polymer clay with red walls and one tiny window. It had a rickety, wood-like, blue roof, and it sat between some thick branches of a weathered tree. On the bottom, in permanent marker, Laney wrote:

"Blake, may this remind you that no matter where you are, you're never too far from your tree house. There's no place like home. Love, Laney 2021."

He smiled softly and looked up at her.

"This is amazing, I love it. I'm so excited to start my own 'ornament of the year' collection. And the best part is that my first one came from you." He leaned over and kissed her on the forehead. "Now it's your turn," he urged.

Laney opened the small brown bag and pulled out something wrapped in tissue paper. A note fell out of the bag at the same time, and Blake snapped it up.

"Save this for later," Blake said to her, placing the note back into the bag.

The weight of the ornament sat heavy in her hands as she unwrapped it. Inside the layers of tissue paper was a beautiful, hand-blown glass starfish. It was aqua, like the Caribbean Sea, and it sparkled, even in the low light.

"So you'll always remember the difference you make in this world— especially to me," Blake said, brushing her hair out her face.

"This is so beautiful, Blake. Thank you so much. It means more to me than you know," she said as she wrapped her arms around his neck and wrapped her arms around him. "You've made a difference in my world, too," she whispered in his ear. "How on earth am I going to be able to leave tomorrow?"

Chapter 12

The first rays of morning light filtered in through the white cotton curtains, stirring Laney from her slumber. The reality of the day clouded over her, and a knot of dread formed in her stomach. She wasted no time in getting dressed before rushing out of her room to find Blake.

"Good morning, Laney," Diane greeted, looking up from her tablet at the kitchen table.

"How did you sleep?"

"Off and on," she replied. "My brain wouldn't stop thinking about the looming dread today would bring." She yawned. "I was hoping that when I woke up, there would be another thing making me stay," she wished. "Like a tree falling in the canyon, another giant storm, a zombie apocalypse…I'm not picky." She grinned wryly.

Diane laughed into her coffee cup. "Oh sweetheart, I hoped for the same thing." She smiled a sad smile, then added with a wink, "Plus, if an apocalypse comes, I'm ready for it."

Laney burst out with a much-needed laugh and poured herself a cup of coffee.

"Have you seen Blake this morning yet?" Laney asked.

"No, I haven't. He might still be asleep," she replied.

"I think I'll go see if he's up," said Laney, carrying her cup of coffee out to the main house.

Down the hall, Blake's door was partially open, and she could see his freshly made bed from the doorway. Laney knocked softly.

"Blake? Are you in here?" she called out.

"Back here! Come on in!"

Laney followed his voice and found him shirtless, shaving at the bathroom sink. He stood with his athletic back facing her, a small towel draped over one of his broad shoulders. The two dimples in his lower back above the waistband of his basketball shorts drew her eyes slowly downward. He looked up in the mirror at her approaching and flashed a smile at her. His superhero physique was even better in person than it was in the movies, now that she could take the time to enjoy it.

Wow. I could never get sick of seeing this, Laney thought to herself as she approached.

He looked over his shoulder at her with a razor streak down his chiseled cheek. The smell of shaving cream filled her nostrils as the rest of Blake filled her eyes. She had briefly seen him shirtless before, but that was all for show. This time, it was just for her eyes, and she intended to see it all instead of turning away.

"Hey, beautiful!" he greeted with a blooming smile, rinsing his razor in the sink. "Did you get any sleep?"

"Not a lot, but some," she said, leaning against the door frame while she sipped her coffee. She couldn't tear her eyes away from him, and she wasn't even subtle about it. It was all she could do not to reach up and touch his soft skin as his back muscles flexed with his arm movements. She studied every razor stroke and expression on his face while he shaved. He focused intently on what he was doing, giving her the freedom to stare a bit too long. Watching a man shave was sexy, and it made her heart race as she memorized him. Although her brain was otherwise engaged, she still managed to squeak out, "Did you?"

"Not really. There was this girl I couldn't get off my mind." He beamed at her through the shaving cream, making her look away. "Come, sit. Talk to me while I finish," he said, patting the counter beside the sink.

She passed behind Blake and sat on the counter as his razor shaved away yesterday's stubble. Every movement was rhythmic and calculated; stroke, stroke, rinse, repeat. It was like a very masculine, very attractive dance, and she was mesmerized. A few stray water droplets ran down his chest and washboard abs, and it was hard for Laney not to be envious of their journey.

Blake saw her watching and handed her the razor. "You look pretty focused there." He laughed. "Wanna try?"

"Oh no," Laney replied, hesitating a bit. "What if I cut your jugular?" She shook her head, pushing the razor back toward him.

"Then it was intentional, nurse." Blake laughed. "Go on, give it a try. Plus, you women shave a lot more risky places than men do. I trust you." With a huge grin, he handed the razor to her again.

"Okaaaaay," she relented, pausing for a moment as she set her coffee cup down and took the razor from his hand. "So, you go with the grain, not against it, right?" she asked as she raised the razor to his gorgeous face. She shaved slowly around his strong jaw, tipping his head back as she went.

Being this close to Blake gave her the opportunity to study every inch of his face. She took in the subtle flecks of green sprinkled throughout his blue eyes. She memorized the curve of his nose, the edges of his cheekbones, the depth of his dimples, and the soft pink of his lips.

He focused intently on her as she touched his face after each razor stroke.

"If you keep looking at me like that, I'm gonna mess up," she warned playfully.

"I can't help it. It's hard to resist when I'm this close to you."

"Resist what?"

"Everything," he whispered as his eyes sparkled with mischief.

"Yeah, well, imagine my plight then, with all this going on." She motioned to his muscular body. "I'm far worse off, distraction-wise."

He looked away and laughed. "Sorry. Continue then. I'll just barely look at you then. Don't slit my throat." He grinned, causing his dimples to dive deep into his cheeks.

He placed his hand on her thigh as she worked. His thumb caressed her knee softly. "It's hard to hold still when your face is this close, you know," he flirted.

Her eyes met his, and they held their stare, neither of them saying anything yet saying everything all at once.

"Well, the only thing keeping me from kissing you is the fact that you have shaving cream all over your face."

"Let's just wipe it all off then. I don't mind a half-shaven face," Blake replied, grabbing at the towel on his shoulder.

Laney laughed. "I'm almost done. Hold on a few minutes longer." She shook her head and smiled at him. "You are nothing but trouble. You know that?"

"I'll take that as a compliment," he said as he moved his focus from her lips to a scar on her forehead.

"How did you get this scar?" he asked, brushing it with his thumb.

"It was from a wild pitch my brother Levi threw me when I was eight years old—it split me right open," Laney recalled with a wince. "The giant goose egg disappeared after a few days, but the urge to run from his fastball never went away." She chuckled. "That was the price I paid for growing up with brothers. I got a lot of bumps and stitches."

Laney turned to the sink and rinsed the razor for the last time. "So, how did I do?" She smiled with satisfaction, running her hands across his smooth face.

"Well, I'm not bleeding to death, so I'd say pretty good!" Blake replied, laughing. "Now for the finishing touch," he breathed as he pulled her close and kissed her softly. "Mmm, that's better."

Laney wiped a remnant of shaving cream from her lip as he rinsed his face and dried off.

"Wanna get some breakfast with me?" she asked.

"Of course!" he replied, splashing a bit of aftershave on. It smelled nice, not overpowering but woodsy and masculine, like a modern-day lumberjack. "Let me throw on a shirt."

"Well, if you must…" she teased as she looked at his chest.

Blake raised an eyebrow and grinned as his cheeks reddened. He ran his fingers demurely through his wild morning hair and pulled a T-shirt over his head.

"What did you have in mind?" he asked. "Do you want to eat here or head to the diner?"

"Can we cook here together one more time?" Laney asked.

"I was hoping you'd say that." He took her hand as they walked down the hall.

Blake and Laney walked through the door of the cottage and saw Diane standing at the sink, washing her coffee cup. She looked up and smiled at the two of them as they took their snowy shoes off at the door.

"Hey, you two! I've got to get to the diner soon, but help yourselves to whatever is in the fridge, okay? Blake, make her one of your famous omelets. Laney, you'll thank me later. His omelets are the best. Come see me at the diner before you leave, will ya, dear? I'll have a bagged lunch ready for your drive." She set her mug on the drying board and headed down the hallway.

"Of course, I will! Thank you for letting me stay," Laney called after her. Then she turned to Blake and said, "An omelet sounds great."

"As you wish," he replied, grinning over his shoulder as he opened the fridge to get the eggs.

Those soft words filled Laney with a sensation she never wanted to fade. He electrified her, causing her blood to rush and her heart to race. She pulled up a barstool and rested her chin on her hand as she watched him prepare her breakfast. He began chopping the ingredients on the counter, his hands making the task look effortless.

"What can I do to help?" she asked.

"Stay right there and keep me company," Blake replied with a wink. "I want to spoil you this morning."

His presence in her life started out as a casual happenstance, but it rapidly grew into everything she never knew she needed. And now she was expected to drive away like he hadn't just stolen her heart, leaving her with a vacant hole in her chest. She swallowed hard, pushing away the ache that rose in her throat.

"So, what are your plans for the holidays?" she asked.

"I plan to wallow in self-pity here at home without you until the new year." Blake let out a low laugh. "But seriously, I need a break from L.A., so I'm going to hang out here for a while."

"Well, if you find yourself wanting to hit the slopes, come see me in Salt Lake. We have the greatest snow on earth, you know," she told him. "And I know a great Lyft driver who could get you around."

"That sounds like fun." He looked up from his cutting board. "I just might take you up on that."

After breakfast was cleaned up, Blake left to get dressed while Laney went back to her room. She wrote a thank you note to Diane for her hospitality, and left it on the dresser. Laney's phone chimed as a text message came in from Angela. There was a photo attached with the message:

Angela: Your secret is out, girl. I'm sorry.

She opened the message to see a photo of her and Blake at the festival. Then another message came in with a link to the tabloid that had posted the photo online.

"*Blake Logan with Mystery Woman!*" the title screamed. She hesitated before clicking on the article. There were several photos of them from the festival that day, smiling at each other, laughing, and having lunch at the diner. Someone had photographed them all over town and outed them to the tabloids. A ball of lead formed in her stomach. She had been betrayed by someone she'd never even met, and although she wasn't exactly surprised by it, it stung. She gripped her phone with shaky hands and ran out to find Blake.

Blake stood out on the patio, his shoulders tense, his knuckles white with anger as he clenched his hand around his phone.

"Shirtless at the airport and tossing autographed clothes to fans is what you're supposed to be photographed doing, Blake! Not looking committed and twitterpated with some wholesome, small-town country bumpkin!" Joe, Blake's manager, yelled over speakerphone.

From her side of the door, the conversation looked heated, so Laney stood there for a moment before opening the door.

Blake's voice grew impatient. "There's nothing going on with me and her, Joe. She was my Lyft driver, that's it. We got stranded in that town for a little while because we had some car trouble, so we wandered around the festival for a bit. The photos were taken way out of context. You know I don't do relationships... Relax, Joe, I have it taken care of. Release a statement saying these photos are a misunderstanding and that it was nothing. Don't worry. It'll blow over. I'll lay low here for a bit and let the dust settle."

Laney felt like she had been kicked in the gut by a horse. Before Blake knew she was there, she pivoted on her heels and rushed back to her room.

Blake heard the door shut and looked over his shoulder to see Laney rushing away. His stomach sunk, and the joy he felt earlier disappeared to make room for the dread that took over. He dropped the phone to his side, but Joe still scolded from the other end of the receiver. Blake's heavy feet dragged as he started to run after her.

"Joe, I gotta go," Blake shouted, hanging up the phone.

Laney stood in her guest room crying as she crammed her belongings into her overnight bag. She refused to look at Blake when he came into the room.

"How much did you hear?" he asked quietly.

"Enough," Laney growled. "How could I be so stupid? I pushed away every nagging thought that this couldn't possibly be real. I gave you the benefit of the doubt and allowed myself to let you in. I am such a fool!" Her tears fell faster than she could catch them, and they soaked her cheeks. "You used me for whatever sick game you were playing. I can't believe I trusted you! This whole time, you promised me authenticity. And you lied," she sobbed.

He reached out to touch her, but she fought hard against him and pushed him away. "Please, Laney, let me explain."

"Oh, you've explained all you need to, to whoever was on the phone. I'm 'just your Lyft driver. Everything else was a misunderstanding,' right? Isn't that what you said?"

"That was Joe, my manager, on the phone. He saw an article with photos of us from the festival, and he called me, all upset. Honestly, it's none of his business what I'm doing here with you, and I don't want him to meddle in my personal life. He thinks everything is a business move. If he had his way, I'd be a single bachelor forever. It's good for both our careers, supposedly. But I don't want that, Laney. Everything that happened between us this weekend *is* real. I didn't lie to you. Everything was real for me. But Joe doesn't need to know that. He wouldn't understand."

"Yeah, well, it was real to me too," she choked. "But how can I trust what you say anymore? This is exactly what I was afraid of, becoming another conquest to you!"

She grabbed her bags and shoved past him, out the front door and into the snow. She fumbled with her keys through the tears, which made it impossible to see the buttons to unlock her car. Blake ran up behind her, panting behind a cloud of steam.

"Please don't go. Not like this. Please, Laney, I can't lose you. Just…will you just wait a minute? Please let me explain," he begged, trying to stop her hand from opening the trunk. He blinked back tears, and he fought frantically to hang on to whatever shred of their relationship was left.

"Don't call me 'Laney'. That name is for people who care about me! And I'm obviously nothing to you!" she shouted as she threw her bags in the trunk and slammed it shut. "And apparently, you were never even mine to lose, so what is the point, Blake?"

Laney pushed past him and flung the driver's side door open and hastily got in and buckled her seatbelt.

"Please, please stop. Don't leave like this. Please just give me five minutes to explain," Blake pleaded.

Ignoring his pleas, Laney yanked the door closed behind her, almost crushing his hand, and started the car. Blake backed away as she threw the car in reverse and stepped on the gas pedal. Her tires spun out on the snow as she tore out of the driveway, and as quickly as she came into his life, she was gone.

Blake stood with tears running down his face as he watched her taillights disappear down the road. "This can't be the way things end," he said aloud before picking up his phone and calling his mom.

"Mom, I messed up. She overheard me talking on the phone to Joe. I told him that the latest tabloid photos of us weren't real, and that it was all a misunderstanding. I didn't know she was standing there. I tried to explain to her why I said those things to him, but she wouldn't listen. Please, if she comes by the diner, please talk to her. I can't let her leave like this. This can't be it."

"I'll do my best, honey," Diane replied with sadness in her tone. "She just pulled up. I've gotta go," she added, hanging up the phone.

Laney stepped into the cafe, red-faced and puffy-eyed. Diane rushed past the counter and wrapped her arms around her.

"Oh sweetheart, I heard what happened. Are you okay?" she asked, ushering her back into the kitchen to talk.

"I don't know what to think, Diane," Laney said, dropping down on an upside-down milk crate next to the fridge. "I thought we had something, you know? Then what I overheard him saying to his manager pulled the rug right out from under me." Diane handed her a napkin from the dispenser and she wiped her tears.

"Laney, listen to me. You two *do* have something special. I have never seen Blake look at anyone the way he looks at you. It was not a misunderstanding. You know it, and Blake knows it. But you have to understand something, sweetheart. A manager like Joe can have a lot of sway over Blake's career. If he doesn't like something Blake does, he can use it to manipulate him. Auditions will get overlooked or 'forgotten,' and he could even be blacklisted if he doesn't toe the line. Unless Joe is happy, no one is happy. But he's good at his job, and he is partially responsible for Blake's success. Until you came along, Blake didn't care about the relationship demands Joe had. Blake hasn't ever had to deal with really caring about someone around Joe yet, and he made a mistake, dear."

"It's just so confusing. I can't kick the thought that this was all an act for Blake," Laney sniffed. "And I look like such a fool…" She buried her head in her hands. "Whether it was true or not, he said it. How can I get past it and forgive him, much less trust him again?"

"Maybe you need to take a few days and breathe," Diane suggested. "Blake's feelings won't change for you that easily. Give yourself some time to think about all this, and you'll understand his reasons for saying them."

"I'm not so sure," Laney muttered. "I don't want to walk away from him like this, but I'm struggling to determine what's real and what's not." "Do what you need to do, Laney. But remember the good more than the bad. The man you spent time with here is real. Every bit of him, just like the boy I raised. And a weekend filled with lovely times together can't possibly be wiped out by a few untrue words. Blake never meant to hurt you, that I know. Take a look at this. This is not pretense; this is real, honey," Diane said, pulling up the photo on her phone of both Blake and Laney asleep on the couch.

Laney took the phone and studied the photo for a minute. She was right; it did look real. She touched the screen, caressing his face with her fingertips. He looked so warm in that golden morning light, so at peace with her in his arms. She pushed the phone back to Diane.

"I need some time to think," Laney whispered, standing up to leave. "Thanks for the advice," she said as Diane handed her a to-go bag. "I really do appreciate all you've done for me this weekend. Thank you," she said again as she hugged her. "I'll see you later."

Laney climbed back in her car and turned the ignition on. Before she let her heart talk her head out of leaving, she sped off down the road toward the canyon. Laney searched through her playlists for music to get her mind off things. The drive would be too long in the silence of her thoughts, but her go-to girl power playlist just reminded her of Blake. And so did the soundtracks and love songs. She threw her phone down on the passenger seat in frustration and resorted to driving in silence. Laney's thoughts rushed back to that morning with Blake. Watching him shave. Laughing with him while he made her the best omelet ever, and sitting together in the sunlight having coffee.

Tears stung her eyes as she drove, and no matter how hard she tried, every train of thought led right back to Blake. She knew she had feelings for him. She knew this was the risk she was taking, yet she did it anyway. That had to count for something, right? Because in the end, she was at least grateful that after all she had been through, she still took a chance on love. The miles dragged on as her mind reeled. No matter how she spun it or which scenarios she thought about, she knew she would still have feelings for Blake. Though she fell fast, she still fell—and hard. But Blake's words to Joe echoed through her mind, and her throat tightened as she tried to quell her emotion. She was angry at herself for letting her guard down so easily. She had allowed him to scale the walls around her heart with ease, leaving her defenseless against his charm. He was a dream come true, everything she'd ever wanted in a relationship—laughter, passion, fun, trust, and respect. He knew more about what was behind the curtain than most, and in one fell swoop, he toppled her house of cards. She was angry at him for taking advantage of her weakened state, then setting fire to her fortress.

The miles stretched on behind her, passing much quicker with good tires and fair weather. Her brain switched to auto-pilot mode, and left her more time to think while she drove. In the quiet, Angela's ringtone suddenly broke the silence from the passenger seat, pulling her from her thoughts. She answered with shaking hands and a raw throat.

"Hey, Ange," she said tearfully.

"Oh no, girl, what's wrong?" Angela replied, her voice filled with concern.

"I'm on my way back home. Everything fell apart this morning before I left," Laney cried. "I've been bawling my eyes out this whole drive. I'm about an hour away, now. Can you meet me at my house so we can talk? I could really use a friend right now."

"Of course, I will. And I'll bring the ice cream," Angela assured her. "See you in a bit, Lane."

Laney hung up the phone and noticed she had three text messages from Blake and one from Diane. Ignoring the messages, she tossed her phone into her unzipped purse and gripped the steering wheel with both hands. Her head pounded from all the crying, but she wiped her eyes and pressed onward.

"**I**'m so glad you're here," Laney said as Angela walked through the front door. "Thanks for coming to help me wallow in self-pity."

"That's what friends are for," Angela replied. "Now come sit down and tell me all about it," she said, patting the couch beside her. She handed Laney her favorite pint of ice cream and a spoon.

"You know when you instantly connect with someone? Like your souls have been familiar long before your eyes ever met? That's how it felt at the festival. He was comfortable with me. We laughed, we shared things strangers don't usually share, and I fell hard. At least I did…" Laney trailed off.

"So, tell me about these photos that were posted," Angela probed, pulling them up on her phone. "You guys look really into each other, Lane. Look at the way you guys are looking at each other! This looks pretty real to me!"

"We got a flat tire in the middle of nowhere on our drive up. The spare was flat too, so we walked to the nearest town. We had to wait for my car to be towed into town, then wait for a new tire. So the mechanic suggested we go check out this little Christmas festival. These photos are from that. I'm not even sure who took them. I know he's a celebrity and that this is normal life for him, but it felt so weird for this small-town nobody to be thrown into that. We thought we were blending in pretty well, and anyone who seemed to recognize him was at least respectful about it, but I guess not." Laney frowned.

"Wow," Angela rasped, surprised. "It's crazy to think that someone would stoop so low. But before everything went pear-shaped, you at least had a great time, right? That has to count for something."

"Ange, he was so amazing!" Laney cried. "We had the best conversations! We laughed and sang in the car, he showed me the quirky socks he wears, and he opened up about his family and his dad's passing. We just—clicked," Laney said, wiping her cheeks with her palms. "I was completely convinced that he cared about me, you know? I feel like such a fool for not being smarter. But he was good, you know? Pulling out all the stops. Playing my favorite song and dancing with me in the middle of the street, cooking for me, holding my hand. And let's not even talk about how it felt when we kissed…"

"Um, yes! Let's do talk about that!" Angela exclaimed.

"Yeah, why not? The wound is still gaping open; let's pour some salt in it." She exhaled sharply and tried to laugh through her tears. "It was seriously like an out-of-body experience. It was that amazing! I'm surprised I didn't float off of the ground." She let out another sigh. "Oh, and I walked in on him shirtless this morning, shaving, so…yeah. That won't be something I'll ever be able to erase from my memory. I could've done my laundry on his washboard abs." Her smile rose at the thought and then fell when she continued. "But then, this morning, his manager Joe called, and he was really mad because of the photos. Apparently, Blake is less marketable if he's not single. So he told Joe that the pictures were nothing but a big misunderstanding and that I was just his Lyft driver." Her chin trembled. "I walked in on the conversation right at that part. It killed me, Ange. And when he realized I'd heard, he tried to backpedal, saying he said those things to get his nosy manager off his back. But I don't know what to believe."

Angela wrapped Laney in a warm, supportive hug. "I'm sorry, Lane. Having the rug pulled out from under you like that is the worst. However, I can't help but think, maybe he was telling the truth. I saw the pictures. You both looked like you were falling hard. Maybe he didn't want Joe to know about you because he really does care about you. Did you ever think about that? From what you've said, I honestly don't think he was lying to you. Maybe he was just trying to protect you." Angela rationalized, making perfect sense to everything but Laney's broken heart.

"Yeah, well, you know as well as I do that I've placed bets on that horse before, Ange. And you know how they turned out."

"That still chaps me," Angela said with a frown. "But I have a feeling Blake is different. You said so yourself that you'd never felt this way before. Have you at least heard from him?"

"I've gotten a few texts, but I haven't dared to read them. I also got one from his mom. I stopped to see her at the diner before I left, and she said the same thing you did. But it's hard not to be skeptical…" Laney trailed off dejectedly.

Angela picked up Laney's phone and opened the text messages. "Oh, Laney, you've gone and broken his heart," she said, handing the phone to Laney.

> **Blake:** Laney (and yes, I am calling you that because I DO care about you), please don't leave like this. Please come back, and let's talk.

> **Blake:** Mom said you came to the diner to see her. I hope you

believe what she said because it's true. This weekend was the best weekend I've had in a long time, and I don't want things to end like this. Please call me.

Blake: Laney, PLEASE answer me! I know you're upset, and you have every right to be, but please just let me explain. Please answer my calls.

Laney's tears spilled down her cheeks. She cared about him more than she wanted to admit. He was a breath of fresh air that she desperately needed, and she wasn't ready to let him go either. She clicked over to the message from Diane. It was simply the photo of them sleeping on the couch, with the added caption:

Diane: You're still carrying the same canoe.

Laney burst into tears again. Angela looked over at the message and smiled. "I'm not sure what this whole canoe thing is about, but this looks like a couple who has feelings for each other to me! Call him! Now!" Angela said to Laney as she handed back her phone. "He deserves to at least explain himself, don't you think?"

"You're right," Laney agreed with a sigh. "Anyway, I'm going to run a hot bath and turn in early." Laney put the lid back on the pint of ice cream and headed toward the freezer.

"Of course I'm right! Promise me you'll call him. And keep me posted, okay?" Angela said as she put on her coat. "Promise?"

"I'll call," Laney told her with hesitation. "Thanks for coming. I don't know what I'd do without you."

"Right back atcha!" Angela said over her shoulder before shutting the door.

The house was eerily quiet, with only the soft ticking of the clock on the wall filling the empty space. Its rhythm pounded in Laney's ears like a kick drum, matching the broken heart beating in her chest. She stared at her phone, almost hitting "reply" several times, but each time, she talked herself out of it. She tossed her phone onto the couch next to her cat, Murphy, and trekked down the hall to unpack her bag.

Back in her room, she unloaded all her clothes. She pulled the tags off the new ones and hung them up before taking all the dirty ones to the laundry room. On top of the pile was her pajama shirt, with Blake's amazing scent still woven into it. She dropped the pile and held that shirt to her face, breathing it in. "This could wait a day or two to be washed," she thought as she laid it over her shoulder. Then, she grabbed her phone from the couch, opened her messages, and replied to Blake:

> **Laney:** Hi. I just wanted you to know that I got home safe. I don't really know what else to say, but I need some time to think.

Blake responded immediately:

> **Blake:** You have no idea how good it feels to hear your message come in. I'm so glad you're safe. I worried about you all day. I miss you, and I'm so sorry this happened.

> **Laney:** I'm sorry too. I've been hurt so much in the past that it's going to take some time before we can talk.

> **Blake:** I understand. I'll wait. I'll give you as much time and space as you need. But know that I was telling you the truth. I care about you so much, and this is killing me. My feelings for you won't change, Laney. You've forever changed my life. I hope to hear from you soon.

After the new year, Blake returned to his home in Los Angeles. The California sunshine should've been a nice change from the Idaho snow. But it just made him feel further away from Laney. They were in two different places with different weather and time zones. They might as well have been on two different planets. His mood had been cloudy and drab for weeks now, so he picked up his phone and messaged the only person who could get him out of his funk.

Blake: Hey, Austin, you in town?

Austin: Hey, man! I sure am! How the heck are ya?

Blake: I'm in need of some good vibes. You got any?

Austin: For you, always! Need a game of pickup?

Blake: More than you know. You tell me when and where, and I'll be there.

Austin: Okay! How about tonight at that fancy executive gym on Pine that you showed me a while back? Say, eight o'clock?

Blake: Perfect. Thanks, man. See you tonight!

After Blake replied, he shoved his phone back into his pocket. It felt good to have plans. He knew if anyone could understand his plight, it was Austin.

Later that evening, Blake parked at the gym and waited in his car for Austin to show up. Austin was about five minutes late, but he brought with him a big smile. When Blake saw him, he got out of the car and waved.

"Hey, Blake! What's new, man?" Austin said, dribbling a ball toward him.

"Hey, Austin," Blake replied.

They greeted each other in true guy fashion with a high five, handshake, back slap ritual, and then headed toward the entrance.

"Mr. Logan, Mr. Graham, welcome!" greeted the front desk receptionist as she scanned their membership cards. "We've got a court set aside for you. Second set of doors on the right," she said in a sing-song voice, pointing down a long hallway. "Enjoy!"

Blake dragged his feet down the brightly-lit hallway and pushed hard on the door handle to their assigned court. When they entered, the motion-sensor lights clicked on, illuminating the freshly-waxed court. Blake dropped his duffle bag with a thud on the floor and the sound echoed through the empty court.

"So, what's the deal, Eeyore?" Austin teased.

"Ugh, I screwed up big-time," Blake said, stealing the ball from Austin and driving to the hoop.

"You? Screw up? No way! You're Hollywood's 'golden boy,'" Austin said with a laugh, rebounding the missed shot.

"Well, not this time. I met this girl, Laney Campbell. She was my Lyft driver up to Idaho when I went to visit my mom and sister for Christmas. We hit it off right away, and I fell hard for her—for real. Joe got super mad when some photos from a festival got leaked to the tabloids. And she overheard me telling him it was nothing, which wasn't true. But now she won't talk to me, and I don't know what I can do to prove to her that I really care about her," Blake said, pulling up for a three-pointer and missing the shot.

"Ah, well, that explains you being off your game!" Austin said as he rebounded the ball and made a basket. "So, what's your plan to get her back?"

"I was kinda hoping you'd help me with that part—since you're the romantic songwriter," Blake said, smirking wryly.

"You've definitely come to the right guy!" Austin laughed. "What always works for me are gestures. They can be big or small, but they've gotta be authentic. Do something to get close to her but still give her space, all while letting her know she is the motivation behind your gestures. Women love to know they've been heard, that you've paid attention to the small details. So find something that means a lot to her, and try it. If she bakes bread, learn to make sourdough. If she's an artist, take a painting class. Stuff like that, you know?"

The wheels in Blake's head whirred and spun. "I have the perfect thing," Blake said, smiling. "Thanks, man."

"I got your back, brother. Now, go after it. But in the meantime, watch me school you on the court!" Austin bragged as he drove to the hoop for a layup.

Blake's plane left LAX for New Orleans, Louisiana, on a rainy, wet January morning. As the plane descended through the clouds, his eyes fixated on the cityscape in the distance and the swamplands below. There were plants and types of trees that he had never seen before, and the muddy Mississippi River stretched on forever.

The humidity hit him like a sauna the moment he left the airplane, instantly making his skin dewy. He gazed out the window of his private car in amazement as they drove through the city to his hotel. Centuries-old buildings stood along both sides of the tiny streets. And the French and Spanish influences in the architecture each had their own stories to tell. His mouth slacked open at the beauty around him, and his heart filled with excitement to explore a city that Laney loved.

Soon, the car came to a stop in front of an old but updated inn with bright white siding and long navy blue shutters. The windows all across the front of the house stretched from top to bottom, and the porch welcomed him with open chairs and ceiling fans on high. Its 1824 architecture stood beautiful and tall, with white columns holding up expansive balconies, perfectly tended gardens, and the best part—privacy.

A young man dressed in a bell-hop uniform greeted him at the door, "Welcome to the Fleur De Lis Mansion, Mr. Logan." His charming southern accent won Blake over immediately. "I'll take those bags for you, sir. We'll get you checked in in no time."

The cool air wrapped Blake in a welcoming hug as he stepped into the lobby. The sun filtering through the windows lit up the entire room full of antique furniture and overstuffed chairs. Blake followed the bellhop up a winding staircase and down a long hallway before stopping in front of a dark blue door.

"Here you are, sir," the bellhop said as he slid a card into the lock and turned the knob. "If you need anything at all, please don't hesitate to ask. We will do our very best to make sure you have a wonderful time here in New Orleans."

Blake tipped the young man and thanked him before letting the door swing shut behind him.

"Wow," Blake gasped as he looked over the room.

Exposed brick adorned the walls in his suite filled with antique furniture and artwork that, no doubt, had history. A large set of tall French doors on the opposite side of the room led to a private balcony. Thick, healthy, potted ferns hung from the eaves, and two weathered rocking chairs begged him to sit. A fresh pitcher of sweet tea sat on a table between the rockers, sweating condensation in the warmth of the day. Somewhere in the distance, he could hear jazz music playing in the street, so he sat back in a rocking chair, poured himself a glass, and listened.

Already, he could see why Laney loved this place. It was a buffet for the senses. The sounds of soulful music echoed down the alleyways. The sunshine filtering through the terrace above rested warmly on his shoulders. And the heavenly smell of beignets frying floated up from the kitchen below. Blake's growling stomach pulled him from his reverie. So he grabbed his baseball cap and sunglasses, and then slipped out into the street.

The French Quarter bustled with life, and it seemed that even strangers were friends in The Big Easy. Loud, happy greetings rang through the narrow streets as friends became lovers and strangers became friends. It's no wonder Laney fell in love with New Orleans—there was no way to resist its charm.

Further down on Frenchman Street, a woman's voice echoed off the old brick buildings around her. It floated up into the air with every beat of the drum and cry of the trumpet that accompanied her. A crowd had stopped to watch, mesmerized by her song, and she sang as if her soul were on the outside of her body. Exposed and raw, her anthem steeped through the skin of her audience. Blake felt a swelling in his chest as he watched this musician's most vulnerable pieces of her heart being given to the world. He stood frozen, unable to pull away from the power of her song. And when the last note echoed off the stone buildings, a new light flickered within him. He breathed deeply and tucked himself away from the crowd, hands curved gently around the flame that grew inside.

A few streets over, artists hung their hearts on the iron gates around Jackson Square to sell to tourists. He explored, looking at all the colorful displays. One painting of a couple kissing in the rain under a red umbrella called out to him, so he bought it and shipped it home. Then, a trumpet's echoing wail drew his attention toward the back of the square at the foot of St. Louis Cathedral. A musician played with an empty case at his feet with a few coins thrown into the bottom. Blake walked up to him, tossed a twenty-dollar bill inside, and put in a request. The beautiful song danced throughout the old buildings, bouncing off ancient iron and stone, straight through to his bones. Blake stood stunned, unable to move—only feel. His heart slowed, keeping beat with the rhythm that captivated him for a few moments in time. He walked along the river as the sun tipped past noon in the sky, and he watched the steamboats pass up and down the Mississippi. Their whistles bellowed as they pulled in and out of port. And the music from a calliope onboard filled the air along the shore. Across the street, a man roasted pecans, filling the air with a sweet, nutty aroma.

He walked the French Market shops and found a music box that played Laney's favorite song. He turned the tiny crank, and it spun out the simple tune of "A Kiss to Build a Dream on." As it played, he felt his heart becoming smashed and mangled through its spiky metal spindles. That song held both joy and sorrow as it clinked through the notes, filling him with a yearning to hold her again. Hoping to have the chance to give it to her someday, he bought it.

The smells of jambalaya and gumbo cooking flooded the streets, and he followed his nose to an outdoor café, where he sat down at a vacant table. He understood more and more with each bite why the way to a man's heart was through his stomach. Food wasn't just a meal in New Orleans but a way of life. It was a whole mixture of flavors that he had never experienced before, and it gave him some great ideas for new dishes to try. The scents of candied pralines, jambalaya, and seafood chased him wherever he went. There wasn't enough time in the day to eat at every place that smelled good, so Blake breathed it all in as best he could. He tucked each memory into his newly-lit heart to keep forever. This place was heaven on earth, just like Laney had said.

He sat on his balcony each night to soak in the city with a glass of mint julep or sweet tea. The music that echoed through the old architecture were by far his favorite part. Because no matter where he was, jazz echoed somewhere nearby. It timed perfectly with the streetcars and carriages, providing a soulful rhythm to live by. He fell in love with the easy, calm, and rich southern perspective that breathed through the city streets. Slowing down rejuvenated his soul and allowed him, for the first time in a long time, to take in all of life's goodness.

He made it a personal mission to drop large bills into the musicians' cases without getting caught. To have genuine interactions with fans who approached him, and slow down and pay attention to the beauty that surrounded him. When he hopped on a plane a few days later to go back to L.A., he was completely recharged. His determination to live more authentically grew with each opportunity to give love to others. He had seen first-hand what it was like to live with joy, no matter what he had, and to focus on the good wherever the road took him. Experiencing New Orleans himself, he finally understood why Laney loved it so much. He, too, had been changed by life in New Orleans.

Laney reluctantly opened the email from her old boss. Dr. Hansen has been trying to get her to come back and work for him for a few months now, but she wasn't quite sure she was ready yet. She missed her coworkers, the intellectual stimulation, and of course, the kids. But to add more weight to her heavy heart might break it completely. She sighed as she scrolled down the message and read:

Dear Laney,

As you may have heard, your replacement, Debra, will be going on maternity leave any day now. I was hoping you might want to come back and cover her shifts for a bit, seeing as how you already know the ropes and the way the office runs. I promise I won't pressure you to stay beyond that if you don't want to, but we could really use the help. Please consider it. We sure do miss you here. Hope to hear from you soon.

-Dr. Hansen

Laney sat back in her chair, the sunlight shining through the kitchen window filtering through her messy ponytail. "It would only be for six weeks or so," she thought to herself. Before she had the time to talk herself out of it, she replied saying,

Dr. Hansen,

That actually sounds awesome. I've been seriously thinking about trying to come back somehow, and this sounds like a good opportunity to ease into things. When do I start? I look forward to seeing everyone again!

-Laney

She smiled into her coffee as the thought of being back in her comfy scrubs for work all day filled her with happiness. Not many people get to work in a uniform that feels like PJs, and not only that, but she'd get to be back around the kids again. That job was hard, but it also brought a lot of joy. Ringing the bell with her patients on their last day of treatment never got old. And neither did sitting alongside Dr. Hansen when he told a patient that they were cancer-free. Focusing on the good things made her excited about nursing again.

The following Thursday, Laney was woken up at 6am. to the sound of Dr. Hansen calling her on her cell phone.

"Laney, it's Dr. Hansen. Can you come in today? Debra went into labor this morning, and I need you if you can swing it."

"Of course!" Laney said excitedly. "I'll see you at nine."

"I knew I could count on you, thank you so much!" Dr. Hansen replied.

Laney climbed out of the covers, put her feet on the cold, wood floor of her bedroom, and took a big, deep breath. Today was the day she'd get back on the horse. She stretched her arms high above her head, focused on the starfish tattoo on her arm, and thought of the promise she made to live deeper. Laney smiled at the memory of Bridget and told herself, "Only good vibes today." She made her bed, neatly stacking the fluffy pillows one-by-one at the headboard. Then, she grabbed her slippers and wandered into the adjoining bathroom to get ready for the big day ahead of her.

Forty minutes later, she was on her way out the door and into the cold January morning. Her breath fogged in front of her as she scraped the snow from her frozen windshield. Although the sun hid behind dreary gray clouds for most of January, nothing could squelch her good mood. She checked the forecast for the day and stared up at the sky, hoping she'd beat the storm coming home tonight. And before she knew it, her thoughts ran off to where the sun always shined. She wondered what the weather was like in L.A. today as Blake started his morning. What was he doing right at that moment? Had he been up working for hours, or was he just rolling out of bed? Laney realized they never really talked about his home in L.A. because he was so excited about showing her his childhood home in Idaho instead. Did he have a favorite sunspot in his kitchen to sip his morning coffee, or was his life so chaotic that he took it to go as he rushed out the door? As she stood in her driveway, lost in thought, she wondered if he thought of her the way she thought of him. If he, too, still kept his ornament out on display, or if it was tucked into a box along with her memory. Did he wear the socks she gave him in the tree house that wonderful night before everything went sideways? Would she ever be able to undo the time that had passed between them? Was it too late to tell him she missed him, and that she still thought of him every time a song they listened to in the car that day came on? Would she ever be able to tell him that she watched all his favorite movies to feel closer to him again? Laney felt ready to forgive Blake and work on trusting him, but she struggled to find the courage to call, or the right words to say.

She shook the thoughts from her mind, tossed her ice scraper in the back seat, and began the half-hour drive to the oncology clinic. The snow-swept miles that she passed usually gave her a lot of time to think. But today, she just needed some good tunes to sing aloud to, without anything heavy or sad. This was a chance at a new beginning, and she was going to make the most of the positivity that swelled within her.

When Laney arrived, she walked through the doors of the clinic to the smiling faces of old friends excited to welcome her back. She already felt the warmth of familiarity enveloping her cold winter shell as she ran to hug her work family.

Dr. Hansen stood toward the back of the crowd and subtly smiled when she met his eye. He was usually a very stoic man, but today, Laney got a genuine smile from him and was welcomed back with open arms and a busy schedule. "We'll be diving right in," Dr. Hansen said to her as he handed her a patient's chart. "The schedule is pretty full, and our first patient is in room ten for his annual scan results and check-up. I'll be there in a minute if you want to go in and start vitals," he added as he stepped into his office.

"Sure thing!" Laney said with a nod as she looped her stethoscope around her neck like old times. She opened the door to the examination room and smiled when she saw and the cartoon paintings that were all around the room to make the kids feel at ease.

"Good morning, my name is—"

"Nurse Laney!" Noah's voice shouted excitedly.

Laney looked up from the chart to see Danielle and Noah sitting on the padded vinyl chairs. She gasped and dropped to her knees just in time to catch the hug that Noah had run to give her. A huge lump immediately rose in her throat, and she couldn't find the words to express how much she ached for them.

"We've sure missed you, Laney," Noah said as he hugged her tightly. "But not as much as Uncle Blake. He got really sad when you left." Noah pulled away enough that he could look Laney straight in the eyes and put his pudgy hands on her cheeks. "Why did you leave? Are you still mad at Uncle Blake? Is he not your special friend anymore?"

Noah rapid-fired questions, and she laughed through the tears in her eyes and said, "I missed you too, Noah. And your Uncle Blake, too. It makes me sad that he was sad, and no, I'm not mad at him anymore. I just don't know what to say to him now. It's kinda complicated." With a small nod and a reassuring grin, Laney lifted Noah onto the examination table. "But what are the odds that on my first day back at work, I get to see you again? This is my lucky day! How have you guys been?" she asked, looking over at Danielle.

"We've been doing good!" Danielle replied. "These yearly checks still make me nervous, but I brought Mom this time to help calm my nerves.

She has the twins in a stroller and is walking around in the hospital while we see Dr. Hansen. She'll be bummed she didn't get to see you. We're going to grab some lunch before heading back home if you'd like to join us. When is your break?"

"I'd love to, but unfortunately, we have a packed schedule today. If I get lunch, it'll be a quick bite at my desk." She frowned. "I would've loved to have lunch with you. You guys are the best. I know I didn't leave in the best of circumstances, and I'm sorry I didn't say goodbye…" Laney sighed as she trailed off. "How is Blake?" Laney asked after a short pause as she took Noah's blood pressure. She felt the nervousness blooming in her core as the words escaped her mouth.

"He misses you, Laney," Danielle said seriously. "Honestly, I'd never seen him so happy before, and right now, he's a little bit lost. He is back in L.A., but we call and talk to him a few times a week. He has been doing some soul-searching. He took a trip all alone to New Orleans a few weeks ago. Did you see his posts on Instagram?"

"No, I've purposefully avoided social media so that I didn't have to face the nosey questions and comments from people," Laney answered. Then, unable to hide her smile, she asked, "He went to New Orleans? Really?"

The thought of him wandering the old streets of NOLA made her warm inside. Kind of like when he first held her hand, or when they laughed in the roadside diner, or when they snuggled together in the tree house. She felt a fire surge within her, one she had tried unsuccessfully for weeks to extinguish. It's amazing how a few words about Blake resurrected feelings she had tried to bury, bringing them right back to the surface again. Only this time, Laney didn't try to push them back down. She let them rise to the surface and bask in the sun, warming her from the inside out.

"I'll have to check it out when I get home tonight," she replied, smiling softly, her fondness for him glowing in her eyes.

"You should give him a call, Laney," Danielle urged gently. "It's obvious that you both still have feelings for each other. Whatever has happened between you can be fixed, but you've got to let go and call him. He misses you."

"I miss him too, regardless of how much I've tried not to," Laney admitted. "But a whole month has passed. What do I say?"

"The truth will do just fine," Danielle said with a smile.

After a soft knock on the door, Dr. Hansen walked into the room. A wide smile spread from ear to ear as he exclaimed, "Noah, buddy!" He greeted Noah with a high-five and said, "Your scans look great, and the bloodwork looks awesome!" Dr. Hansen then turned to Danielle and continued. "As long as Noah is feeling great and not experiencing any of the symptoms we've talked about in previous visits, we don't have to see you again until next year!"

The relief that crossed Danielle's face was what made this job so rewarding. Laney said a little prayer of gratitude in her heart for the good news they got to hear today, and how once again, fate stepped in and connected Blake to her. Seeing Danielle and Noah gave her the courage to finally call him. Laney hugged them both as they left to find Diane and the twins. And she swallowed the lump forming in her throat as Noah wildly waved goodbye over his shoulder.

Laney's thoughts drifted all day about what she would say. *Should I send him a message so I don't say anything stupid? Or should I just bite the bullet and call him?* The rest of the day went in slow motion until she could finally call and hear Blake's voice after she was done with work. The nagging thoughts that she was too late were loud and obnoxious, but she shoved them away and trusted what Danielle had said. He missed her, just like she missed him. As she clocked out for the day, Dr. Hansen called down the hall to her and said, "Remember, our office is closed on Fridays. Have a nice weekend, and we'll see you on Monday! Thanks again for your help!"

"It's nice to be back. See you Monday!" Laney called over her shoulder as she pulled on her coat, slung her purse over her shoulder, and left through the front door.

Climbing into her car for the drive back home, Laney took a deep breath to steady herself. She sat in the driver's seat and stared intently at her phone for a few minutes while the car warmed up. The whole time she was apart from Blake, she thought of everything she would say to him when this moment came. And now that it had, her mind was blank. She tossed her phone into her purse in frustration and decided to think a bit more about what to say as she drove home.

Laney struggled half of the night to find the words to say to him, but ultimately, her message to him sat unfinished and unsent. How could she come up with the words that would convey how she felt inside? Did he really miss her as much as Danielle said he did or had he moved on? Laney tossed and turned, thinking about the perfect thing to say, but ended up falling asleep with her phone still in her hand.

Chapter 15

Laney turned on the TV the next morning, then stared at her pantry, trying to decide between pancakes, scrambled eggs with salsa, or an omelet. As she pulled mixing bowls and a pan from the cabinet, she thought about her time in the kitchen with Blake. In fact, she thought of him every morning while she made breakfast, and she wondered if he ever did the same.

She grabbed her phone from the counter, her thumb hovering above the Instagram app on her phone. She had avoided social media like the plague the last few weeks while she licked her wounds. But she couldn't hide under a rock forever, could she?

The moment the app loaded, Blake's stories popped up on her feed, sending a tsunami of nerves rushing through her. She closed her eyes, took a deep breath, clicked on his profile, and dove in.

She scanned through his photos but stopped when she recognized his location. He was smiling next to the wrought-iron railing of a balcony with a mint julep in his hand. His eyes had a sort of contentment about them, and she could almost hear the music echoing around him.

"He did go to New Orleans," she whispered to herself. A bittersweet knot formed in her stomach as she scrolled through his photos, taken in her favorite place.

A video began to play under her thumb, and she turned up the sound. Blake grinned from under a navy blue baseball cap and aviator sunglasses as he strolled among the street performers in Jackson Square. His voice held a grateful tone as he spoke about the beautiful people, the amazing food, and, of course, the music. Then, the video cut away from him and showed a trumpet player in the square, playing her favorite song. She laughed through her tears and quickly messaged Angela to take a look, to which Angela replied:

> **Angela:** Girl, call him already! You KNOW he cares about you if he goes all the way to NOLA to experience a closeness to you.

> **Laney:** I know. But I'm afraid it might be too late. What do I say?

> **Angela:** It's never too late for love, Lane. Just swallow your pride and call him! He told you he'd wait for you to figure stuff out. But don't keep that gorgeous man waiting any longer!

Suddenly, a familiar voice came through on the TV, and it pulled her attention away from her messages. After the shock of seeing him right there on her TV, she sent Angela another message:

> **Laney:** Ange, turn on channel four! He's on Good Day, USA.

There he was, sitting casually on the couch of the early morning news program, being interviewed about his cookbook releasing soon. He laughed with the hostess, talked about his inspiration for writing the book, and even did a live cooking segment. Laney followed along, but she still couldn't get her omelet quite like he made them. But it gave her more closeness to him than she'd felt in a while. That familiar ache to be cooking together again in the same kitchen and fighting over the correct sauces for eggs returned in full force. But the thing she noticed most was that he had softened from his usual Hollywood persona. This time, he laughed, shared stories about his family, and listened intently to the hostess when she spoke. This interview was more genuine and grateful than he had ever been in the public eye, and his answers were honest and real.

Then, flashing a tabloid photo of him and Laney, the hostess turned to him and said, "Now, I know practically everyone in the country right now is wondering who this is. Care to clear up the mystery?"

Blake took the photo from her and smiled sadly at it.

"Well, I'm sorry to disappoint everyone out there, but she is a part of my private life, and I want to keep it that way."

"All I know is that every woman in the world wants to be looked at exactly like this by the man of her dreams, am I right, ladies?" the hostess grinned. Blake laughed softly and looked down at the photo, then up at the hostess as he responded,

"Every woman deserves to be." Then, looking directly into the camera, he added, "So don't settle for anything less."

The conversation about his upcoming cookbook drew to a close. Blake adjusted in his seat a bit and crossed one foot over his knee, exposing the pair of pineapple socks that Laney had given him for Christmas. He rested his hand on the cuff of his pant leg as if to draw her attention to them. She let out a small gasp, and in her mind, she heard his voice say again, "I wear them when I start to miss home. It helps me take a little piece of her and my mom with me wherever I am."

"He misses me," she thought to herself. "He still misses me." And for the first time in a month, she was confident in the timing to reach out to him.

Laney rushed to finish getting ready that morning, and her mind raced with what she would say to him when she called. She stood in front of her dresser and put on her earrings, but her shaking hands didn't have normal dexterity, and she dropped one on the floor. As she peeked under the dresser to retrieve it, a folded-up piece of paper caught her eye. The ink smudges and smears showed that it was hastily written, but when she opened and read it, the words were clearly thought out.

Dear Laney,

There is so much I want to say to you, but I don't know how to find the words. Especially since you're waiting for me to go back to the tree house, I have to make this quick. You are amazing in every way. You have breathed life back into my broken heart, and you are the joy that I never knew was missing. I have learned more and felt more in this short weekend with you than I have in the past few years. I am so grateful that I got into your car that day. It's crazy to me how such a simple choice can change a person's whole trajectory. You made me feel found at a time when I thought I'd be lost forever. Thank you.

-Blake

Laney held her breath as she read those words, rereading them over and over again. With shaky hands, she set the letter down, picked up her phone, and dialed his number.

Chapter 16

Blake's phone rang several times, each time sending bursts of adrenaline throughout Laney's body as the sound pulsed in her ear. Just when she was about to hang up, a voice broke the monotonous tones:

"Hi, you've reached Blake. I'm not available at the moment but leave me a message, and I will call you back as soon as possible. If you don't leave a message, then I'll always wonder who you were and why you called. So don't do that to me." Blake laughed. "Here's the beep!"

The loud, high-pitched beeping flustered Laney, and she lost her words and her nerve. But gripping her phone tightly, she took a deep, steadying breath.

"Uh, Blake. Hi. It's Laney," she stammered. "I just called to talk. Um, call me back when you can, I guess. Okay, bye."

Laney slapped her forehead as she ended the call and sighed. "Ugh, I sounded like such an idiot. Totally choked," she chastised herself. "After weeks of trying to come up with something eloquent and flowery to say to him, that's what you come up with, Laney?" She groaned and threw herself face down onto her bed. But the ball was in his court now, and waiting to hear back from him would make time pass backward.

After a few minutes of self-loathing, a Lyft alert for a ride to Park City broke the silence. "I might as well stay busy while I wait," Laney thought to herself as she accepted the job. She got up from her bed, smoothed her hair and clothes, and grabbed her coat and purse on her way out the door.

After the TV show that morning, Blake went straight to a radio interview with a popular podcaster in the L.A. scene. Instead of sauntering in and answering the questions with a cocky, half-smile on his face, he made a conscious effort to be more real. He smiled when it was genuine and took the interview as a chance to give his fans a piece of the real Blake Logan. Joe's wild pantomiming in the booth to be suaver was hard to ignore, so Blake purposefully avoided eye contact with him while Joe waved like a lunatic. The interview was going well without all the usual fanfare, and Blake grew more and more confident that being himself was enough.

When Blake left the radio station, the afternoon sun shone warmly on his face, and he had a slight pep in his step as he walked out to his car.

All of a sudden, the station door slammed further behind him, and Joe ran past the photographers toward Blake.

"Dude! What was that all about?" Joe huffed as he caught up and grabbed Blake's arm.

"What do you mean, Joe?" Blake asked sternly, ripping himself from Joe's grasp.

"You—going rogue today. First, Good Day USA, and now this? We had a plan. Who was that guy?"

"'That guy' was me, Joe. I'm tired of playing games. I don't want to pretend to be something I'm not every minute of every day. I've been so worried about being someone who pleases you and everyone else that I've completely lost who I am. I'm done pretending."

The paparazzi began to swarm as their conversation got louder.

"You see them?" Joe pointed at the flashing bulbs. "You work for them. If they don't like you, no one will."

"No, Joe. That's where you're wrong. They work for me, and so do you. And my job is to be authentic. If you can't get on board with that, then maybe your part needs to change. I'm miserable, and I lost the greatest thing that could've ever happened to me because I was so worried about pleasing you and them. But no more!"

With that, Blake pushed past Joe and picked up the pace to his car.

"Nice guys are boring, Blake! Think about it for a few days before you make a stupid decision like this!" Joe called out to Blake as he got further away.

"Nice guys get the girl, Joe! My mind's made up. Get on board or swim!" Blake called over his shoulder as he pulled his keys and phone from his pocket.

A missed call and a voicemail notification from Laney illuminated his phone, sending jolts of lightning through his body. He had been waiting for so long for this moment, yet all he could do was stand there and stare at the screen. *What if she's calling to say she was ready to talk? What if she was calling to say it's over?* The waiting and uncertainty was something he had gotten used to. Like an old, unwelcome visitor that stayed too long and rifled through his bathroom cabinet. But at least it was familiar. This new prospect staring him right in the face made him sick inside. Because now the waiting was over, and the uncertainty was about to become certain.

His hands shook as he shoved his phone back into his jacket pocket and picked up his stride toward his waiting car. It was the longest walk in history. The parking lot seemed to stretch on for miles, and time went in slow motion. As he quickened his steps, so did the paparazzi, shouting questions at him as he ran.

Reaching his matte-black Audi R8, he unlocked it with the key fob and ducked inside, shutting out all the chaos surrounding him. The smell of the leather interior soothed his nerves a bit, and the driver's seat cradled him perfectly as he buckled his seatbelt. He gripped the steering wheel with one hand—his thumb hovering over the bright red "Start" button—and clutched his phone with the other. As soon as the silence inside the car enveloped him, he unlocked his phone and stared at the notification waiting for him. Blake took a long, deep, calming breath. *This is it. Does she want me or not?* He exhaled sharply, started the car and clicked on the voicemail before he lost his nerve.

The engine purred in the background as Laney's voice jumped from his phone to the surrounding speakers, inundating him with the recording. *She sounds nervous. Is that good or bad?*

"Uh, Blake. Hi. It's Laney," she stammered. "I just called to talk. Um, call me back when you can, I guess. Okay, bye."

Blake's countenance fell. Although it felt so good to hear her voice, her message was vague, and it gave him no indication of her feelings for him. He listened to it again, trying to read between the lines before giving up. The only way he'd be able to get an answer is to call her back, but what would he say? What would *she* say? He put the car in reverse and hit the call back button. Each time the phone rang, he wound tighter and tighter. He had never been more anxious in his entire life than he was at this moment. Grateful that he had to focus partially on driving, he used it as an anchor to keep his thoughts from running away from him. After three rings, Laney's cheerful voice broke the silence and said:

"Hi, you've reached Laney Campbell. I'm sorry I couldn't answer your call. Leave me a message, and I'll get back to you as soon as I can! Have a great day!"

Blake sighed, cleared his throat, and spoke after the beep, "Hey, Laney, I'm sorry I missed your call. Things have been crazy lately. It was really nice to hear your voice. Call me back. I'm anxious to talk."

He hung up the phone and tossed it on the seat next to him as he entered the freeway on-ramp. He drove around for miles, trying to make sense of Laney's message. Danielle had given him hope when she called about running into Laney at Noah's appointment. But after hearing Laney's voicemail, he wasn't so sure anymore. After passing his exit three times, he decided to take matters into his own hands. No more waiting patiently. He had serious feelings for this woman, and he wasn't going down without a fight, so he changed lanes and headed toward LAX airport.

He sped down the 405 freeway, zipping in and out of traffic, his stress increasing with every nerve-wracking mile. Blake called his personal assistant as he neared the exit toward the airport.

"Hey, Adam, I'm leaving for Salt Lake City, and parking my car at LAX long-term parking. Can you please come pick it up, and bring it back to the house? I don't want to leave it here all weekend. Oh, and by the way, can you go online right now and get a plane ticket for me? Thanks!"

He pulled into the parking lot and sent a pin of his car's location to his assistant. As it finished sending, an email came in with his QR code for a flight that would leave in an hour.

His thumbs flew across the screen as he texted one last message:

Blake: Thanks, man, I owe you one. I just sent you a pin so that the car will be easier to find. The spare key is hanging in the cabinet in the kitchen. Thanks for your help. Have a good weekend.

Blake grabbed his newly packed emergency overnight bag from the trunk and locked the car with the key fob. As he ran through the airport, a boldness grew inside him, pouring like melted wax into the cracks that doubt had created.

Today was a great day to be Blake Logan because the VIP line at the security checkpoint moved twice as fast as the regular line. He threw his shoes back on and stuffed his belongings into his pockets at lightning speed, barely making it to the gate in time. On the plane, he flopped down in his first-class seat, relieved and out of breath from running.

"Welcome aboard, Mr. Logan," the flight attendant greeted him in a sing-song voice. "What can I get you to make your flight more comfortable?"

"Just a few bottles of water, please," Blake replied with relief in his voice as he wiped the sweat from his brow. "Thank you."

Chapter 17

Blake spent the majority of the flight staring out the window, watching the misty clouds rush by. He gazed at the shadowy patterns they painted on the ground below and wondered about Laney. *How will I ever find her, and what will I say to her if I do? Is there even a chance that we get a happily ever after to this whole thing?* He jumped head-first into the deep end for Laney, and he wasn't about to drown now. He didn't care that he had no plan. For the first time in a long time, he was acting spontaneously, and it was thrilling.

Everything happened so quickly that it gave him a rush when he thought about their whirlwind romance. She had stolen his heart like a thief in the night, and he never wanted it back. He wanted to make sure that she knew it. Sure, there was a strong possibility of things backfiring, and he'd feel like a fool. But the chance of getting to spend the rest of his life with a woman like Laney drove him forward. Past every doubt, every obstacle, and every nay-sayer. He knew, now more than ever, that he loved her. And if she'd let him back in, he'd spend the rest of his life trying to make her as happy as she made him.

Soon, the plane began its gradual descent below the clouds, revealing a picturesque mountain valley blanketed in a fresh coat of snow. Salt Lake City was a breathtaking place, and he couldn't help but stare in awe at the massive Rocky Mountains that welcomed him with open arms. The scenery below was a delicately painted canvas from the air. The snow glistened off the jagged mountain ridges, and sharp purple edges sat exposed where the sun had kissed them. The evening sun was starting to tip toward the mountains in the West, illuminating a few sailboats on the Great Salt Lake. He'd definitely be okay with spending more time here—maybe even call it home someday.

The moment the pilot announced that they would be landing in a couple of minutes, Blake rushed to collect his belongings and threw them in his bag. So many unknowns lay ahead, his stomach twisted and turned like a child's does on the first day of school. This day could either go undeniably right or horribly wrong, and he was anxious to find out what the outcome would be.

Blake weaved in and out of the crowds through the airport terminal, laser-focused on winning back Laney's heart. He had no plan, just a hired car waiting for him to hop into, and would figure out the rest later. He depended on Fate to help guide him through the next steps back to Laney's arms, and he didn't care how ridiculous it seemed. His heart pounded like his feet on the cement floors as he neared the sliding glass doors to the parking lot. The black SUV Adam had hired waited patiently for him, but in his haste, he almost missed his golden opportunity. Parked a few car lengths in front of his ride was a little gray SUV just like Laney's.

No way, Blake thought as he slowed his pace, shocked. *It can't be that easy…* He glanced over at a little old lady shuffling with her suitcase toward the gray SUV. He followed her gaze to see Laney in the driver's seat, typing a message on her phone. Suddenly, a text message came in on Blake's phone:

Laney: Hey. I have one more pickup for the night, and I'll call you afterward. I'm not sure what to say, but I miss you.

Blake shoved his phone into his back pocket and ran after the little old lady. He softly tapped her on the shoulder. "Excuse me," he said politely. "Can I help you with your bags?"

The lady stopped, her face turning from a smile to shock as she recognized the young man who was offering to help her.

"In fact, is that your Lyft ride right there?" he asked, pointing in Laney's direction.

"Why, yes, it is." She smiled. "Thank you for your help, young man," she added with a wink.

Blake smiled his winning, star-studded smile and said, "Tell you what? How about you take a ride in style tonight…" He nodded toward his hired car. "…And I'll take yours." The sweet old lady straightened up and a sly grin crossed her face. "Fifty bucks, and you've got yourself a deal, Mr. Logan."

"Done," Blake agreed, chuckling.

He pulled her suitcase up to the hired car and then heaved the heavy suitcase into the trunk. Giving the sweet little old lady a hand into the backseat, he leaned in and told the driver, "This is my special guest. Please take her wherever she needs to go and bill me for the tab." He handed the driver a folded-up tip and patted him on the shoulder. Then, turning to the lady, he smiled at her through the open back window. He handed her a fifty-dollar bill, and said, "Thanks. You saved my life." As the Tahoe drove away, he turned toward Laney's car.

She stood near her open trunk in anticipation of her passenger showing up and scanned the crowd with one hand raised to shade her eyes. Her blond hair caught the sunshine and a breeze blew it delicately in her face, making his heart skip. She was even more beautiful than he remembered, and a sense of calm poured over him like hot fudge on a sundae.

Blake took a big, deep breath in an attempt to quell the nerves building up inside him. Seeing her again after so long made him more excited than scared now, and he started toward her.

"Laney!" he shouted as he neared her car, his footsteps slowing as he approached. She froze, then slowly turned toward the familiar voice yelling her name. She searched the crowd for the source and saw him as he paused a few feet in front of her. His blue eyes shone in the sunshine as they pierced into hers. Shock covered Laney's face, wiping from her mind anything cognitive. Blake's heart raced, and her breath hitched as she stood in disbelief. He dropped his bag on the ground in the parking lot, wrapped his hands around her waist, and pulled her against him.

"I've missed you too," he said as he leaned in breathlessly and kissed her. Their lips touched with a hunger that had gone unfed for weeks, sending a jolt of electricity from his head to his toes. He held her firmly with one hand at the small of her back and gently cupped the nape of her neck with the other. Laney's hands ran up his athletic back to his muscular shoulder blades and pulled him closer. Blake's hands slipped into her hair, combing her curls and sending chills across her scalp as he kissed her—intensely at first, then long and slow. Laney's hands under his jacket were warm on his back, and he felt her relax into his body, molding perfectly into his embrace. Laney Campbell—a strong, independent, warrior had been disarmed, dropping her sword and shield at his feet. A star like him could have any woman he wanted, but he didn't want just any woman. He wanted her—a small-town girl with a big heart and a feisty attitude. And she wanted him right back.

Her surprise softened into surrender as he unguardedly kissed her right there in the airport parking lot. He held nothing back this time, completely giving in to reckless abandon. No secrets, no sneaking, no fears of paparazzi leaking photos, and no concerns of his manager finding out. He was free to love her, and he didn't care who knew. Laney had given him more than he ever thought possible. She was exactly what he wanted and everything he needed, and he would never let her go again.

A camera flash broke up the moment, bringing them both back to earth. Blake leaned his forehead against hers, breathing a sigh of relief that she was once again in his arms.

"Let's get out of here, shall we?" he whispered, caressing her cheek with his thumb.

"Please," Laney replied with a small breath. "Although I'm not sure if my knees will hold me." She giggled and cupped his face in her hands. "I still can't believe you're here!"

"I know exactly what you mean," he said, kissing her forehead. Blake grabbed his bag and tossed it into the trunk as a crowd gathered around them with cell phone cameras clicking.

"Looks like a great time to make an exit." He looked at her and beamed. "By the way, I kinda paid off your passenger and gave her my ride instead."

"You did what?"

"She was a nice little old lady, but she drove a hard bargain. Cost me fifty bucks," he told her, laughing.

"I'm flattered you went to such lengths to get into my car," she said, impressed. As he sat down in the front seat, he smiled at her before saying, "I hope you don't mind if I sit up here with you. I hate sitting in the back when being driven alone. It feels so impersonal."

"That's fine, but if you have a lousy taste in music, I'll hit the ejection seat button," Laney replied, playing along. Then they left the scene at the airport in the rearview mirror.

Chapter 18

Blake grabbed Laney's hand and laced his fingers into hers. The engine hummed quietly in the background as they drove down the highway, and the radio playing on low volume was the only noise in the car. Laney was the first to break the silence between them.

"You grew a beard. I like it; it suits you."

"Thanks," Blake replied, rubbing the trimmed hairs along his jawline. "Shaving became too hard for a while there. It brought up a memory of you I couldn't face, and then before I knew it, there was a beard. So I kept it."

"I saw your interview this morning. You wore my socks." She smiled shyly and glanced in his direction.

"I've worn them weekly since you left," he told her with a grin, pulling up his pant leg to show her.

"Please tell me you've washed them, or it's a deal-breaker for me," Laney bird free into the outside air. She watched it fly away, never to return to its cage within her mind. At last, she was safe with him, and she let herself be completely vulnerable for the first time in years. It felt good to tell him she loved him, and she decided it was something she could do every day for the rest of her life.

said, laughing. Blake laughed too. "Man, it's good to hear you laugh. It's felt like a million years," Blake admitted. "And yes, I've washed them."

"I'm sorry it took me so long to call," Laney muttered nervously. "I wasn't quite sure what to say, and I had to figure out which story to believe—the one we lived, or the one you told Joe. Then I saw Danielle and Noah, and they gave me the courage to call. Noah said you were pretty miserable, huh?" Laney teased a bit.

"I can't believe my wingman outed me so hard." Blake chaffed, running a hand through his hair. "Yeah, I was a pretty big mess. I wish you would've come back and let me explain things in person," Blake said sadly. "I hated being so far away from you, not knowing what you were thinking or if I'd ever see you again."

"I know, but I was so hurt and mad at you that I couldn't think straight. It was for your own good—trust me." Laney grinned and shot him a teasing glance.

"Oh really?" Blake teased back. "Were you going to force me to my knees like you did that cab driver?"

"Maybe." She laughed. "You should've learned from his mistakes."

"Truth be told, you brought me to my knees anyway when you left," Blake confessed. "You have more power over me than you realize, Laney."

The sun dropped below the horizon, and the last brilliant color in the sky faded to black as the first of the stars began to shine. The car came to a stoplight, the red glare illuminating their faces through the windshield. Laney glanced down, saddened at the thought of Blake hurting because of her. He had shown her his true colors, and she had so easily forgotten that. She turned to him, meeting his gaze and seeing a heartache in his eyes that matched her own. She gingerly caressed his hand in hers.

"I'm sorry that I hurt you when I left. I felt like my trust in you had been betrayed—and it was a feeling I was way too familiar with. I just got scared and ran. I wanted to hear you out, but the doubts in my head were too loud. I needed them to quiet down before I could believe you, but I'm ready now." She cleared her throat. "You can thank your wingman for that one." Blake felt gratefulness bubble up inside him, and he smiled at the thought of Noah. He owed him—big time. "Will you please let me explain why I said what I did to Joe?" Blake asked softly.

Laney nodded as the light turned green. She turned West from the exit ramp and accelerated, heading toward home.

"You know that life in the spotlight is kinda weird. I'm who my fans think I am, and then there's the real me. Some of it overlaps, but you know the whole 'eligible bachelor, cocky womanizer' thing is not me at all. I went along with it at first because Joe told me it would make my career more successful, and I didn't see the harm in it. After all, it was just another part to play. It wasn't who I was inside. But after it started affecting my relationships, I began to resent it. Joe pushed away anyone I got close to because it made his job harder. I didn't want that to happen to you. I didn't want him exposing you to the press so you'd get overwhelmed and leave. I didn't want him to try to pay you to break things off. Needless to say, I didn't want him anywhere near you. Hollywood sucks the life out of me sometimes. And I didn't want that to happen to you because I care about you a lot, Laney. Honestly, it's none of Joe's business who I date! After you left, I told him that, and I also said that if he couldn't get on board with it, then I'd fire him."

"Wow! Did you really?" Laney exclaimed.

"Yeah, I did. I'm tired of letting him control both my public life and private one. But I need you to know that I am sincere, Laney. If you doubt me at all, this won't work. I'll do whatever it takes, for as long as it takes, to prove to you how much you mean to me. I love you, Laney," he spilled, and then slammed his mouth shut, surprised that those words left his lips without consulting with his brain first.

Deep down, Laney knew that his feelings for her were stronger than a weekend fling—her gut told her that a month ago. But to hear the words 'I love you, Laney' left her stunned. It was like he took off his leather jacket, warmed by his own body, and wrapped it around her broken heart. It emanated outward, thawing all the frozen gates that surrounded her. She knew she loved him too but didn't know if or when she would ever tell him. But seeing Blake step out into the open, completely exposed and unprotected, made her feel safe enough to join him. Laney swerved the car to the shoulder of the road, and the gravel crunched under the tires as she skidded to a stop. She put the car in park and turned in her seat to face him. Then, she reached up and touched his face, feeling the texture of his newly grown beard under her fingertips. He leaned his face into her hand and gently kissed her palm and held his breath in anticipation of what she might say next.

"I love you too," she whispered in return. "And I've been trying for days to try and figure out how to tell you that—or if I would *ever* tell you that. I could never find the words that explained my heart, especially after so much time had passed. I was afraid and a coward for waiting so long, and I'm sorry for hurting you. I needed help being brave. And then you jumped first." She smiled at him with tears in her eyes.

Relief flooded Blake's face when he realized that his love would not be unrequited, and she watched the worry fade from his blue eyes.

Laney brought his hand up to her soft, pink lips and kissed each of his fingertips. Blake watched her in awe as she robbed him blind of every insecurity he ever had—without so much as a whisper. She never needed a weapon because he gave everything to her willingly, and he had never felt so free. He caressed her cheek and tucked her hair behind her ear, letting his hand rest on the back of her neck. Pulling her to him, he delicately tasted the lips of the woman he loved, knowing she loved him in return.

Laney surrendered all doubt to Blake, letting go of it like a chil

Chapter 19

*A*round 7 p.m. that evening, Laney's headlights illuminated the driveway of her quaint gray cottage. Her little farmhouse out in the country was humble but updated, with a bright red door and white plantation shutters. One lonely porch light glowed in the darkness, silhouetting the white picket fence and mature trees that outlined the front yard.

"Welcome to my home," she said, squeezing Blake's hand. "It's nothing fancy, but I fixed it up from a beat-up old thing when I bought it a few years ago, and I love every old board and brick."

"You did all this yourself?" Blake asked, impressed.

"Well, a lot of it. Although my dad and brothers helped with some of the heavy lifting and the roof."

"That's incredible! You're incredible! I can't wait to see the inside," he enthused as he kissed her hand.

The front porch squeaked under the weight of their feet as Laney unlocked the door and swung it open. They stepped inside and were greeted by her orange tabby running figure eights around their feet. Picking up her greeter, Laney extended his paw out to Blake.

"Blake, this is Murphy. Murphy, this is Blake," Laney introduced.

Blake shook Murphy's fluffy pad and laughed. "It's nice to meet you, buddy."

"I found him as a kitten by the dumpster at the hospital. I couldn't bear to leave him, so I scooped up this muddy little furball and took him home with me. What I didn't realize was that I needed him as much as he needed me, and we've been rescuing each other ever since." With an endearing smile, she kissed Murphy between his triangle ears and set him down.

Laney hung her purse and coat on a hook by the door and led Blake down the hallway to the guest room.

"I'm not sure how long you get to stay, but the guest room is yours for as long as you want it. Although, you may have to share it with Murphy because, technically, this is his man cave." She laughed, flipping on the light switch.

The room was bright and airy, painted a light gray with subtle pink floral accents. With a meow, Murphy jumped up and settled down on the pile of decorative pillows on the bed, claiming his spot for the night.

Laney looked down and blushed. "It's not exactly 'manly,' but he doesn't seem to mind."

Blake laughed, setting his overnight bag on a soft pink overstuffed armchair in the corner. "It's perfect," he said, pulling her close. "Besides, real men wear pink, right? I can totally stay in a pink flowery room, especially if that means getting to hang out with you all weekend," he added as he kissed her on her head.

Laney sighed as she relaxed against him, something she'd missed more than she realized. "I still can't believe you're standing here, hugging me in my house! One minute I was leaving you a voicemail, and the next, we're face to face at the airport. You sure know how to surprise a girl. I can't stop smiling." She rubbed her cheeks.

"Looks like being more spontaneous pays off," he announced proudly. "Someone taught me that embracing life changes everything, so I thought I'd give it a go."

"I'm so glad you came," Laney said, nuzzling into his chest. "So, are you hungry? We could grab a late dinner somewhere, but the Friday night rush will probably still be crazy. Or we could do dinner in…"

"Dinner in sounds great. I haven't been able to eat all day, and I'm starving!" Blake said as they headed down the hallway to the kitchen.

Laney's brightly-lit kitchen was humble yet updated, with white cabinets and granite countertops, gray walls, and a farmhouse-chic decor. It reminded Blake of his mom's cottage, and he instantly felt at home.

"Can we make anything good with what's here?" Laney asked, opening the refrigerator door. "I don't want to go to the store tonight if we don't have to."

"You forgot who raised me. My mom could make something out of nothing, remember? Let's see, oh yeah. I've got an idea," Blake replied as he grabbed ingredients.

"I'll put on some music," Laney said over her shoulder as she headed to the record player in the corner.

"Ooh, I like your style! There's no better sound than a vinyl!" Blake smiled. "I have a whole collection at home."

"Great minds think alike! What's your favorite album?"

"That's a tough one," Blake answered. "I'd have to say, Queen's Greatest Hits. You can't listen to that one without singing at the top of your lungs."

"Yes! I love that one!" Laney beamed. "Mine is The Beatles, The Red Album. There isn't one song I'd skip. But this one is my go-to for singing and dancing in the kitchen," she said, smiling as she set the needle delicately down on Journey's Greatest Hits.

Blake grabbed a wooden spoon and flipped it like a drumstick when "Don't Stop Believing" came on and then began singing into it. Laney chimed in, grabbing a spatula. They danced around the kitchen in socks, standing back to back like band members, belting out an off-tune rendition while they prepped. Blake's air guitar put Neal Schon to shame, but it couldn't beat Laney's counter-top piano solo. When the famous line at the end came, they put all their efforts into the performance, singing, "Don't stop, believin'!" at the top of their lungs.

Murphy's ears flattened as he jumped down from his window perch and ran into another room.

"Everyone is a critic, I guess," Blake snickered.

"Whatever. We sounded awesome. Murphy doesn't know what's up."

The cracking and popping of the record advancing filled the silence between songs as "Faithfully" started to play. Blake slowed, set his wooden spoon down, turned the burner on low, and took Laney's spatula from her unsuspecting hand.

"This is the perfect time to let things simmer," he said as he stepped away from the pot on the stove and spun her into to middle of the living room. He wrapped his arm around her waist and swayed gently to the music. The lyrics sunk into Blake's bones as he more fully understood the words of the song after being apart from someone he loved.

The ominous fact that they would have to separate again soon hung thick in the air, but there, in that very moment, was exactly the kind of love Laney had always dreamed of. Finding someone to dance with in the kitchen made every tear she had ever cried and every heartbreak worth it. As she swayed along with him, contentment filled her once-shattered heart and smoothed its jagged edges.

"So," Laney began when the song ended and they wandered back toward the stove, "how long do you get to stay?"

"I don't have a return ticket yet, but I should probably head back on Tuesday. I've got a packed schedule on Wednesday until the end of the week."

"Since you've talked to Danielle, I suppose you know I went back to the oncology practice."

"Yeah, I think that's great, Laney. You can make such an impact on the kids there—I know you did for Noah." Blake smiled at her from over his shoulder.

"Well, I have to work on Monday, but only until two o'clock. Do you mind hanging out here while I'm gone? I have a giant movie collection, and there's a lot of peace and quiet…" Laney trailed off.

Before answering her, Blake poured a ladleful of beef stew into bowls and then brought them to the table. Laney grabbed two wine glasses and a bottle of wine and took a seat across from him.

"That sounds nice," Blake finally replied. "But I think I have a better idea." Then he smiled at her inquisitive gaze and raised an eyebrow over his wine glass.

After dinner, he got on the phone with his assistant while Laney started the dishes. "Hey, Adam, I have a huge favor to ask of you," he said, looking over his shoulder as he disappeared into his guest room.

Chapter

20

The morning sun peeking through the sheer curtains in Blake's room cast a perfectly filtered light on his bare shoulders. He rolled over, stretched, and lay there in the quiet, soaking in the solitude while Murphy slept curled up into a donut shape at his feet. The aromas of fresh coffee and bacon sizzling crept into his room, awakening his senses, and he lay there smiling at the thought of being able to wrap Laney in his arms again. He decided that the real thing was better than the dream, so he climbed out of bed. The room had a cool, crispness that only a late winter morning can bring, and the floor was cold on his bare feet. He pulled a T-shirt on over his head and fixed his hair in the mirror on the wall before stepping into the hallway.

Laney hadn't heard him get up yet, so he leaned up against the wall, quietly hidden in the hallway, and watched her. Her bed hair was disheveled yet sexy, pulled up into a messy bun on top of her head. She wore a worn Rolling Stones T-shirt that hung loosely over her tight black leggings, and she had bright pink cat slippers on her feet. Music played from her phone on the counter, and she sang softly to herself as she prepared breakfast. Blake felt a tug in his chest as he watched her, natural and one hundred percent herself. The most honest parts of people come from observing them when they don't know they're being watched. And Laney, she was even more beautiful to him as each minute passed. He loved seeing the truest parts of her and knowing she was the real deal. The women he had dated the past few years would've never allowed for a moment like this. Yet there she was, dancing in her kitchen, raw and exposed and beautiful.

She poured two cups of coffee into mugs that said, "Good Morning, Lovely," and "Hello There, Gorgeous," added creamer to hers, and left Blake's black. Piling the mugs and two plates with a breakfast spread onto a bed tray, she squealed under her breath as she headed toward Blake's room.

Looking around sharply, he pivoted on his heels, rushed to his room, and threw himself back into bed. He barely made it back under the covers before she knocked on his partially open door.

Laughing to himself, he called out, "It's open!"

Laney's face was lit up with joy when she sauntered into the room with his breakfast-in-bed surprise. He sat up against the headboard, propping up pillows for her to join him. Murphy perked up at the smell of bacon but decided that it was too early—even for food.

"I made you breakfast," she said with a childlike grin.

"And you remembered the salsa!" Blake laughed. "Thank you! Come! Sit with me!" He patted the bed next to him.

"And the ketchup!" Laney added, giggling. Sitting cross-legged on the bed facing Blake, she set the tray down between them.

"This looks amazing," Blake admired.

"Well, it's no 'Blake Logan Omelet,' but the bacon is cooked to perfection." She grinned proudly. "How'd you sleep?" she asked as she lifted a forkful of eggs to her mouth.

"Like a rock! It's so quiet here in the country, and the night was so still. It was like being lulled to sleep by the stars themselves."

"I'm so glad," she said, sighing happily. "And Murphy ditched me for you. I hope he didn't bother you."

"Oh no, he kept my feet nice and warm. Sorry I was an accessory to his treason. But he must've known that this California guy needed some extra warmth out here. I haven't done this much winter in a long time!"

Laney smiled, petting Murphy behind the ears. "Ah, he's forgiven. I'd rather you be kept warm." She glanced up at Blake, her eyes shining.

"I have something for you," Blake said, handing her a tiny box from his nightstand.

"What's this?" She rotated the box in her fingers.

"Open it," he said with a huge smile.

Inside was the tiny wood music box he had bought in New Orleans. Laney's eyes brightened as she turned the metal crank on the side.

"It's my song!" Her face filled with joy as she listened to the notes being plucked one by one. "Thank you!" She threw her arms around him and said, "This is the most thoughtful gift ever!"

"I'm glad you like it. I found it in a little shop in New Orleans," he told her as he studied the joy on her face.

"I love it," she whispered, clutching it tightly to her heart. "I saw you went to NOLA. So what did you think?"

"It was the most beautiful and interesting city I have ever seen!" Blake's face lit up as he told her all about his trip.

"It truly is an amazing place, and I'd love to go there with you someday," she said, already dreaming about it. "Hey! I have an idea," Laney suddenly added. "You game for an adventure today?"

"Always," he replied. "What did you have in mind?"

"You'll just have to trust me."

"Oh really?" he teased. "I'm intrigued."

"Good. I want to do something fun while you're here. And although it's in public, no one will know it's you," she reassured him, taking a bite of bacon.

"Now you've got me curious," he said, grinning. "What are you up to, Campbell?"

She smiled coyly, milking it for all it was worth.

"You'll have to wait and see! Get dressed—as warmly as you can," Laney said, looking Blake up and down, wondering if he'd be warm enough.

She disappeared with the tray down the hallway to the kitchen, and Blake could overhear her on the phone with someone. He got up to change into warm clothes, wondering what on earth she was planning. As he dressed, a message came in on his phone from his assistant, Adam.

Adam: Hey boss! I shipped it. Should arrive early Monday morning.

"Perfect," Blake said aloud, smiling covertly.

"You ready to go yet?" Laney called from down the hall a few minutes later. "We have a stop to make on our way. Shouldn't take long."

"I hope so!" Blake called back, throwing on his leather jacket as he met her in the front room.

"You are definitely going to need something warmer than that," she said, looking at what he was wearing. "Come on, let's go." She grabbed him by the hand and led him into the garage.

While Laney drove down the tiny, snow-covered streets of town, Blake watched out the window as they passed by an old school movie theater with missing letters in its marquee, brightly-painted gas stations, and the worn-out brick high school. The only traffic light in town hung across the street, and it blinked yellow, but everyone in town drove slow anyway, regardless of its warning.

When Laney turned down a long, gravel road at the end of town and followed it to someone's driveway, Blake's face betrayed his thoughts of confusion.

"This is my brother Levi's house. He's the one married to my best friend, Angela. It'll just be a second, come on."

Angela whipped the door open and greeted Laney with a tight hug, unable to hide her enthusiasm. "I'm so happy that you two finally got your-selves together again! That took FOREVER!" Angela emphasized her exasperation at the two of them with a huge smile on her face.

"Ange, this is Blake. Blake, this is Angela, my best friend since first grade and now my sister-in-law too."

Angela shook his hand vigorously. "Thank you for making my bestie glow with joy!" she exclaimed, then she pulled Blake in and squeezed him as well.

Slightly taken aback, Blake laughed and replied, "Believe me, she does way more for me than I do for her. I'm the lucky one." He winked at Laney from over Angela's shoulder.

Levi overheard the conversation from the other room, and he came in with an armful of winter gear piled so high that they could only see his eyes.

"Hey, DeeDee!" He dropped the gear on the couch and hugged his sister. Laney smiled over his shoulder. "Hey, big brother," she greeted with a laugh, wrapping her arms around him.

Laney was the closest to Levi out of all her brothers. When the others would run away from her, Levi stayed behind. He was the one who taught her to play baseball, who had tea parties with her, and the one she could always turn to when she needed brotherly advice or a shoulder to cry on. Their bond ran deep, and when Laney came home from Idaho with a broken heart, Levi and Angela were the ones who helped her pick up the pieces again.

"Levi, this is Blake. Blake, this is my favorite big brother, Levi." She looked up at her brother, beaming at him.

"Nice to meet you," Blake said, shaking Levi's hand. "So you're the one I come to when I need dirt on Laney, huh?"

"Haha. Very funny. We aren't here to embarrass Laney. We are here to borrow some gear. We're hitting the slopes today," she said to Blake giddily. "So let's make sure all this fits before you end up in knee-deep snow with floods on."

Levi grabbed the equipment on the couch, and Blake tried things on, piece by piece. It helped that Levi was about the same height as Blake, though not as built. The coat was a bit snug, but it would do the job, and Laney kind of liked the way it hugged him.

Thanking Angela and Levi over their shoulders, they headed back out to the car. Laney strapped the boards to the roof rack and piled the rest of the gear into the trunk.

"Hey, Dee, are you guys coming to dinner at Mom and Dad's tomorrow night?" Levi called out into the driveway.

"I'll have to think about that one." Laney smirked. "I don't want you all to scare him off with one Sunday dinner," she joked, climbing into the driver's seat. Levi and Angela stood on the porch and waved until they drove away.

"So, 'DeeDee,' huh?" Blake teased.

Laney chuckled. "Yeah, he couldn't say Delaney when I was born, so the name sort of stuck. I allow it since he's my favorite brother," Laney said as they pulled onto the highway. "What did you think of them?"

"He's nice! And he didn't pound me for hurting you, so that's a plus!" Blake chuckled. "Angela's cool too. I can see why you two have been friends for so long. She really cheers you on, doesn't she?"

"Yeah, we've been through everything from bras to boys together. It's hard to break a bond of sisterhood like that."

The drive up the canyon was winding and slow, which gave Blake the perfect speed to gawk at the gorgeous scenery around them. The pine trees held frost perfectly on their needles while their boughs shouldered the weight of a plentiful year of powder. It was like being in a live Bob Ross painting with no "Happy Little Mistakes" anywhere, and he rode most of the way with his mouth open in awe. He had an effervescent, boyish charm that he buried from a lot of the world, but he never hid it from Laney.

The parking lot at the ski resort was covered in packed snow, making the lines for the stalls impossible to distinguish. Laney pulled her car into a good guess of where stall lines might be and killed the engine.

"Have you ever been snowboarding before?" Laney asked Blake as they put on their gear and gathered the boards from the top of the car.

"Of course! That was my friends and mine's favorite thing to do when we skipped class in the winter. But I have to admit I haven't boarded in quite a few years," Blake said.

"We'll take a few practice runs down the smaller slopes until your muscle memory comes back," she told him and patted his arm. "You'll do great. Now, the best part is that you'll be incognito with your beard and these goggles, so nobody will recognize you," she added as she pulled them over his head.

Sitting in the snow at the top of the bunny hill, Laney buckled her boots into her bindings, and Blake did the same. Then, she tipped up onto her feet and offered her hands to Blake. His first attempt to stand was as graceful as Bambi's first time on ice, and his weight distribution quickly overpowered hers. She toppled down into the snow next to him, laughing. The sound of joy coming from her warmed his heart in the frigid snow, and he laughed hard along with her.

"Okay, let's try this another way." She giggled, turning over onto her knees and popping up.

After practicing on the smaller slopes for an hour, they decided to head up the ski lift.

"The ride up is just as great as the ride down," Laney said as she deeply inhaled the scent of pine all around her.

The golden sun peeked in and out of clouds, warming their pink cheeks while making the snow below them sparkle like diamonds. Below them, boarders carved the mountainside, the snow softly giving way as they weaved like falling leaves down the run. Each rider painted their own beautiful strokes on a community canvas, making everyone an artist.

"I can see why," Blake replied in awe, putting his arm around her as they rode the ski lift. "This is God's creation right here."

"It sure is," she agreed. "I haven't been up here for a long time. Angela and I used to get season passes and come up two to three times a week in high school. But ever since I went to nursing school and she married my brother, we haven't had a lot of time to come."

"Well, I'm glad you brought me. This has already been a fun day," Blake said, smiling from under his goggles. "And the best part is that not only do I get to spend time with you, but I get to do it out in the open where no one knows who I am. It's nice to have a day with you without any interruptions."

The end of the lift was nearing them, so they readied themselves for a quick escape. As they strapped their boards on, a sudden scream came from further down the slope. It sounded like a child's voice, scared and calling for help. Without hesitation, Blake hopped on his board and took off after the voice. Laney was right on his heels, although she couldn't ride fast enough to catch up to him. He zigzagged in and out of the crowd with ease, floating over the snow like he had been doing it for years. She watched as he neared the out-of-control child, grabbed her hand, and helped to slow her to a stop. Then, he sat her down in the snow to calm her down and listened as she told the story of being left behind by her big brother and his friends.

"Well, don't you worry," he reassured the young girl. "My friend Laney and I will stick with you until we get to the bottom, okay? Then we will find your brother."

"My mom is in the lodge waiting for us. I didn't know this run was so big, and I'm not that good yet, so I got scared," she cried.

Laney rode up as Blake was helping the girl back onto her feet.

"We will do this nice and slowly, okay?" Blake said, coaching her along until they reached the lodge.

"That's my mom right there," she said in a slightly shaky voice, pointing to a woman scolding an older boy. "Thanks for the help today, mister," she expressed gratefully before walking away with her board in her hand.

"So he saves the day in real life, too?" Laney whispered as they unhooked their boots. His smile pushed his cheeks up under his goggles. "A good superhero never passes up an opportune moment." And with that, he leaned closer and dropped a snowball down the back of her coat.

Laney squealed, "Oh, I'll show you 'opportune moment!'" She scooped up some ammunition and threw a snowball at him. Blake burst out laughing and wrestled the next round from her hand and smashed it on the top of her head.

"You just wait. I'll get my revenge," she threatened playfully, tackling him down into the snow.

"I'm looking forward to it." He laughed and wrapped his arms around her.

As he gazed at Laney, his hand went to the nape of her neck, and he leaned in closer, which made Laney drop the last of her snowballs and surrender. His soft breath was warm on her cheek as she anticipated his lips on hers. But the sound of their goggles colliding interrupted the mood and made them both open their eyes. There was no getting around them no matter what they tried, inducing a fit of laughter from them both as they lay in the snow.

"Let's just put a pin in this for now," Blake whispered, stroking her pink cheeks with his glove. "Do you have another run or two left in you?"

"Absolutely," Laney said as Blake helped her to her feet.

The gravelly snow crunched under the tires of Laney's car as they drove to her parents' house at the end of a dark country lane. It stood alone—the nearest neighbors were several acres away—but close enough to be a community. An American flag attached to the eaves on the porch blew lazily in the light evening breeze, casting shadows from the porch light onto a blanket of snow.

"Looks like the whole gang came tonight," Laney said, nodding toward the driveway filled with minivans and sedans. "My brothers each have three kids—except for Levi and Angela, who are basically still newlyweds—so it's about to get wild."

A kaleidoscope butterflies erupted in Blake's stomach, and he was so preoccupied with the thought of meeting Laney's whole family that he tangled up his seatbelt trying to get out, then slammed it in the car door. As soon as he recovered, he forced a smile and took the pie he made from Laney's cold hands, so she could hold onto his arm while they walked up the salted sidewalk. When Laney and Blake neared the front door, the commotion in the house that ebbed and flowed through the light-filled windows grew louder. Laney paused on the doorstep and turned to face him, lacing her shaking hand with his.

"Are you sure you're up for this? I mean, we could turn tail right now, and they'd never even know we came."

"Hey, I'm supposed to be the anxious one, remember?" Blake laughed nervously, juggling the freshly-baked cherry pie he'd made in one hand while holding tight to her hand with the other. Fear settled in his eyes, and his shoulders held a rigid pose. He looked more like a deer in headlights than the cool, calm, and collected guy he normally was. "I got this! What do five brothers and the father of the only girl in the house have that I can't handle? It's fine! I'll be fine!" His words convinced no one. "But if I start to get in over my head, throw me a rope, okay?"

"We need a code word—one we can use if either of us feels overwhelmed," she said. "I'm pretty sure you're going to get mauled in there." Laney laughed when his smile tightened. "I'm kidding. They're going to love you," she reassured him. "How about, 'pie?' That's a good code word. If you need a life preserver, say, 'pie,' and I'll come to your rescue."

"'Pie,' it is," he said, his voice cracking as she reached for the doorknob.

The light from inside flooded the porch as the front door opened, illuminating the panic on Blake's face. Laney laughed and squeezed his hand as she led him into the foyer. Laney's mother, Eliza, met them in the hallway with a big smile and a motherly hug.

"Mama, this is Blake. Blake, this is my mama, Eliza."

"It's a pleasure to meet you, Mrs. Campbell," Blake replied respectfully.

"Oh, you can call me Eliza." She smiled the same smile Laney was born with as she hugged Blake. "This smells amazing. Thank you for baking us one of your famous pies. Laney has raved about it since you met," Eliza said as she took the shaking pie from Blake. "Come on in and meet everyone else—that is, if you're up for it," she teased.

A small boy with a towel for a cape raced past them in the hallway. "Mom! The Sentinel is eating dinner with us tonight! Can he sit with us at the kids' table?" he shouted before disappearing with a rowdy group of his cousins.

The volume in the dining room erupted when Laney and Blake walked in. Hugs were exchanged between siblings and in-laws, and they all lined up to meet Blake.

"Everyone, this is Blake. Blake, this is everyone. We can do the name game later." She looked over at him and smiled. "But I want to take you to meet my dad. He's out on the patio." Laney grabbed his hand and led him through the sea of people. "Daddy," she said softly as she slid the glass door open. "I want you to meet Blake."

Laney's dad turned from the smoker and set his tongs down. "Robert Campbell," he said, shaking Blake's hand firmly. "It's nice to meet you, Blake."

"The pleasure's mine, sir," Blake said with a smile, returning the handshake.

"We've sure heard a lot about you. Laney tells us that you live in L.A. Is that right?"

"Yes, sir," Blake replied humbly.

"We watched all your movies after you and Laney met. You do all right, kid."

Blake rubbed the back of his neck nervously. "Thank you. It's a blessing to get to do what I love for a living." Then, Blake turned to the smoker and breathed deeply. "This meat smells amazing! What are you cooking in there?"

"Oh yeah, these are pork roasts. Been smoking them all day long! The neighbors have even stopped on their way past, wondering what the delicious smell is." He laughed. "I hope it doesn't disappoint."

"Well, if they taste as good as they smell, odds are in your favor. I love to cook, but I've never smoked meat. Have you been doing it for a long time?" Blake asked. "I'd love to get into it myself."

"While you boys talk shop, I'm going inside to help Mom with prep," Laney said over her shoulder as she walked back through the door. She smiled through the glass at Blake and her dad shooting the bull, grateful that a tough nut to crack like her father was going easy on him.

The kitchen hummed with female voices and dishes clanking, and the occasional yell came from the family room where the brothers were watching a basketball game. Angela sidled up next to Laney, potato peeler in hand, and nudged her hip.

"So...tell me all about your time with Captain Handsome," Angela pressed Laney while they peeled potatoes. "I love his beard. Very sophisticated."

Laney looked excitedly at her best friend, unable to squelch a squeal.

"He surprised me at the airport on Friday," she swooned. "He paid off my little old lady passenger to take her place and gave her his private car to take instead. I was so shocked to see him standing there that I couldn't even speak! Then he kissed me as I've never been kissed before—and it was like we hadn't been apart."

They giggled together over a bowl of potato peels about a boy, like a couple of teenagers.

"He looks really cute and so nervous!" Angela laughed, looking over at Blake and Robert through the glass doors.

"We are a bit overwhelming," Laney admitted. "He's doing pretty good, considering the crowd tonight."

Angela laughed. "Well, when everyone found out they could potentially meet *the* Blake Logan, they all clamored over."

Out on the patio, the mood shifted from cooking tips to a more serious tone. Robert looked up from the smoker and met Blake's eyes.

"I know this sounds cliché, but I have to ask. What are your intentions with my daughter, Blake? I know your lifestyle in L.A. is probably full of beautiful women, and I don't want to see my Laney get hurt again," Robert said, basting the roasts.

"You're right. Life in L.A. is full of fancy parties and beautiful women. But that's not what I want out of life, sir. I grew up in a small town in Idaho with good parents and strong values. I'm not here on conquest, and she isn't a trophy to win." Blake paused before continuing, "I love Laney, sir. And I want to do everything in my power to show her how loved she is every day. I know our meeting and relationship are unconventional, but I also believe fate played a big part in guiding us together. I don't take it lightly that she is the best thing that has ever happened to me. I will treat her like I'm grateful for her every day." Glancing over his shoulder at Laney and Angela laughing in the kitchen, he rubbed at the tug in his chest.

"Well, that's nice to hear, son. Because, with the way she looks at you, I can tell she is pretty head over heels for you too. And I know if you hurt her, she'll take good care of it before her brothers or I ever could." He snorted.

"Oh yeah." Blake laughed. "My first time seeing her was when she was handing it to some cab driver who was giving her trouble at the airport. I knew right then and there that she wasn't like any woman I'd ever met before. She is definitely something special, that's for sure." He looked back and gazed at her through the window.

Robert smiled and closed the lid to the smoker. "A couple more minutes, and they'll be perfect!" he said with satisfaction. "Thanks for visiting out here with me. It was nice to talk to you without the ladies around. They're outnumbered, but they tend to steer the conversations around here," he joked and patted Blake on the back as they went into the house.

Dinner was loud and full of laughter around a large farmhouse table. The food was as good as the company, and Blake's anxiety melted away like the butter on the mashed potatoes. Laney's family was as amazing as she had said they were, and he felt right at home amidst the chaos.

Laney leaned over and whispered in his ear, "I think I'm going to go check on the *pie*. Can you come and help me in the kitchen?" Her words sent pleasant chills down his neck and arms.

Blake excused himself from the table and placed his plate in the dishwasher before following her down the hallway. Laney grabbed their coats from the rack by the front door on her way past and headed up a long staircase.

"Where are you taking me?" he whispered up the stairs to her.

She smiled over her shoulder and put a finger to her lips. "Shh! The kids will hear you and follow us!" She grinned widely. "Now hustle before they realize we're gone."

She scurried through a long hallway full of doors on each side and stopped at one with pink flowers painted on it.

"This was my old room. I wanted to show you my rooftop spot," she said as the door creaked open. "Now, be careful. The exercise equipment doesn't feel too great to slam your shins against."

They weaved their way through the dark room to the only light source and opened the curtains. A rush of cold air hit them both as she slid the window up and climbed onto a stool. Throwing her coat over her shoulders, she dared him to follow.

The snow on the rooftop had mostly melted away, with only a few drifts remaining on the shingles where the sun never touched. Laney sat beside the attic-style window and waited for Blake to emerge.

The moment he climbed out the window, Blake's eyes cast heavenward, and his jaw slacked open at the expanse of space above. The cold night sky was filled with sparkling diamonds that spilled from God's gemology desk and scattered across His floor. From the dusty Milky Way to the large and mighty, the stars dazzled, waiting to fill their minds with the wisdom of the universe. He took a deep breath, letting the cool air fill his lungs, and breathed out the steam his body was done with.

"Wow! This is incredible! Now I get it. This is so worth the fear of falling to my death," he half-joked, looking down toward the ground.

"I know it is! It's perfection!" she agreed. "Even if the potential to die is there," she teased, lacing her hand into his.

They sat in silence for a while before his voice, barely above a whisper, broke the quiet.

"Laney, are you happy? And I don't mean like 'today is a good day' kind of happy. I mean, deep down, in your heart of hearts, is your life everything you've wanted it to be?" She thought for a moment, then replied in her own hushed tone, "Most of the time, yeah. It is. Is it perfect? Not exactly. But is it perfectly tailored for me to learn and grow the best I can? Absolutely. I have good friends, a good family, jobs I love, a home to feel at peace in, and a heart full of love. I don't know if there's much more a girl could ask for…" She paused. "Except maybe someone to share the journey with and a crazy brood to keep me on my toes. Yeah, that would set me up for life."

Blake smiled. The idea of rocking chairs on a wooden porch while the kids ran and played with the dog in the yard sounded pretty dang good. The whole "white picket fence" thing was hard for Blake to understand as a teenager. But after he'd had the adventure he craved, the wild oats were sown, and the dreams were captured; what was left? What was next on the horizon? What would bring his life real meaning? Was it an academy award like Joe pushed for, or someone to love by his side? Was it millions of dollars and a fancy mansion in Malibu, or the warmth of a woman with a heart of gold that drove him further? Now, the urge to grow old with someone that gave him purpose grew wildly in his soul like ivy until it consumed everything else.

"What about you? Are you genuinely happy?" she asked in return.

"You know, there were times when I thought I was. When I had dreams to chase, and I surpassed the goals I set for myself and my career, I thought I had it made. But then I'd leave the set, or the fancy parties, and come home to a dark house. Alone. With no one to add light to my life and no one to share things with. And it suddenly felt so hollow. After my dad died, I realized how successfully empty my life had become, and I ached for any human connection that was more than skin-deep. And until I met you, I had lost hope that it existed for me. You plunged me into the deep end, and at first, I didn't know how to come up for air. I was out of my element and lost—but found—all at the same time. I've never forgotten it. And I'll never be content with less." He looked over at her.

"Now *that's* incredible," she whispered. "And here I was, worried I was a cheap thrill for a fancy celebrity."

"You are not a cheap thrill. You are the real deal, Laney Campbell. I'm just glad I was smart enough to recognize it when I first laid eyes on you—beating up a big, hairy dude and all." He laughed.

She elbowed his ribs playfully.

"Well, I'm glad we got together at his expense then. It was worth it for me—although the cab driver might feel differently."

Blake laughed again, his face filled with genuine joy.

"Now, will you kiss me before my face freezes off, and my family eats all your pie?" she grinned and ran her fingers through his hair, pulling him close. "Thought you'd never ask," he whispered before acquiescing her request.

L **aney** rolled into work that Monday morning with a smile that covered her entire face. The time she had spent with Blake that weekend had been like a dream, solidifying her feelings for him exponentially with each day they spent together.

"This could be it," she said to Trish, her coworker, that afternoon at her workstation. "I can't wipe the smile off of my face!" Laney tried, unsuccessfully.

"I just can't believe you're living the fairytale in real life!" Trish grinned. "You know every woman on the planet wants to be in your shoes, right?"

"It still doesn't feel real, but he's so different from how he's portrayed in the magazines. I never thought something like this would happen to me. I can't stop smiling, and my face hurts so bad." She rubbed her cheeks.

Trish laughed over her shoulder as she grabbed a chart from the wall and disappeared into an examination room.

Suddenly, a familiar voice spoke in the distance, and Laney paused what she was doing to focus on it.

"Excuse me, do you know where I can find Delaney Campbell?" the voice asked the receptionist down the hallway.

Laney leaned around the corner in her chair to confirm that the voice she heard was, in fact, her Sentinel in combat boots. A hush of disbelief settled over the foyer before whispers started. Because there, at the end of the hallway, was Blake, dressed in his Sentinel costume. The thick navy blue fabric hugged him in all the right places, accentuating his broad shoulders and strong arms. He was built like a train, solid and unstoppable, from his perfectly messy hair to his chunky black combat boots. And the clean, horizontal, gray stripes and insignia across his chest highlighted his pectoral muscles. Diagonal stripes traveled from his ribcage to a dark leather utility belt slung low around his waist, leading her eyes to his washboard abs. An over-the-shoulder gun-holster circled his shoulders, and a matching holster was strapped to his right thigh. A thin gray stripe ran down the outside of each muscular leg to black combat boots, and fingerless leather gloves finished off his look.

Laney snapped a photo of him and typed a message to Angela:

Laney: Look who showed up at work today. That wardrobe department needs a raise after the homerun they hit on this one.

Laney giggled to herself as she hit send.

He was more than a tall, handsome drink of water—and she knew that. But man, was he nice to look at from across the room. Everything about him started a fire inside her, and she found herself so focused on him that she forgot about the wheeled chair she was tipped in. Laney quickly went from discreet to crumpled on the floor as her chair toppled over and dumped her out of it.

The commotion drew Blake's attention from the receptionist to the end of the long hallway. He ran to her, laughing hysterically as he picked her up off the floor.

"Well, that's one way to get my attention!" He laughed. "Are you okay?"

"Nothing but my pride is bruised," Laney said, blushing as she dusted off her soft pink scrubs. "You look incredible!" She stepped back, taking him in. "What are you doing here?"

"I had my assistant ship my uniform to me overnight. I thought I could come and visit the kids." His eyes shined with this excitement. "I've always wanted to do this, and I thought today would be a perfect day to do it. Will you help me?"

"Of course, I will!" Laney grinned from ear to ear. "This is going to be awesome! And I know just where to start!" She grabbed his hand and took him to Dr. Hansen's office.

"Dr. Hansen," Laney called out, knocking on the door frame. "Blake has come dressed up as The Sentinel today to see the kids. I wanted him to meet you first before I take him around the peds unit if that's okay."

Dr. Hansen's stoic persona disappeared as stood up from his desk with a huge smile on his face, thrust his hand out, and shook Blake's enthusiastically.

"I think I'm as big of a fan as my patients are." Dr. Hansen chuckled. "Superheroes were my thing as a kid, and I still have my collection at home. But who am I kidding, I *still* love them." He beamed with boyish excitement. "Can I get a photo and an autograph?" he asked, handing Blake his prescription pad and a sharpie.

"It would be an honor," Blake replied as he signed:

To Dr. Hansen—an unsung hero.

Blake Logan

Blake handed the pad and sharpie back to Dr. Hansen and stepped next to him while Laney took a photo with his cell phone.

"I don't know if Laney told you, but you treated my nephew, Noah, a few years ago. I appreciate you so much for what you did for my family. Thank you," Blake said graciously. "You have no idea how grateful we are for you and your staff."

"I am extremely proud to have the people behind me that I do. We love what we do here." Dr. Hansen smiled as he shoved his hands into the pockets of his lab coat. "It's very nice to meet you. Thanks for coming down, and have a great time in the unit. The kids will be thrilled!" Dr. Hansen shook Blake's hand again before he and Laney left.

"Dr. Hansen is a big kid at heart. Thanks for meeting him." Laney squeezed Blake's hand. "Now, let's go make some dreams come true."

In the pediatric oncology unit, Blake took the time to meet every child who wanted to see him. He took photos, played games, and read stories, giving his full attention to each patient. Laney watched him with a huge lump in her throat as he interacted with the tiny bald warriors. Blake's face was as lit up as the kids' faces were, and she could see what a difference his animated conversations made in the very glum days for some. For a moment, their frail and sick bodies were filled with hope and joy instead of nausea and weakness. They were no longer cancer patients but sidekicks to the biggest superhero they had ever known. Blake's eyes sparkled with wonder as he visited with each child, and Laney fell harder and harder in love with him with every high five, smile, and hug he gave. It was no wonder he had scaled her walls so easily. He was made of goodness and light. He was as beautiful within as he was without, and she had never seen a more gorgeous soul.

The evening sun painted the sky orange as it dipped below the horizon on their walk to Laney's car, and Blake's excitement turned serious. She could feel the energy change as they climbed into the front seats. Blake buried his face in his hands as soon as they were alone in the cold silence. Then, he took a deep breath and sobbed. Laney wrapped him in her arms and cried alongside him, knowing the weight that a day like that carried.

"Those kids are stronger than I will ever be," he wept. "Now I know what you meant about your job taking your whole heart. That was the most inspiring yet heartbreaking experience I have ever had," he said as he wiped his tears. "They have such positive attitudes while going through a hell a child should never have to face. They were so brave. I am nothing compared to them—nothing." He hung his head.

Laney wiped his face with her fingers. Taking his chin in her hands, she looked deep into his sad eyes. She spoke softly, but her words hit him like a tsunami.

"You have no idea what you have given those kids today. They will remember those moments with you forever. You have given some of them another reason to stay positive, and some of them the courage to keep fighting when they want to give up. I could see the fire turn back on in their eyes. They are warriors, and you just gave them another reason to stand with courage and fight for another day. That's not something to take lightly, and I am so proud of you!" She wiped her own tears away and kissed his forehead.

"This day is definitely going down as one that changed my life forever." He gazed out at the sunset through the windshield as they drove away from the hospital. "I had no idea how much good I could do with this." He put his hands on the insignia on his chest. "For those moments, I wasn't Blake Logan. I *was* The Sentinel—for real. Changing one tiny corner of the world. It felt incredible!" He smiled proudly. "This was a good day. Thank you. I can't wait to call and tell my family about it."

Early the next morning, on her way to work, Laney dropped Blake off at the Salt Lake City airport. They parked in the farthest spot they could find, where jet engines coming and going would be the only disruptions. Blake dropped his black duffle bag at his feet and opened his leather jacket to share his warmth with her, enveloping her like a cozy morning sunspot. Laney leaned into him as he held her against his chest, taking in every scent, every heartbeat, every frosty breath. She hugged him tightly, melting into his firm yet gentle embrace, feeling more at home than she was in her own living room.

He kissed the top of her head and sighed. "This weekend was everything I needed, right before the chaos begins," he spoke softly. "Thank you."

"Agreed. I don't want it to end," she lamented. "I loved having you here, meeting my family, seeing those kids. I don't want to go back to the way it was without you."

"After my book tour is over, will you come to L.A. and see me? I want to show you my home there, and maybe you can meet a few of my friends. Can you get some time off?"

"Of course! Dr. Hansen actually has a few oncology conferences pretty soon, so I will have some time off then. Say when and where, and I'll be there."

"Perfect. I'll look at my calendar when I get back home, and we can make plans, okay? But I don't want to think about that right now," he said, tightening his grip around her. "I want to focus on this, on you, on right now, for just a few more minutes." His voice reverberated through his chest and into her ears like music.

An announcement over the PA reminded him that he had a flight to catch and a life in L.A. to get back to. He pulled away from her slowly, easing himself into a life with her at a distance. He kissed her forehead and brushed her hair behind her ear.

"I'll see you soon, okay?" He kissed her cheeks, her frozen nose, and her lips one last time. Then, he donned a New Orleans Saints baseball cap and put on his aviator sunglasses. "I am ridiculously in love with you, Laney

Campbell, and it's going to take every ounce of strength I have to walk away from you right now. So give me a little push, will ya?" He laughed wistfully.

"I don't think so." She frowned a little and locked her hands around him. "And for the record, I'm ridiculously in love with you too." She left a kiss on his cheek before stepping backward. "Now hurry, so you don't miss your flight," she said, handing him his duffle bag. "The sooner we say goodbye, the sooner we get to say hello again." She let go of his hand.

"Not goodbye, just 'see you later.' 'I'll call you tonight," he said as he turned and walked away.

He stopped before the doors opened and looked over his shoulder at her. He smiled sadly and waved across the parking lot to the girl in soft pink scrubs who held his heart in her hands. She waved back and blew a kiss as the automatic doors shut behind him, and he disappeared into a crowd.

Chapter 23

The next few weeks were spent trying to connect over the distance. And although texts and video chats weren't quite the same as being together, they made the best of it.

"I can't wait to see you tomorrow!" Laney squealed over FaceTime as she pulled out a suitcase from under her bed. "What is the weather in L.A. like in the springtime? I have no idea what to bring!"

"Well, it's definitely warmer here than it is there, but pretty unpredictable. Bring both shorts and a jacket. You'll probably need both," he replied from her phone on the dresser.

"I'm glad it will be warm. I haven't seen the sunshine in forever."

"You'll have plenty of time to soak it up. Hey, listen. I've gotta get going to a meeting with the studio, but I'll be at the airport tomorrow to get you, okay? I love you."

"Sounds good! I love you too!" she shouted from her open closet, blowing him a kiss.

"I'm so anxious about seeing him again!" she confessed to Angela on the way to the airport. "It's been hard to be so far away from him. What if things are different?"

"It's going to be fine. You guys are made for each other. I'm going to miss you, girl, and I'm worried about you. What if I can't get a hold of you for some reason? What if you have too much fun without me?" Angela pouted.

"I make no promises about the fun, but don't worry—I'll be careful. And if it will make you feel better, I'll give you Blake's number in case of emergencies, okay? But remember, emergencies only! Don't give my boyfriend's private number to the tabloids, you hear me?" She laughed, programming in Blake's number on Angela's phone.

"So after this visit, then what, Lane?" Angela asked. "You're not going to move away from me now, are you?"

"I'm not sure of anything that far into the future. I'm just trying to take it one day at a time because the rest as a whole is too daunting to think about. But even with all the uncertainty, one thing is for sure. I love him," she said, smiling widely. "He is the best thing that has ever happened to me."

"Hey!" Angela contested.

"Well, besides you, of course."

Angela grinned smugly, satisfied that Blake hadn't taken her place—yet.

"I'm not sure what will happen. But I know I have to try with my whole heart, or I'll regret it forever."

They pulled up curbside at the airport, and Laney hugged Angela goodbye, hopped out excitedly, and ran to the trunk to grab her bags.

"I'll see you in a few days. Don't do anything that I wouldn't!" Angela yelled out the open window as Laney walked away, pulling her suitcase behind her.

"That leaves it pretty open!" Laney yelled back, laughing as she disappeared through the automatic doors.

Laney's plane touched down in sunny California just before noon, and her insides fluttered like a jar full of butterflies, making it impossible to focus. She had a smile that crossed her whole face as she pulled her luggage through the airport. Her phone chimed as a message came in from Blake:

> **Blake:** I'm out in the pickup line but hurry. I was followed, and the vultures are circling.

Laney picked up her speed to a low jog, weaving through the crowds of travelers and hurrying toward the doors. Up ahead, a commotion waited for her outside. She pushed her way through the crowds to Blake's car, surrounded by paparazzi. They swarmed like a colony of bees, shouting questions and taking video and photos of him through the car windows. When Blake saw her, he jumped out of his car to come to her rescue. He helped her into the passenger seat and tossed her suitcase into the trunk. Slamming the hood, he yelled at the photographers to step back as he climbed into his car, put it in drive, and sped off impatiently.

"Hi, I'm so sorry. That's not the greeting you were supposed to get. Welcome to L.A.," Blake said with a tired sigh.

"That was crazy," Laney exclaimed, catching her breath. "I knew red carpets were swarming with paparazzi, but the airport too?"

"Around here, yeah. Now you know why I was so happy to hang out in Utah and Idaho with you. Because it's near impossible to avoid them here if someone outs you," he said, running his fingers through his hair. "But I have a nice, chill weekend planned. So don't worry, okay?" He reached over and took her hand.

The tension hung in the car like a pair of fuzzy dice hanging from a rearview mirror as they left the chaos behind, but his touch made her feel a bit better. Laney took a deep breath and kissed the back of his hand in hers. His face relaxed, and the stress left his shoulders.

"You smell nice," she purred, resting her head on his arm while he drove.

"You're going to make me crash," he warned with a laugh, looking at her lips mere inches away from his.

"Please don't. I'm betting this car cost as much as my house did." She laughed. "So, what is the plan while I'm here?"

"That part is a surprise." He grinned. "I do have an event that was sprung on me last minute, and I was hoping to take you if you don't mind. It's a wrap party for a friend's movie that he directed. We just have to make an appearance. If it's too overwhelming, we can leave at any time. Want to go?"

"I'm game, but I didn't bring a nice dress. What kind of party is it?"

"It's cocktail attire, but don't worry about that. We can go get you a nice dress. In fact, let's go now while we're close to the shopping district. There's an outdoor mall I like pretty close by." He turned on his blinker and checked his blindspot. "And then we can have a relaxing night in tonight."

He exited the freeway and headed toward a swanky shopping complex. Blake pulled the car into the valet parking lot and came around to open Laney's door.

"Rodeo Drive is a bit too stuffy for me, so I hope you'll like this place a little bit better." He offered her a hand and helped her out. "Plus, they're really great about keeping paparazzi out, which is nice." He checked over his shoulder to see if they were still being followed as he handed his key to the valet.

Laney's eyes opened wide when she saw the gorgeous designer shops lining the mall. In the center stood a modern theater with an old Hollywood twist and a giant fountain in front of it. The waters danced to Frank Sinatra, waving hello to a bright green, double-decker trolley that chimed as it rolled past.

The alleyways that branched off from the main square were lined with shops reminiscent of old European cities with cobblestone streets. Each storefront was unique in design and color, but it all tied into the architecture.

"I really like this designer," Blake said, leading her into a store. "He makes amazing suits, so I'm sure we can find the perfect dress in here for you too."

Laney's jaw dropped when she stepped inside the brightly lit store. Mirrors every few feet reflected the white lights hanging above and the natural light coming in from the large display windows. Headless mannequins were placed all over, wearing the most gorgeous clothes she had ever seen. Clean, modern furniture peppered the store, resting atop bold, brightly patterned area rugs. The walls held shelves of handbags that were perfectly color-coordinated with the clothes.

"Wow! This is a person with OCD's organizational dream! And I thought Target was fun!" She looked over at Blake with eyes glittering from the bright lights.

"Pick out whatever you want. Shoes, accessories—the works. I want to spoil you today," Blake said, beaming at her.

"Oh, I couldn't possibly…" she trailed off with her jaw slacked open.

"Sure you can! Please let me do this for you." He pulled her close and kissed the top of her head. "I want to."

Laney hesitated for a moment until a little black dress on a mannequin beckoned to her from across the store. She was completely drawn to its sleek lines and off-the-shoulder neckline.

"Can I try that one?" she asked timidly.

"Of course! Let me get a saleswoman over here to help you find your size." Blake disappeared behind a corner and came back with three women chatting excitedly. "These ladies are here to help you with whatever you need. I'm just going to hang out here on the couch while you try stuff on," he said, taking her purse and settling in.

The women went to work on Laney, grabbing dresses, accessories, shoes, and handbags for her to try on. The chatter surrounded her in the small dressing room, and hands and arms and voices flew all around her as she changed. Her focus swirled, but even with the chaos, Laney couldn't stop smiling. She stood in front of the dressing room mirror, surprised at herself. She looked amazing, and although she wasn't much for fancy clothes and shoes, she couldn't deny the 'million bucks' feeling that swelled inside. She spun in front of the mirror and looked at herself from all angles, confident that her first impression in Blake's world would be perfect. Laney peeked out of the dressing room door and said, "I think this is it! Just let me get unzipped."

The ladies rushed to get everything organized and settled before Laney had even finished getting dressed. Blake was waiting outside on the couch with his arms full of bags by the time she came out.

"Did you find some things you liked?" he asked through his grin.

"Oh yes! But I'm feeling guilty because I got a peek at one of the price tags." She cringed.

"Don't you dare. Let me do something nice for the woman I love, okay?"

"I feel like Julia Roberts in Pretty Woman. Well, minus the whole, being humiliated by snobby store clerks part, and the fact that our careers vary quite a bit—of course." Laney's smile stretched from ear to ear as she beamed at him. "I can't wait to show you—I've never worn a more gorgeous dress in my life."

Blake pulled through the wrought-iron gate that stood at the end of a long, winding driveway. His house nestled on five acres of land in Beverly Hills, surrounded by lush green trees and a large stone privacy wall. The two-story, modern-style home had immaculate gardens to welcome visitors, and floor-to-ceiling windows across the living room, facing the valley below. Laney's jaw dropped when she stepped through the door and crossed the stone floors to take in the view. Blake's shiny black grand piano sat in an alcove surrounded by windows, and the golden light from the setting sun wrapped around its beautiful curves.

Although the home was filled with sharp modern lines and angles, it felt cozy and warm. The furnishings were inviting and colored in neutral grays and black leather, with bright accent pillows and artwork to top it off.

Blake's backyard overlooked the whole valley, and a giant infinity pool ran the length of a basketball court. A brick patio stood alongside the pool, with a sitting area for entertaining.

"Your house is incredible!" gasped Laney.

"Thanks," Blake replied humbly. "Let me show you my favorite part!" He took her hand and led her into the backyard.

On the far end, an outdoor kitchen stood next to a fire pit and a living area filled with tables and padded patio furniture.

"I want to cook dinner out here for you tonight. What sounds good to you?" Blake asked, taking both her hands in his and pulling her close.

"Hmmmm," she thought out loud. "Can I have an old firehouse favorite?"

He smiled and leaned in for a kiss. "Absolutely."

The time they had spent apart melted away between them like a popsicle left out in the sun. Whatever tension they felt at Laney's arrival faded away with the sunset behind them, and they were right back to where they'd left off in Salt Lake City.

Blake operated the grill while Laney poured them each a glass of wine.

She sat with one leg tucked under her in a chair that enveloped her as she watched him work.

"This patio furniture is more comfortable than my regular furniture." She laughed. "I love this! The whole ambiance is so relaxing," she said with a long exhale, looking out over the valley lights as the sun dipped below the horizon.

"I thought the same thing when I bought this house. I wanted a place I could feel at peace in. A place that was a sanctuary from the chaos out there during the day. And honestly, I'd pick staying home over going out all the time because I love it so much, but it can be lonely sometimes too. Peace is hard to come by, so I'm taking full advantage of the fact that I have it here." Laney walked up behind him and wrapped her arms around his chest. "And here," he said quietly, putting his hand over hers. He rocked gently side to side, swaying with her to imaginary music that only they could hear.

The moment in time was perfection—the aroma of steak kebabs on the grill, the sounds of birds settling down to sleep, and her arms wrapped around him. Blake took a deep breath, soaking up the importance of the here and now, committing it to memory to sustain him later. He had found a calm amidst the storm around him, and he would do whatever he could to hold onto it.

"That reminds me," he said, turning to look at Laney, "I sent you a 'Blake & Laney Mixtape' playlist while you were trying on clothes."

"Oh yay! I can't wait to listen to it!" Laney exclaimed, grabbing her phone from the table. "I need to text Angela and my mom to let them know I arrived safely. The second I saw you today, my brain wiped clean, and I completely forgot. That kind of distraction tends to happen a lot when you're around," she flirted.

Blake and Laney spent the evening on the patio, having dinner and listening to the music in their playlist. They laughed and danced and spent the night just being together—the little things they longed for when they were apart.

"So, we can do a movie night in, or we can hang out under the stars. Although they're not anywhere near as bright as the ones in the country," Blake said as the last of the dishes were dried and put away.

"Hmmm. I think a night in with a bucket of popcorn is exactly what we need," Laney replied, heading up to her room to change.

"Perfect! I'll meet you down here in a few," he called over his shoulder.

Chapter

24

The next morning, Laney woke up early. The sun hadn't fully risen yet, so she slipped down the stairs to make a pot of coffee. The morning light was starting to creep its way above the hillside around Blake's house, filling his living room with soft, golden tones. She tip-toed out the back door with her mug and found a place to sit and bask in the rising sun. The soft breeze blew around her as she listened to the birds sing about what a glorious morning it was. She could understand why Blake craved this calm after the chaotic experience they had at the airport yesterday. He dealt with a lot more than she realized, and it was a heavy load to bear.

Blake woke up to morning light filtering through his window. He breathed deeply, and the aroma of fresh-brewed coffee filled his nose. He stretched then excitedly flew out of bed when he realized Laney was already up. He threw on a T-shirt and headed out into the kitchen. The evidence that she had been there was apparent, but she was nowhere to be seen. He headed up the steep staircase to her guest room, only to find it empty. As he neared the railing, he spotted her outside on the patio, soaking up the sunshine like a reptile on a rock. He paused to watch her—folded up on the chaise lounge, eyes closed, the sunlight dancing in her hair. He snapped a photo of her through the window before stepping outside to join her.

"Good morning!" she greeted him with a smile.

"Hey beautiful, how'd you sleep?"

"Like a rock! The bed upstairs is so comfortable!"

"I'm glad. So, I have a question for you," Blake said, sitting down next to her. "Tonight is the wrap party. Would you like me to ask my hair and makeup friends to come and help you get ready, or do you want to do it on your own?"

"Well, I don't want to be a bother," she replied, biting her lip. "But it does sound kind of fun to get pampered a bit!"

"Perfect! Then I'll get it arranged." Laney sighed and molded into Blake's shape on the chaise. "This has been such a gorgeous morning. Do you sit out here a lot?"

"Not nearly as much as I should, but I will definitely make it a point to do it more," he said, sighing contentedly.

That afternoon, a swarm of people filled the house to get Blake and Laney ready for the party. Laney was surprised at how much effort it took to glam up for things, and she felt a bit overwhelmed by it all. But when she spun in front of the mirror, she couldn't deny that the hair and makeup team made her look and feel amazing.

As the team left the house, Blake waited for her patiently at the piano, dressed in his designer suit, his fingers softly playing "A Kiss to Build a Dream On." The anticipation ebbed and flowed inside him, and the anxiety caused his hands to tremble on the keys.

Laney stopped at the top of the stairs and took a deep breath. From her colorful floral pumps to her perfectly pinned up-do, she felt incredible. She loved the way the crew enhanced her features, and that, when they were done, she was still able to recognize herself. She gripped her bright red envelope clutch, transferring her nerves through her hands and into the purse. Tonight would help determine whether she could hack it in Los Angeles. Whether she would be accepted as a foreigner in this exclusive world, and whether or not Blake would even want her there. She wanted so desperately to fit into this part of Blake's life, but her self-doubt turned from a whisper to a roar when she saw him at the piano. He was everything to her, but a persistent thought at the back of her mind questioned if she would be enough for him here. She placed one hand on the railing and took a deep, self-assuring breath as she descended the staircase.

Blake turned toward the sound of her heels clicking on the stone steps, and when he saw her, his fingers lingered on a note, his mouth slacking open in awe. As she climbed down the stairs, he studied her inch by inch, sweeping his eyes from her head to her heels. He slowly got up from the bench and made his way to the bottom of the stairs to take her hand.

"Wow," he finally managed to whisper, his voice hoarse. "You clean up nice, Campbell."

"You're not so bad yourself, Logan," she flirted, taking his hand. He spun her on the stone floor to take her all in.

"I can't think of any other words but 'wow.'" He laughed lightly.

"Thank you. Your team did a great job," she said, blushing.

"They're talented for sure. But this is all you." He looked deep into her whiskey-brown eyes as he pulled her in close and left a soft kiss next to her red lips.

"Don't want to smear your lipstick," he said with a wink.

"I'd rather you ruin my lipstick than my mascara." She winked back and walked ahead of him to the car.

Blake stayed two steps behind her on purpose, enjoying the smooth way she walked in her heels.

Laney's stomach flipped and flopped the whole drive to the party. Feeling nervous and overwhelmed, she clasped her hands tightly in her lap to keep them from shaking.

"You're awfully quiet," Blake whispered. "You okay?"

"Yeah. Just nervous. I really want this to go well."

"It will. Just stick with me. You'll do great."

The drive was far too short for Laney's liking, and when they pulled into the driveway, Laney took a deep breath and exhaled slowly.

The valet opened her door and offered her a hand, and she forced a smile as Blake met her at the hood.

The bass pumped outside the house with pulsing neon lights that danced to the beat of the music. Crowds of fancy people dressed to the nines filled every room. Conversations buzzed below the music as Blake and Laney weaved their way through. However, a noticeable tension hung in the air between them after they were surrounded by "The Cream of the Crop." Blake's persona switched to one she had only briefly seen while he was greeting fans the day they met. His whole demeanor had changed, but she was the only one who seemed to notice. He laughed differently and at things she knew he didn't find funny. He talked too loud and kept the company of people she knew he couldn't stand. His body language was stiff as he schmoozed directors and studio executives, and he came off superior to those below his level. The air surrounding him smothered her, and her face hurt from faking a smile all night long. Blake had morphed into his celebrity self. And in the company of his Hollywood peers, it made sense. How could she expect him to be as vulnerable as he was with her? Yet, in her heart of hearts, it bothered her. Seeing him change who he was to fit in with the crowd gave her a knot in the pit of her stomach.

After a few minutes of uncomfortable chatter with the cast from the movie, Laney excused herself to the restroom. She stood in front of the mirror, examining her makeup and checking her teeth for lipstick—pushing down the nagging feelings that hovered below the surface.

Taking a deep breath, she told her reflection, "You can do this. It doesn't matter who he is around others. It only matters who he is with you. He loves you, and you love him. The real him. You'll have to fight to belong in his world, but you're a fighter," she whispered as she dismissed the anxiety rising in her chest and pulled the heavy door open.

As she stepped back out into the party, she came face to face with Alexandra Chase—the star of the movie and the woman on every magazine cover. Every man wanted to date her, and every woman wanted to be her, and as Laney recovered from the shock of running into her, she understood why. Alexandra stood in the hallway looking like she had just stepped out of a photo shoot. Her long legs ended in four-inch stilettos, and a slinky red dress hugged every curve. Alexandra tossed her jet-black hair over her shoulder and placed a hand on her hip. Laney smiled politely and stepped to the side to get by. Alexandra stepped the same way, and Laney laughed at the awkwardness of it.

"Sorry, I've never been good at dancing," Laney said with a giggle before stepping aside again.

"Imagine doing it in stilettos." Alexandra forced a smile and glanced down at her dangerous shoes. "How are you associated with the movie? Intern? Assistant?" Alexandra asked.

"No, I'm here as Blake Logan's guest," Laney said, extending her hand. "I'm Delaney." Alexandra's smile faded as heavy tension settled between them. She offered Laney a limp-fish handshake and narrowed her green eyes.

"So you're the flavor of the week, hmm? Where did he pick you up, a second-hand store?" she mocked.

"Excuse me?" Laney shook her head in shock.

"You know Blake could have any woman he wanted, right?" she moved her hand back to her hip, crowding the hallway. "He might make you feel special now, but just when you fall hard for him, he'll get bored and drop you faster than it takes that bargain lipstick to wear off. Ask most of the women here, they'll tell you the same story. Besides, this world isn't for outsiders like you. So enjoy the ball while it lasts, Cinderella, because midnight is fast-approaching," she scoffed.

Alexandra's words dumbfounded her, and Laney stood there in utter disbelief.

"What's the matter, honey? Did you really think he'd choose a tacky woman like you over someone like me?" Alexandra laughed. "That's cute."

Laney's inner-fighter kicked in, and before her brain could stop her mouth, she replied, "Well, some of us are tacky on the outside, and some of us are tacky on the inside." Laney spotted an abandoned, almost-empty glass of wine on the small vanity table outside the bathroom. She picked it up and dumped it down the front of Alexandra's designer dress, smiling mockingly. "Oops! Looks like you're both now. You really should put some club soda on that. Wine stains, you know." Then, with a determined look, Laney pushed past, leaving Alexandra with a ruined dress and a gaped-open mouth.

Laney fought to breathe. The panic within her chest expanded and pushed out any air left inside her lungs. Blake stood at the other end of the room, engulfed in a loud conversation with a portly man she didn't know, completely oblivious to Laney's world collapsing. *What has gotten into me tonight?* She blinked back the tears that stung her eyes. As the room swirled around her and the music pounded in her ears, all she could focus on was getting a gulp of fresh air. She fought frantically through the sea of people—like a drowning man clawing his way to the surface —and slipped out the back door.

After Laney didn't return to the conversation, Blake scanned the crowd for her. Coming up empty, he headed outside into the salty night air. A few small groups chatted on patio furniture, but Laney was nowhere to be seen. Blake leaned over the balcony outside and scanned the beach, finally noticing one set of footprints that disappeared into the dark.

Laney sat in the sand a few hundred yards down the beach. Far from the obnoxiously loud music, far from fake Blake and his fake laugh, and far from Alexandra and her insults. But most importantly, far away from the person that she was ashamed she became when the pressure was too much. Even in the most expensive clothes, designer shoes, and fancy makeup, she felt as cheap as the shots Alexandra took at her—and the shots she threw back in return. Tears streamed down her face as she relived that moment in the hallway. She hung her head and wouldn't look up when Blake approached.

"What are you doing out here? Are you okay?" Blake asked, offering his hand to her. When she refused his help, he joined her in the sand.

"What's the matter?" Blake asked insistently, removing the pocket square from his jacket, unfolding it, and wiping her mascara-streaked face.

"I met your friend Alexandra," she squeaked between sobs. "She's definitely not as lovely as they make her out to be, that's for sure."

"What did she say to you?" His brow furrowed into stone.

"That I was your flavor of the week, that I was tacky, and that I'd never fit in this world with you. And you know what? She's right. I will never fit in. I can put on all the fancy clothes and makeup to play the part, but deep down, we both know I don't belong here. But the worst part? The worst part was the response I gave in return. I'm not sure exactly what came over me, but I'm not proud of myself right now. When I stood up to that cabbie, I was defending myself against a man who was trying to intimidate and dominate me. But when I stood up to Alexandra, all I did was stoop to her level. It was as if being accepted by her and the others here tonight would prove to me that I was worthy of you. I shouldn't need her approval, but I wanted it. And when I didn't get it, I panicked. I should've let it go and walked away. But now I'll never live down what I did, and I probably need to pay a dry-cleaning bill for her dress that I ruined."

"You don't need their approval, Laney. I don't care what they think of you, and neither should you. Honestly, you not being just like everyone else is what drew me to you in the first place. Your depth, joy, and authenticity are what I love about you. She doesn't know me any better than the tabloids do, Laney. Do you really think I'd ever let a woman like that see any shred of my true self? She's basing everything on what she thinks I'm like, whereas you should be basing your opinion of me on what you know." "That's the other thing, Blake. I *do* know the real you, and that is who I love. That other guy in there…is definitely not you, and I know the reason why you act that way, but it's still hard to see you change into a person I barely recognize. I guess this environment brings that out in both of us, doesn't it?"

Blake scooped a handful of sand and let it flow through his fist. "I never thought about it like that before. I'm so used to playing the part that I didn't even consider how it would affect you. I love making movies so much, and I guess sometimes the good outweighs the bad, and sometimes it doesn't. And I'm sorry about Alexandra. Although I wouldn't be surprised if that was the first time someone put her in her place. She probably passed out from shock." He laughed. "Don't worry about her. She's just jealous of you."

"There is no way a woman like that is jealous of me," Laney scoffed, nodding toward the beach house in the distance.

"It's true. She may be beautiful, but she lacks substance and depth. And she hates to see someone else getting what she wants."

"You mean, she wants you?"

"Well, she's the costar I wouldn't date for publicity, which I think always rubbed her the wrong way. She's used to getting everything she wants, and rejection isn't in her vocabulary. She views people as conquests or collateral, and I refused to play her games. So, please, don't listen to her. I don't want you to blend in here. I want you to stand out—because that's what makes you so amazing."

Laney stared out at the ebbing and flowing ocean, the moon providing the spotlight for its graceful dance. Being reminded of how small she was compared to both the vastness of the water in front of her and the expansive stretch of the sky above her re-centered her breathing. She inhaled the salty air, filling her lungs with a grateful breath. Then, she buried her feet into the sand—feeling each grain sift between her toes—and allowed the sensation to anchor her in that moment. Her heart slowed, her tears stopped, and she found within herself her fractured courage.

"I don't know what I was trying to prove here tonight. I tried so hard to play the part, Blake. All dressed up, I look it, but underneath the designer clothes, I'm still a nobody from a small Utah town. I'm flawed, untrusting, and rough around the edges in this world of people who are perfectly smooth and polished. It's a lot to live up to, and at what cost? Do I have to hide who I really am and become someone I'm not, just to be accepted in a world of fallacy?"

"You're right," Blake ceded with a sigh. "At first, it bothered me a lot, too. But after a while of playing along with what Joe wanted just became sort of numb to it. I was getting more and more roles and bigger and bigger parts. And before I knew it, I was a household name, but I barely recognized my own reflection. When you came into my life, you opened up my eyes again to what I was doing. And although I knew I didn't want to pretend like I was someone else anymore, it's hard not to fall back into old habits, you know? It's so easy to get caught up in the riptide of fame, and for what? For the approval of people, some of whom I don't even like? It sounds ridiculous, and I know it is. I just sometimes forget how strong the pull is to become someone else. And the funny thing is, sometimes even a fake persona isn't enough. To live here, I always have to be chasing an unattainable goal, never good enough to be who I am. It's exhausting. And you…you deserve more than that." He glanced over at her, a glint of sadness in his bright blue eyes.

"So do you, Blake," she whispered, the waves almost drowning out the softness in her voice. She rested her head on his shoulder and sighed, the events of the day setting its lead-weight onto both of them. "There's got to be a way for you to do what you love and still be who you are."

They sat there in silence for a while, the sea hypnotizing them with its rhythmic waves crashing onto the shoreline. Laney's exposed shoulders began to shiver in the misty breeze, so Blake took off his suit coat and wrapped it around her. His body warmth transferred to her, and the subtle scent of his cologne and the salty air mingled in her senses. She felt oddly-shaped and rough in a smooth world of perfection, but at that moment, she believed his words. Down the beach, a faint flashbulb went off, and Blake knew the paparazzi would discover them soon—if they hadn't already. His voice broke the stillness.

"How about we get out of here? I've had enough of the L.A. life tonight. Can we go back home to tranquility? Just you, me, comfy clothes, and a nice fire out on the patio?"

The picture he painted was music to her ears.

"Yes, please," she replied happily. "But I've got a small problem. I rolled my ankle when I was running away. Can you help me up?" she asked, extending her hand.

"I'll do you one better than that." He smiled and swept her up into his sturdy arms. They whispered and laughed as Blake carried her back to the house, oblivious to the threat hovering above them. On the deck, Alexandra glared through narrowed eyes at their joy as she stirred the olive in her martini, and watched with disdain as they walked beneath her. She vowed that she would do everything possible to make sure that Laney never came to L.A.

again. With a malicious smirk, she snapped a few quick photos on her phone and sent them to her favorite gossip columnist with the message:

Alexandra: Let's ruin this wannabe's life!!

Then, she smiled smugly and waltzed back into the party, the music rising and falling through the door as it opened and closed.

Chapter 25

*T*he ride back to Blake's house in the hills was a quiet one, but Laney's thoughts of the evening screamed in her mind. She tugged uncomfortably on her dress, anxious to unmask herself from the person she pretended to be. She kicked off her shoes on the floorboards, pulled the pins out of her hair, and took a deep breath as her head tipped back against the headrest. This visit with Blake certainly wasn't what she had expected it to be like. Sure, she knew there would be photographers following him since that's pretty standard for someone of Blake's caliber. But what she wasn't prepared for was the way Alexandra had treated her and how she responded in return. It's one thing to be mistreated by others who didn't even know who she was, but quite another to become someone her own eyes didn't even recognize. She glanced over at Blake in the driver's seat. His face was wrought with concern too, and she wondered if he was as disappointed in her as she was in herself.

"Penny for your thoughts?" she voiced softly, laying her hand on top of his on the gear shift.

His face softened, and he managed to push a smile to the corners of his mouth. He met her eyes briefly before he spoke, choosing wisely the words he wanted to say.

"Honestly, I'm just really sorry..." he trailed off. "The way Alexandra treated you tonight is embarrassing, and I wish I could say it was uncommon. But truth be told, I've seen people who would stab you in the back for far less, and I hate that your first experience here forced you to deal with that."

The headlights from passing cars momentarily lit his burdened face before fading into the darkness. Blake hoped she wouldn't see the severity of the worry in his eyes, but the energy between them made her afraid of the unknown running around in his brain. She squeezed his hand and forced a smile.

"It's not your fault, Blake. You can't control the actions of others. She obviously has some hang-ups that got to her, and you are in nowise responsible. I, on the other hand, had full control of my response to her, and I'm definitely not proud of it."

"Well, I brought you there like a lamb to the slaughter, knowing full well people there aren't kind like you are. And I'm sorry she hurt you. You didn't deserve that."

Blake glanced over at Laney and wondered if she believed him. She had such a fresh, clean, bright soul, and tonight, it was tainted by a side of her that he had never seen before. She wiped the last of the mascara tracks from her cheeks, and a faint sparkle in her eyes returned.

"At the end of the day, they're all still just people too, right? We all make mistakes. I would like the chance to make things right with Alexandra if I can. That was just not me…"

"I'll see what I can do, but I doubt she'll want to talk to either of us." He rubbed the back of his neck. "But enough of letting Alexandra ruin any more of our night. That offer for a fire on the patio still stands if you're up for it." Blake smiled in her direction.

She sighed. "Sounds like perfection."

Blake was outside getting the fire pit ready when Laney came down the staircase. She could see him through the floor-to-ceiling windows, and she paused to watch him work. The way he could look amazing in both a perfectly tailored suit and a pair of sweats and a T-shirt made her grin like a fool. She memorized the way he moved, his body language, his physique—so natural and comfortable compared to the man he was earlier. He had been two different people tonight—Blake Logan, the movie star, and Blake Logan, the man she knew. After all, he was the man everyone wanted, but no one understood, and he had given his heart to her. Delaney Campbell. A "nobody" from a small town with a big heart and a warrior's soul. Because at the end of the day, it didn't matter that she stood there bare-faced in leggings and a T-shirt. He made her feel like the most beautiful girl in the world. And coming from a man who lived in a world of perfection, it meant more to her than he would ever know.

Laney stepped out onto the patio, her hair falling softly on her shoulders. All the fancy makeup from the day had been rinsed down the drain, the shoes kicked off by her bed, and the designer dress packed up to send to the cleaners. Grateful to slough off the heaviness of the day, Laney joined Blake by the fire. He handed her a glass of wine, and she started toward her favorite chaise.

"I had someplace else in mind tonight," the Blake she knew deep down smiled and said, gesturing toward the other end of the patio. Laney laughed when she saw the two-person hammock in the corner; its arching stands stretching the fabric taut.

"I'm not sure I have enough coordination for a hammock. You do remember the chair-toppling incident at my work, right? I can be about as graceful as a bad joke delivered at the wrong time."

"What's the harm in trying?" Blake teased with a laugh as he set his glass on the stone wall to help her into the soft cocoon.

"Well, I could go head over feet onto a stone patio and bruise both my butt and my pride…But what the heck." She finished her wine, handed him her empty glass and climbed in.

He stepped around the other side and jostled next to her.

"Unnecessary roughness! Flag on the play!" She gripped the edges and squealed. "If I go down, I'm taking you with me!"

He nestled in next to her, laughing to himself.

"Oh, you think you're funny, do you?" she teased.

"Oh, I do. I'm hilarious."

"Well, at least one of us thinks so," she lovingly jabbed.

"Ouch. That hurts me deeply." He laughed, feigning a hurt look while clutching his chest like she had just broken his heart.

Laney laughed and molded against his contour, sharing his blanket and warmth. He wrapped his free arm around her to keep her as close as possible and sighed. His body next to hers made her feel like she was home again as the scent of his faded cologne filled her senses. As they swayed, the heaviness of the day floated away on the breeze, like autumn leaves in a storm.

The two of them lay in silence, gazing up at the night sky, and although the lights from the city below upstaged many of the stars, the brightest and boldest stood strong against their competition.

"There aren't a lot of secrets to be told tonight," Laney whispered as if they would be caught eavesdropping. "We will have to listen extra hard to hear the stars." She smiled.

"The night sky out here is definitely less of a show than it is back at home, that's for sure," he agreed.

"Sure, but that just means we will have to pay closer attention. What are they saying to you?" Laney asked after a few minutes of silence.

"That, in a room full of stars, you are my Polaris. You shine the brightest, you're the most constant, and you guide me home like the North Star does a lost sailor." Blake hugged her tighter. "What do yours say?"

"Mine are saying…" she paused thoughtfully, "…to stay the course no matter the storm."

Blake smiled at her words, grateful that she no longer seemed weighed down by the events of the evening. He had never experienced a love like hers. A love that didn't want his name next to hers for publicity but for the partnership. A love that made him feel like home no matter where he was in the world. The mere thought of her took him right back to safety, to peace. And he needed that desperately. He held her as tightly as he could—as if she'd float away from him in the breeze should he fall asleep—and absorbed every ounce of good vibes she gave off.

The buzzing vibrations and constant chiming from her phone on the nightstand stirred Laney from a night of restless sleep. The morning sun had begun to trickle in through her window as she rubbed the sleep from her eyes and grabbed her phone to silence it. Her notification screen was so long that she had to scroll several times to see it all. Her social media had been swamped with comments and DMs, and her text app had triple-digit numbers of unread messages. She opened the message from Angela first to see a link to a gossip website headlining a photo of her and Blake from last night. The photo was grainy and dark, but she could easily make out their laughing faces. Her arms were wrapped around Blake's shoulders as he carried her up the beach, his suit coat still draped over her. The perspective was from above, possibly from a balcony, and she immediately knew that

Alexandra was behind whatever charade was being pulled. The headline screamed in big, bold letters:

Blake Logan Cheats on Alexandra Chase with Mystery Woman!

Laney's hand flew to her mouth in disbelief. Another notification chimed, ripping her from her shock. Reluctantly, Laney clicked on it, and it brought her to a Facebook inbox full of hate messages from people she'd never met.

HOW DARE YOU BREAK UP MY FAVORITE CELEBRITY COUPLE! YOU'RE NOT WORTH THE AIR YOU BREATHE, HOMEWRECKER!

WHY BLAKE WOULD CHEAT ON THE BEAUTIFUL ALEXANDRA CHASE WITH A NOBODY LIKE YOU IS MIND-BOGGLING. GO BACK TO WHATEVER HOLE YOU CRAWLED OUT OF AND LEAVE THEM ALONE.

The messages, each filled with poison and ignorance, continued to file in. Laney couldn't change her privacy settings fast enough. Her face was all over the internet, being blasted as the woman who broke up "America's Sweethearts." Tears stung her eyes as she watched her world turn to ash and cinder around her. She jumped up from her bed, and her feet pounded the stone steps on her way downstairs. Hearing her footsteps, Blake turned his attention from the rain pelting the windows to her panicked face. His defeated shoulders carried the burden forced upon him, and his brow wrinkled in concern. She paused at the bottom of the stairs, wiping her tears with the hem of her pajamas.

As she approached, he stood stiffly and forced a smile on his face. Laney did nothing to hide the turmoil she felt but left it raw and open, like a fresh wound.

"I'm assuming you saw this too?" The first words spoken for the day scratched in her throat as she held up her phone.

"Yeah, I did. Joe sent it to me a little while ago. I'm so sorry. I will fix it. I already issued a statement with Joe, but the gossip sites are sitting on it so the drama can turn into an inferno. I can't believe she'd stoop this low," he growled, running a hand through his messy hair.

"So what do I do about the death threats and attacks on social media?"

"The what? You're kidding me! They found you?"

"Yeah, and my inbox is filled with toxic messages. They don't even know the truth, and yet they hate me. I know I'm not perfect, but I certainly don't deserve this." She buried her face in her hands.

Blake took Laney's phone and deleted all the messages before she could read any more.

"Did you tighten up your privacy settings on all your accounts? I should've had you do it long ago. I'm so sorry…" Heavy guilt shadowed his red-rimmed eyes as he avoided eye contact.

"I have now, but I haven't even dared to open my Instagram yet."

"Let me do it. I'm used to having to deal with this crap, so I should be the one who cleans it all up," he said as he went to work on her phone. "We need to adjust your email filters too. There are going to be reporters all over this, trying to contact you for a statement. Say nothing. It will all blow over in a few days. In the meantime, you need to lay low and stay here. I'm afraid if you go back home, they will hound you and your family until you break. Call your family and warn them too."

Laney sat quietly next to him on the couch with her legs tucked up under her elbows. His words didn't seem real. They felt far away and inaudible. Her brain couldn't process what had happened, much less what would happen next. Blake got up and poured them each a cup of coffee.

"This will help take the edge off." He offered her a steaming cup, made just how she liked it.

"Thanks," she muttered, letting it warm her hands, then her insides as it trickled down her throat.

"I'm so sorry. I can't believe Alexandra would do this—why she felt the need to lie, to destroy you, to destroy us. I knew she sunk low, but I never even imagined she'd do something like this." He shook his head. "Please say something. I can't read you right now."

"I really don't know what to feel, or think, or say," she said, still feeling shocked. "This doesn't feel real, and yet it feels one-hundred percent real, all at the same time."

"I know. It's like an earthquake hit, and now we have to wait for the aftershocks, then the Tsunami that's coming next." He put his arm around her shoulders.

Instead of melting into him like she normally did, Laney stiffened at his touch. It was ever so slightly, but he noticed it. He knew, at that moment, that irreparable damage had been done to this beautiful woman, and it was all because of him. His role was to make her feel safe, and yet she was now unarmed and exposed to the whole world. He had heaped this upon her and exposed her to a life of poison and pain, all the while knowing he had no antidote that could save her. He moved from the sofa to the table in front of her and took her shaking hands in his. He forced himself to look into her eyes, where the most agonizing lesson he would ever learn resided. Her sorrow was the reason why he would never be able to fully love anyone, ever. The woman who held his heart would always be subjected to the radiation of his stardom. The highest of highs came at a cost that no one should ever have to pay just to love him. There was no middle ground. No normal. No peace. It was all a façade to lure in the unsuspecting and trusting before the floor dropped out from under them when they let themselves love him. He was a curse that had no end, and he would never forgive himself for exposing her beautiful soul to this hell.

He lifted her chin slowly, her eyes the last to rise to the level of his face. And there it was—the absence of joy. The absence of hope, love, and light. Her brown eyes were red, swollen, and blank. Her beautiful light was flickering in his hurricane with inadequate shutters to keep the storm out. Bit by bit, her heart was being ripped apart. And it was his fault. He was naïve to think he could ever be loved by someone with the gentle depth she had and be able to preserve it. Her light would never survive a storm like his life.

"Talk to me," he begged.

"I don't know what to say," she replied sorrowfully. "I don't understand why someone would be so cruel. And for what? What does Alexandra get out of this?"

"She gets the satisfaction of knowing that if she can't have me, no one can. Which will still not be enough for someone like her." Blake sighed. "This is all my fault. You don't deserve this. Any of this.

"All I wanted was to love you, that's it. I don't care about the spotlight or the cameras. I don't care about your fame or popularity. I just want you."

"What can I do to fix this?" he cried out desperately. "I can't lose you, not again."

"I think we both need to decide if this is really the best for the both of us. I know I love you. I have never felt about anyone the way I feel about you. But I'm not sure any love can survive a lifetime of events like this. Love needs sunshine and joy along with the rain in order to thrive. And this place seems to bring out the worst in both of us. This world is cold and cruel and void of real light. I honestly don't know how your beautiful heart has survived so long." She laid her hand on his tear-stained cheek, wiping it with her thumb.

Her eyes tracked Blake's tears and met his gaze again. As he looked into her eyes, he could see a slight flicker of her sparkle remaining. She still loved him. But how much she was willing to fight for him, he would have to wait and see. He would fight for that tiny flame until it became a roaring bonfire if it meant he could still have her heart.

The weight of stress pressed heavily on their shoulders for the next few days. Neither of them went anywhere outside the house, and the only comings and goings were the cleaning crews, Blake's assistant, and his manager. Life continued outside in the world, but it stood stiflingly still within the walls of his home.

Alexandra continued her relentless rumor mill turning, posting multiple times a day about how hurt she was. She completely took advantage of the sympathy offered from unknowing fans. The drama was a catalyst for her fury, and she was coarsely satisfied with the trouble she was causing in Blake's world. She sneered at the mud being slung, turning her minions loose on her victim and laughing as they took over most of the dirty work. The situation spiraled out of control—just the way she liked it—and Alexandra stood at the center of it all, soaking up the spotlight.

Laney woke up on day three of the mess and began packing her bags. She needed a place where she could breathe, a place she could go for a walk and clear her head without a crowd of people following her. Somewhere she could step back from the whirlwind whipping around her and collect her thoughts. Somewhere far away from this world, far away from the reminders, and far away from Blake. She couldn't think clearly around him, with his strong arms and blue eyes swaying her. He begged her to stay with each kiss, and she wanted to. But her confidence waned in her ability to keep her head clear when his mere presence clouded her judgment.

"What are you doing?" Blake's voice came from the doorway. "Are you…are you leaving?"

"I just need some time to think. I need some peace in my heart to figure this whole thing out," she replied, avoiding his influential blue eyes.

"What do you mean?" he asked, while the beginnings of fear and loss welled up within him.

"We both know this lifestyle brings out things in us that are less than desirable," she started. "I know I love you more than I've ever loved anyone before, and I would give up so much to be with you. My privacy, my home…" she trailed off. "But becoming someone I'm not proud of was definitely unexpected, and it got me thinking about what I was willing to give up to try and fit into this life with you."

"What are you saying, Laney? You're leaving for good? Forever?" The hurt in his voice dripped from his words.

"I don't know what it is I'm trying to say, Blake. I just know I can't breathe, much less think when my whole world is tumbling and falling apart."

"So stay, and we will figure this out together. I know we haven't dug in and really attacked this, but I want to. We can figure this out."

"I'm afraid…" she whispered, trailing off.

"Of what?" His voice rose. "I love you, and you love me. The rest can be worked out."

"I do love you, Blake. But how do I know I'm not going to be standing next to a stranger in public for the rest of my life? The man you are away from the public eye is who I love. But the man you become out there…is a stranger to me. He's the one I read about in magazines and gossip columns. I was fully prepared to love the real you forever. But so much of your life is being the man in the spotlight, and I've seen you morph into someone I barely recognize. Let's just call it what it is. I'm not sure I'm equipped for this life, and I can't ask you to give up your dreams for me."

Blake's shoulders fell. He had seen the toll this trip had taken on her, and although he would rather ignore it, she forced him to stare it in the face. She deserved more than a man playing a part, and he knew that.

"How can I fix this?" he asked.

"I want to stand here with my heart in my hands and plead with you to choose me. To run away to a place where you can be you and I can be me, and that's all that would matter. I want to stand back-to-back in the trenches with you and fight the whole world—"

"These are the trenches, Laney!" he interrupted. "These are the trenches I fight against every day to do what I love! You say you want to fight alongside me, but at the first sign of trouble, you want to run. What is it? Are you a fighter or a runner?"

His words stung. Not because they hurt but because they were true, and they caught in her throat. "You and I both know this lifestyle is not conducive to vulnerability and kindness. And I need that. And you need your job and your dreams, and with those things comes sacrifices you have to make to be successful."

"So we are at an impasse, I suppose," he whispered hoarsely.

"I can't give up who I am to become someone I'm not, Blake."

"And I'd never ask you to. I just can't understand why this is how it has to be."

Her honey eyes glistened with tears, and her hands shook as she zipped her bag.

"You're the man I'll always love but can never keep. And you'll sit in the back of my mind in a place that'll always make me wonder, What if? We're so good together—but not in this world."

She crossed the room with her suitcase and cupped his face in her hand.

He leaned into her touch and pulled her close, his heart pounding in her ears. "I can't believe you're giving up so quickly. I know I can't ask you to stop being who you are, Laney, because that's what I love most about you. But I honestly thought you had more fight in you than this. I thought that what we have between us would be enough—and it is for me—but I guess it's not for you." He sighed and ran a frustrated hand through his hair. "I can't make you stay if you don't want to. Just know that you're making a huge mistake. We can figure this out if you stay. But if you go, you will always be the one who got away for me, and nothing else will ever come close to how I feel for you."

With a sad sigh, he tipped her chin and kissed her lips with all the emotion their goodbye deserved, sending a shockwave through her whole body.

"And there you go trying to convince me to stay." She smiled weakly at him. "You always were good at that part."

"I don't know how to let you go," he whispered as he squeezed her tighter. "I want to beg you to stay, but your beautiful heart deserves so much more than this."

"Please don't forget that the life you have here loves the person you pretend to be, not the person you really are, Blake. I hope for your sake you're not swallowed up by a life lived only on the surface and that you find a way to have both deep roots and strong wings."

Her phone chimed.

When she looked at her phone, her breath hitched. "My Lyft is here at the gate. I'm so sorry."

Blake dejectedly carried her suitcase down the long staircase and to the front door. "I'm sorry too, but as much as this hurts, I'll never regret loving you," he confessed.

"Neither will I," she whispered and stepped outside.

As she pulled the door closed, a resistance made her turn back. Blake stood, holding the knob, tears welling in his blue eyes that begged her to stay without saying a word. Letting out a tiny sob, she flew back into his arms and breathed him in one last time.

"You are a bird, and I am a fish. But I wish more than anything that fishes could fly," he cried into her hair.

"Me too. Goodbye, Blake," she said, forcing the words out through the lump in her throat. "I will never forget the colors you taught me to see. And my world will never be the same."

Before Blake could say anything else, she pulled her suitcase off the porch, and the slow clicking of it on the stone walkway faded around the corner.

Blake stood frozen on the porch, unable to wrap his mind around what had happened. He shook his head and fought the tears that flooded his eyes. How could he possibly let the woman he loved walk out of his life again?

Her words lingered in the air like the hot ashes from a beach bonfire. They floated away from love's charred remains between them, threatening to fall any moment and destroy whatever they touched.

He blinked hard, spilling tears down his cheeks, no longer wanting to be strong and hide them. With a heart-wrenching sob, he grabbed an empty pot from the table by the door and threw it angrily against the stone wall, the pieces of clay shattering like his heart. How could he be so stupid, exchanging the best thing that had ever happened to him for a life that could walk away anytime and never look back? The severity of it all hit him in the chest like a wrecking ball, and he crumbled to the ground like an old, dilapidated brick building.

"What have I done?" Blake whispered abjectly to himself. Aching to run after her, he forced himself to stay on the cold, hard cement. He did love her—more than he loved anything or anyone else—which is why he had to let her go. The life he lived in L.A. corroded away people's happiness like rust on a weathered pier. He couldn't watch her spirit be broken the way his spirit was. He couldn't ask her to give up her joy in exchange for a life that even he despised at times. So, instead of chasing after the woman he loved like the hero at the end of a romantic movie, he wept alone and heartbroken on the cold, hard ground in a world he resented.

Laney held her composure as she walked away from Blake's house, feeling weaker with every breath she fought for. Her lungs tightened and refused to expand, and the lump in her throat grew too large to swallow. This was not how the weekend was supposed to go, and *certainly* not the way her relationship with Blake was supposed to be. Laney thought she had finally found a man worth keeping—her partner to dance with in the kitchen. Someone she could finally trust to protect her scarred heart. Was she wrong to let herself love him? She could've avoided this whole painfully wonderful thing if she had guarded her heart instead of dropping her defenses. She ached to turn back time and do things differently. Yet, if one thing had changed, everything else would be different. No, she didn't regret loving him even as she crumpled like a house of cards, but she wondered if she would ever love that deeply again.

Her sorrow hung hotly in the air on her way to the airport, suffocating her in the steel cage she was trapped in. She didn't try to wipe her tears now. She just let them race down her cheeks—unashamed of the heartbreak she was feeling. Her head spun as she stepped out of the car, and as the trunk slammed and her ride drove away, she stood alone in a crowd of strangers.

A rush of people flooded the automatic doors as she pulled her suitcase through, drowning her in a sea of flashbulbs and shouting paparazzi. Laney shielded her face with a raised hand, thinking she'd been followed for their next big break in the scandal. That is until she saw her. Alexandra Chase strutted through the airport, holding a dog almost too small to be real in her perfectly manicured hands. Her entourage juggled coffee cups and expensive suitcases, dragging the weight of her entitlement behind them. The whole scene was chaotic, to say the least, but at that moment, her eyes locked with Alexandra's, and a wave of courage came over her. She squared her shoulders and wiped her wet cheeks. As soon as the paparazzi recognized the gold mine of gossip news they had walked into, the bustle quieted. Laney held her chin high, looking up at the long-legged mean girl towering in front of her. Alexandra smiled a wicked, venomous grin and stepped too close for Laney's comfort.

"Throwing in the towel a little soon, aren't we, sweetheart? That was an easy win," Alexandra whispered low in Laney's ear. Looking down at Laney, Alexandra's demeanor went from villain to victim and she wiped a fake tear. "I still can't believe what you did to me. All I ever wanted was to love Blake, and you took that away from me," she whined as the substantiating displeasure from the crowd echoed around them.

Every camera and eye fell on Laney. Her pulse pounded in her ears, crowding out the loud silence around her. She knew this was her one shot to put Alexandra in her place, so she took a long, hollow breath before she spoke. Her heart raced, her palms were sweating, and thoughts of everything she'd ever wanted to say—given this moment—tore through her brain. But a rush of clarity forced everything unimportant away, and a fierceness overtook her nerves.

"Alexandra, I'm really sorry I ruined your dress. I'm sorry I stooped to your level. I'm sorry that when it mattered most, I lost sight of who I was. The girl who threw wine on you was not me, and I'm not proud of it. Please accept my apologies and let me pay your dry-cleaning bill," Laney said as she slipped a twenty-dollar bill into Alexandra's hand.

"Seriously? That's all you've got to say for yourself? After all that you've done?" Alexandra crumpled the twenty and let it fall to the floor, playing up the dramatics perfectly.

Laney sighed. "I don't care what lies you tell the media, Alexandra. We both know the truth, and that's enough for me. You have everything going for you: a great career, men falling all over you, and a gorgeous face. A woman like you could be so influential for good. But you'd rather use all your energy to spin lies and be mean. And the worst part is, you're capable of so much better if you'd only get out of your own way. I don't consider this a 'win' for any of us. I lose Blake, he loses a chance to have real happiness, and you lose a chance to give love instead of hate. We all lose this time." Laney stood firmly in place, never breaking eye contact with her rom-com villain. "Now, if you'll excuse me, I've got a plane to catch." Laney reached up and tousled the ear of the fluff ball in Alexandra's arms. "Cute dog," she said before grabbing the handle of her suitcase.

Laney pushed past a stunned Alexandra, the gaping mouths of her entourage, and a sea of clicking and flashing cameras as she made her exit. Her chest swelled with pride as she left the crowd of people in her wake, and it took every ounce of control she had to stifle a squeal rising up inside her. The tears that now welled in her eyes were ones of both sorrow and accomplishment, mixing together in a bittersweet mess. She may have lost Blake, but at least Laney had one last chance to clear the air before she left Los Angeles. Her heart hurt a little less after speaking her piece, numbing the sting of her goodbye.

After boarding, she messaged Angela to let her know she was coming home early and then stared out the window as the plane took off.

The plane ride home felt eerily similar to the drive back home from Idaho a few months prior. A tempest of unknowns swirled inside her, draining her of any effort besides the simplicity of survival. She looked back at the California valleys below and said a silent goodbye to the life she thought she'd have with the man she'd always love. She rested her head against the window and wondered what would become of Blake. But she was sure of one thing: regardless of her circumstances, she was in control of her own happiness. She had walked this beaten trail before. She knew every pebble, every tree root waiting to make her stumble, and every wrong turn. She knew what would become of her if she chose to wallow in self-pity again, so she decided to take a new path instead. One in which she got to be the heroine of her own story. Where she was in charge of the way the book ended. So, in that very moment, she chose to pick herself up, dust herself off, and go forward with courage—no matter how hard it would be.

.

The video of Laney standing up to Alexandra had circulated the internet for weeks before it was finally buried by more "breaking celebrity news." Laney went home to find a stir of chaos everywhere she went, but she clung to the hope that it would die down sooner or later, as all celebrity gossip does. She quickly learned how to lay low and blend in but couldn't shake the thoughts that wandered off to L.A. after Blake. She rarely used social media after the comments that berated her, and she avoided the news altogether. Most of her time was spent at work or staying safe in the sanctuary of home and family. It was only with her patients that she could slough off all her troubles and focus on making someone else's life better. Work was her therapy because the only mending her heart did was while she was in the service of others. After walking in his very public shoes, she finally understood why Blake sought the solitude he did.

But at night, when the world was quiet and still, she sat in her window seat with Murphy purring in her lap and looked up at the stars, wondering if Blake ever did the same. She pictured him standing outside on his patio, casting his eyes heavenward, aching for her the way she did for him. Some nights, the memories that flooded back gave her heart peace. But most of the time, though, her heart throbbed so deeply that pain filled her chest and overflowed, sliding down her arms and settling into her hands. The poisonous ache of a broken heart changed as much as the moon that floated through the sky in all its phases. Some nights it was blaring, bright, and full, forcing her to acknowledge it. But other nights, it stayed back in the edges of her mind and lay just over the mountain tops in a crescent-shaped sliver, ever-present in her world and never fully disappearing, but changing with the days.

Back in L.A., Blake waded through his heartache alone. The video of Laney went viral almost immediately, and he watched it more times than he would ever admit. He missed her terribly, and the video only made it worse. But each time, he was filled with pride as his beautiful country girl found her voice. The fierceness in her that stole his heart in the first place continued to do so long after he'd let her go. He loved the fire in her eyes as she spoke to Alexandra, and it made him ache to be near her again.

He woke up every morning with the resolve to leave her in the past, but with each passing day, it became evident that he never would. Her ever-present absence ached in his bones, imprinting her memory in his whole existence, and he wasn't sure if it would ever leave or if he even wanted it to.

Late at night, he'd go out on the patio, lay in his hammock like they had done together the night of the wrap party, and listen to the stars. The breeze rustled leaves in the trees, and crickets sang softly in the gardens around him as he swayed back and forth. His eyes searched the sky for answers he so desperately needed, but the bright city lights drowned out the stars' glow, making them almost impossible to hear. Yet, there was always one constant: Polaris. It never left him stranded, and on the nights when he needed the most guidance, it was there, pointing the way north. The rest of the stars spoke too softly in the cacophony of his life, and without Laney to interpret them, he couldn't tune in well enough to hear their words of wisdom. He began to resent them for withholding their secrets from him—and the moon, too—whose phases reminded him that life goes on whether he was ready or not.

After a while, he stopped listening to the sky, the ocean, and anything else that reminded him of her—the woman he would always love but could never have.

Blake withdrew further and further inside himself, becoming a solitary creature and less of a man. He still went to the parties and events he was obligated to go to, but always alone. He wore a forced smile and an unkempt beard, and the heaviness in his eyes replaced the sparkle that once resided there. He stayed at the back of the crowd, hoping to float in and out unnoticed, watching the world around him swirl while he stood motionless. The mask he wore so loudly in the past was too great a burden to bear, and it made him hate himself more and more. He craved Laney's depth and light in the dark valleys where he stood. Life without her next to him was chaotic and hollow, and he ached for her to calm the storms again, though he knew it wasn't fair to her. She didn't deserve to have her life be put into a fishbowl with nowhere to find refuge from the eyes of the world. He suffered alone without her so she could have the life she deserved. But what Blake didn't realize through all of it was how much she yearned for him too. They suffered alongside each other in a split-screen montage but in two different worlds. Their universes were opposite in every way, except in the parallels of their loneliness.

Blake was deep in thought and staring at the bottom of his empty glass when someone sat beside him and slapped him on the back. The music from the party became unbearably loud again as he was ripped back to reality.

"Hey, man! Whatcha lookin' for in there?" the voice chuckled.

Blake turned to see Austin Grant smiling over the top of a red plastic cup. Austin leaned in close to Blake as he spoke, looking him right in the eyes, one hand still resting on his shoulder.

"How about a game of pick-up?" Austin smiled gently, but his tone grew serious when he saw how bad of shape Blake was in. "I saw a court out the back. How about you tell me what's going on while I beat you at hoops?"

Austin took the empty glass from Blake and set it down on the bar. Blake's eyes lowered as he nodded, and they weaved through the crowd and out into the summer night.

While Blake removed his navy suit coat and laid it across the back of a patio chair, Austin found a basketball and dribbled it rhythmically on the cement. He was just about ready to shoot when Blake slapped the ball from his hand and headed down to the opposite hoop. There, Blake made an easy layup, rebounded the ball, and checked it back to Austin.

"Okay, so you're playing mad, huh?" Austin let out a short laugh and quirked an eyebrow at Blake.

"Yeah. I guess so." Blake shrugged. "I don't know what I feel anymore. Though I know for sure, it's not happy." Blake forced a wry grin.

"So what are you going to do about it then?" Austin pressed. "You look terrible, and you can't stay like this forever. Something has to give, man." Austin shot and missed a three-pointer, the ball bouncing hard off the rim and into the bushes.

"I don't know. I mean, I know what would make me happy, but it's much more complicated than that."

"You talking about Laney?" Austin passed the ball from the shrubs back to Blake.

"Yeah. I can't get her out of my mind. It's been three months since we broke up, and there isn't a day that goes by that I don't regret letting her go. I've never been that happy in my life. And I doubt I ever will again at this rate."

"So then go get her, man!" Austin encouraged. "That's not complicated at all."

"I want to more than anything! But she deserves better than what this life can give her, and I'm not even sure she wants me anymore." Blake's countenance fell.

"So you're telling me that she doesn't deserve your love because it comes with a bit of chaos too?" Austin stopped dribbling the ball. "What needs to happen in order for her to take you back?"

"Well, I've been working on being more authentic despite the pushback I keep getting from Joe, which is fine. He's coming around to it. But what then? I'd have to take quite a few steps away from this lifestyle to get her back—if she'd even take me. But how do I know she's not already being loved by some schmuck who could give her a life of normalcy, you know?"

"The way I see it, your choices are, stay here in L.A. and be miserable and alone, or go after the woman you love and be happy." Austin held his hands up like a scale and tried to balance them.

"You make it seem so easy, so black and white." Blake sighed. "What am I supposed to do about my career then? My dreams?"

"Keep making movies if it's what you love to do, but do it your way. You can chase a new dream too, man. Life is too short to pass up on love. It's like, you're on this crazy train, and everything is blurring past you—so fast that you can't focus on anything but the ride. And it's amazing and exhilarating. But once in a while, you need to stop, get off at the nearest station, and look around to see what comes into focus. Only then will you know what's most important," Austin advised. "When you let love lead, things have a way of working themselves out."

"Ugh, I don't know. She's too amazing to still be single."

"Well, it's definitely a no if you don't try at all. If she loved you as much as I think she did, then she's probably just as miserable as you are. Now, what are you going to do? Live stubbornly in misery, or eat crow and chase after your girl?"

"You're right," Blake admitted, pulling up and landing a three-pointer. "I can't keep doing this, that I know for sure."

"Agreed. Cause you look awful," Austin confessed with a smirk. "If she's what will pull you out of this slump, then go get her, man!" Austin's brow furrowed in focus as he rebounded the ball, but he missed his shot. "Don't let her become the one that got away."

"Your advice is on point tonight, thanks." Blake slapped him on the back. "Your game, on the other hand, hurts me to watch," Blake said with a laugh, shaking Austin's hand.

"Ouch, you cut me deep." Austin laughed along but clutched his chest. "Oh, and Blake?" he yelled as Blake walked away. "Don't forget to feed the soul."

Blake walked off the court and grabbed his suit coat from the patio chair. "You got it, man. Thanks."

His gait had an upbeat rhythm as he made his way back through the party. His spirits lifted against the heavy emotional cloak he wore, sending it crashing to the floor. He finally felt like he was in control of his own life again as he set off on a mission to go after Laney. Hope had picked him up, dusted him off, and shoved him back into the rear seat. This was the fading out of one chapter as it grew into the beginning of a new one. He couldn't wait to watch the story unfold.

As he pulled open the front door to leave, Alexandra Chase stood on the other side, a hand poised to turn the knob. Blake's expression went from surprised to angry as he came face to face with the woman who single-handedly ruined his life. He tried to shove past her, but she stood firm in his way. For a brief moment, her eyes flashed with regret. Her face softened, and she glanced over her shoulder at her entourage walking up the driveway before speaking.

"I've been so awful to you and Delaney, and I'm sorry." Her voice was low and hushed, cautious about who would overhear. "She said something to me that day at the airport that stuck with me, and it got me thinking about how badly I treated people. She also made me realize that I have so much potential for good, and I'm trying to do better about that. I know an apology doesn't fix all I've done, but I want you to know I truly am sorry for hurting you." She brushed her jet-black hair behind her ears, exposing tear-filled eyes. Her gaze shifted from his and fell to her shaking hands.

For the first time, Blake saw the sincerity in her, and his tensed shoulders fell. Instead of anger, he now felt compassion. He smiled gently and placed a hand on her shoulder.

"Thank you. You have no idea how much I needed to hear that. If I ever see Laney again, I'll pass the message along. She'll be glad to know that her words had such a profound effect on you. She has a tendency to bring out the best in people, that's for sure." Blake smiled nostalgically at the thought of Laney. "I hope you continue to improve yourself. Genuine is a good look for you." He stepped aside and held the door as she passed.

"Thank you." She spoke so low that it was almost a whisper. Then, she disappeared into the crowd, her entourage scurrying in behind her like rats following the Pied Piper.

The engine purring under the pressure of the gas pedal was the only sound in Blake's ears as he drove home. His mind churned with ideas on what he would say to Laney when he saw her again. His thoughts wandered so far off the beaten path that when he reached his driveway, he wondered how he'd even gotten there. The next steps for his life weighed heavily on his heart, and he knew they were not to be taken lightly. *If I walk away from this career and life in L.A. to be with Laney, what else would I do? Would she even have me? And if I chose to keep my career and asked her to come back, would she be able to live in a world of chaos if I stayed genuine?* He had some big choices to make, but so did she. He was about to take a head-first plunge into the waters without knowing their depths, gambling on the fact that she was even still around. She said she'd always love him, but would she really? What if she came to realize that she was better off without him? He had everything to lose but also everything to gain.

Chapter

28

*A*s soon as Blake made the decision to win Laney back, the universe chimed in as if it were patiently lying in wait for him to be ready. The day after his pick-up game with Austin, he got a text message on his phone:

> **Angela:** Hi Blake, it's Angela. I know I promised Laney that I'd never use your number for anything but emergencies, but my best friend's happiness is at stake here. And if you ask me, that's a pretty big emergency. It's been three months, and she is still as miserable as the day she came home. She is a shell of the person she used to be, and she is getting worse and worse at hiding her sorrow. If you ever loved her at all, or still do, please respond to me.

Blake reread her message a dozen times before replying. This was the first contact he'd had with anyone close to Laney since she walked away. His hands shook, and his heart pounded in his ears as he typed:

Blake: I'm so glad you reached out to me. I'm miserable too, and I miss her more than I ever thought possible. Every day since she left, I've regretted letting her go. I'm not sure what to do. Or if she'll even talk to me, much less take me back. I love her, and I want her to be happy. If there's even a small chance I can fix this, I'll do whatever I can. What do you suggest?

A few minutes later, she replied.

Angela: Let me put the feelers out there with her, and I'll get back to you. :)

Angela punctuated her message with a happy face—which had to be a good sign, right? Blake's hope hung on that tiny emoji, and for the first time in a long time, he allowed himself to reminisce and not hurt.

A few days went by with no word from Angela. He tried to stay busy, but his mind always wandered back to Laney. She had wrapped herself throughout every aspect of his life in such a short time, and he struggled to focus on much else.

While searching through his closet for a suit, his hands found an old dry-cleaning bag buried in the back. He pulled the bag over the hanger as he laid it on his bed and uncovered the stunning black dress that Laney wore the night of the wrap party. He was instantly taken back to that night, her heels clicking on the stone steps as she floated down the stairs. He could still clearly recall everything about that moment—the sun's golden light dancing on her shoulders, her soft eyes full of nerves, and the scent of jasmine that pulsed from her pretty neck. He never wanted any of it to fade. He voluntarily laid his sword at her feet that night when she took his hand and smiled. But the scars of that memory stung around the edges like a wound that wouldn't heal, making it too difficult to completely revisit.

He held the dress out in front of him and studied its form. It looked so empty on a hanger, such a contrast from when it wrapped around her body. Blake wanted so badly to hold it close to his face and breathe in Laney's scent. But like the rest of his life, she had mostly been erased from it. He ached to have the fruity bouquet of her hair fill his senses each time he hugged her. To hear the sound of her laugh again. And to look over at the passenger seat in his car and see her riding shotgun, her shoes kicked off on the floorboards.

He sighed—the longing crowding out his logic—and hung her dress on a hook on the door instead of pushing it back to the darkest corner of his closet. He needed it to have a bigger presence in his life. Something he'd see out the corner of his eye when he got ready in the morning and something that reminded him of a happier time to suture his broken heart. The reminder of her hanging around would give him the shot of courage he needed to make his next move, whatever it would be.

That night, Blake had a dream. He was standing in a huge crowd of people dressed in his Sentinel uniform, and everyone buzzed around and through him like he was a ghost. He stood motionless, wavering against the bumping of the crowd, unable to move. He fought to get somewhere, but the crowd weaved so tightly around him that he finally succumbed to their forces and began to fade into nothing.

That's when a delicate hand touched him on the shoulder, giving rise to an existence he thought he'd lost. The crowd moved further and further away as Laney looked him in the eyes, creating a wide space around them. Piece by piece, she removed his disguise, never saying a word, just seeing him when no one else did. Her hands pulled at the back of his neck until a mask of himself was removed. She smoothed her fingers through his hair like she used to, and smiled.

"There you are. I've been looking everywhere for you."

Blake sat straight up in bed, running his hands through his hair just like she had done. It felt so real that he could've sworn she was there, but as he sat alone in the darkness, reality quickly settled in.

That dream consumed his thoughts and haunted him for days. When he thought he had figured out what it meant and what to do with it, he wound up back at square one, confused and listless.

A few nights later, he dreamt of her again. But this time, she was standing in his kitchen in an apron, stirring something on the stove.

"Hey, honey," she called over her shoulder. "Can you come and taste this? I just can't get your sauce right."

He walked over to the stove and tasted the sauce on the end of her wooden spoon. The savory, slightly tart sauce tickled his taste buds, and he closed his eyes in thought.

"A tiny bit more oregano," he said.

"I can make this a hundred times, and it's still not as good as when you do it blindfolded." She said with a laugh. "People would pay for this, you know."

His eyes flew open, and at that very moment, the clarity he needed hit him like a freight train. When the sun came up that morning, Blake dialed some contacts he had and set the ball in motion for the greatest Hail Mary pass in history.

Angela stepped through the door of Laney's house to find her rage-cleaning a hallway closet. She was on her hands and knees, halfway hidden by the closet door, violently throwing things out and breathing hard between sobs.

Laney knew that no amount of cleaning was going to erase Blake's memory from her life because he had crept into the quietest, loveliest corners and stretched his roots into her heart. What used to feel as good as the morning sun after a midnight thunderstorm now burned too brightly in the eyes of someone left in the dark for too long.

She felt completely out of control with her emotions, hating the fact that she still missed him so much after all this time. Most days, she worked hard to hide the pain, but today, she left the wound open, gaping wide and exposed to the world. She took a long look in the mirror—knowing she wouldn't win the battle today—and let herself cry. Instead of tucking her sorrow away behind a forced smile, she honored her grief by opening the faucet and letting it all go. Laney heard the door open, but she was too buried in the moment to care who had come in. It wasn't until Angela put a calming hand on her back that Laney finally stopped throwing things and turned into a puddle on the floor.

"Wanna tell me what this is about, Lane?" Angela asked, already knowing the answer.

"I can't shake him, Ange!" she wept angrily, holding Levi's coat that Blake wore when he went snowboarding with her. "Every time I think I'm over him, his memory creeps back in again! I found this when I was digging for vacuum bags." Laney threw the coat across the room. "Why did I let this happen? Did I honestly think this was going to end well? Am I that big of a fool that I ran away from the best thing that ever happened to me? I know things weren't ideal, but I didn't even put up a fight. I hate myself for being such a chicken. Every day I wake up and hope it will fade, and every night I cry myself to sleep because I can't forget him." Laney buried her face in her hands and curled her legs in against her chest.

"Oh, honey." Angela moved next to Laney on the cold floor and wrapped her arms around Laney's shaking shoulders. "Maybe he misses you as much as you miss him," Angela consoled.

"Yeah, right. He's probably off on some yacht with ten supermodels around him, having the time of his life." Laney wiped tears from her puffy, red eyes. "I bet I'm the last thing he thinks about. I'm so far in his rearview that he could walk right by me and not recall a thing."

Angela frowned at Laney but laughed internally at the thought, knowing what she knew about how Blake really felt. But her intuition told her to keep their latest conversation to herself for the time being. So she scooped Laney up off the floor, helped her to her favorite spot on the couch, gave her a blanket and a bowl of her favorite ice cream, then began boxing up the mess that littered the hallway.

Murphy hopped up next to Laney on the sofa and rubbed against her arms, purring.

"Sure, now you come to make me feel better because I have ice cream!" Laney chuckled at the eager kitty in her lap and stroked his head gingerly. "Thanks for coming over and putting me back together." She looked up at Angela across the room. "I don't know if I'll ever be the same, Ange. I'm trying so hard to move on, but I feel like no matter how hard I work at it, I'll never free myself from his grip around my heart. I went on a date for the first time since the breakup last night, and I couldn't get home fast enough. It hurt so bad to be out there again. I couldn't do it."

"Well, maybe you just need some closure, Lane. Have you tried talking to him? Telling him that you regret running?"

"Oh no." She shook her head. "Not with the way things ended. I'm not sure there will ever be a resolution to this, except maybe that I become a crazy cat lady. That's what my future holds because he set the bar so unfairly high for anyone else to measure up to."

"Understandably so, but you do still love him, right?"

"Completely against my will, yes. And I'm ready for it to go away anytime. Then it can settle into the dark corners on a bookshelf of memories in my mind, where it can gather dust and be forgotten." Laney began to cry again.

"You'll move on when the time is right, Lane. Until then, allow yourself to feel everything you need to so that this experience can flow through you completely, changing all the parts that need changing. That way, you'll be a better version of yourself on the other side." Angela took a seat next to Laney on the sofa, tucking her feet under her. "In the meantime, I'll be here to scoop your ice cream."

Heavy machinery whirred and clunked in the background as Blake walked around with a design team carrying landscaping plans and paperwork to review. Their hard hats cast a shadow on their faces as they stared into the sunshine at all the work being done. The dust rose and settled on a new dream, one he hoped to share with the woman he loved. The remodeling for his new restaurant had gone off without a hitch, and every day he became more and more excited to go after Laney. Angela's messages about Laney still caring about him drove Blake forward through doubt and fear. And he felt more prepared than ever to take on a new adventure. The grand opening was a few weeks away, and Laney didn't even know Blake was in town yet. He needed to show her how committed he was to her and how he'd fight for her, but he struggled to find the words he longed to say. Would she even take him back? What if he'd missed his chance because he waited too long? He dialed Angela's number with shaking hands, his whole inner being feeling jittery.

"Angela, it's Blake. Do you have a second to talk? I need your help with something." He glanced around, drawing designs in the dirt with his dusty shoes. Twenty minutes later, after talking to Angela and setting some plans in motion, she sent him a message.

Angela: She's about to drop off her last passenger. Good luck! I hope it works!

Blake hastily opened his Lyft app and requested a ride. Over and over again, he was assigned to other drivers. He laughed at his misfortune and canceled each one until his request was accepted by her. He smiled to himself as he ripped off his hard hat and combed through his hair with his fingers. Using the reflection in the restaurant window, he dusted himself off and tried his best to look presentable. Then, all he could do afterward was wait. His chest pounded as he thought of the right words to say. But it was all a huge waste of time because the moment she pulled up to the curb, every thought fled his mind like a bird escaping its cage, leaving behind an empty vessel, incomplete without its prisoner. He blinked into the sun, took a deep breath to fill himself with courage, and approached Laney's SUV.

Laney watched as her passenger approached the side of the car, seeing only jeans and a torso through the window. The door clicked open, and she heard a familiar voice speak familiar words.

"I hope you don't mind if I sit up here with you. I hate sitting in the back when being driven alone. It feels so impersonal." Blake smiled nervously as he lowered into the seat next to her.

Her breath hitched, and while her mind filled up with things to say, nothing came out of her mouth. Her already vulnerable paper heart ripped along the taped seams that she fought so hard to repair. Blake gently shut the door behind him and sat beside her in silence for what seemed like an eternity. As if to jolt herself back to reality, she shook her head and blinked.

"Blake. W-what are you doing here?" Laney stammered, her face covered with the shock that fluttered throughout her body.

"Do you know how many drivers I had to cancel before I finally got you to accept my ride request?" He chuckled nervously. "More than I care to admit."

"Well, you're definitely not the 'Rose Nylund' I was expecting to pick up..." She glanced at her phone, looked at the fake profile, and chuckled. "Golden Girls. I should've seen it coming. That was a nice touch." She shook her head at her naiveté.

Blake moved his gaze from his wringing hands to Laney's face. She was even more beautiful than he remembered, which didn't help his nerves. "I had to see you. I've needed to talk to you, but I wanted to be ready with a game plan first." He gestured out the window at the restaurant. "I decided a while ago to branch out a bit, and I'm opening a restaurant here in Salt Lake City in a few weeks."

"You gave up on acting? But you love making movies," Laney protested.

"No, I didn't completely give up acting. I'm just going to be a bit pickier about roles I take and how much time I spend away from loved ones." His eyes met hers as if to say she was still included in that category. "You showed me that although I enjoyed my life, I wasn't happy being someone I wasn't anymore, so I started chasing a new dream." As he looked at his restaurant, his eyes beamed with pride. "It's called 'The Firehouse.'"

"In honor of your dad…" Laney smiled at the thought. For a moment, they were transported right back to the first day they met. The bridge that burned between them extinguished, and they were once again just two people with a feeling that their souls had met before. But in the air hung a stiff, awkward feeling that needed more than a surface conversation to be cleared. Laney felt the old familiar heartache climb to the surface as she met his blue eyes.

"So you up and left your whole life in L.A. behind? Why?"

"I didn't up and leave it. I just re-prioritized things that mattered. I learned there is more to life than fame, and when you find something or someone that makes you better, you should never let it go. I never should've let you walk out of my life, Laney." His voice cracked under the pressure of the tears he was holding back. "I was so wrong, and I have regretted it every day since. I realized that life—even one with dreams fulfilled—isn't worth much without someone to share it with. I can't ever be the same man I was before I knew you. You came into my life at a time when I was missing something, and I didn't even know it. Without even looking for you, I found exactly what I needed to feel complete. And I was such an idiot to let you walk away, not once, but twice." Blake closed his eyes and shook his head in frustration at his foolishness.

"You chose a façade over a real life with me." Her voice shook, straining under the tears welling up in her eyes. She fought hard to keep them at bay, but it was impossible to hide the pain she felt at his mercy. "How can I be sure you won't do it again?" Laney took a ragged breath to try and quell the sobs rising inside her. The bitterness of that day stung her insides as sharply as the first time.

"I know, and it was the biggest mistake of my entire life," Blake confessed, his breath struggling to fill his lungs. "I thought that by letting you go, I was protecting you from a life of exposure and criticism. I didn't want your beautiful light to fade because of me." His eyes shifted downward.

"Yet that's exactly what happened anyway," she rebutted, her voice low as her sorrow turned to anger. Laney looked away out the windshield as tears of frustration soaked her face.

"I know. I was so incredibly stupid. I wish I could take it all back and change what happened. I never wanted to hurt you, Laney. I loved you…I still do. I know I don't deserve your forgiveness, and I know I'm not worthy of your love anymore. But when you left, my world went dark. It's like the sun went down with you and never rose again. I was stuck with a hole in my chest that I was forced to ignore—to just pretend it didn't exist. But I couldn't continue on and go back to the way things were when I wasn't even the same person I was before. I was lost, and I've been half a man for months without you. There has been no joy in my life. No laughter, no peace. I couldn't even look up at the night sky without missing you." The thought of all those lonely nights crept to the front of his mind and singed the edges of his soul while his facial expression deepened to a sorrow Laney had never seen on him. "You infused yourself into my life so quickly, so deeply, that everything reminds me of you. And all the things that brought me joy when you were there brought me sorrow without you. I know things won't be easy, but I need you, Laney. And I'm pretty sure that behind the defenses you've put up, you still need me too."

Blake's heart pounded as it battled with the possibility that she may not need him anymore. She was strong and independent and guarded. He felt the weight of her silence like lead on his chest.

Laney looked across the middle console of her car to the broken man sitting next to her. The banks of his bloodshot eyes ran over, and he did nothing to hide it from her. The guilt from turning her back on him instead of fighting for him ate away at her insides, yet her pride stood between him and her apology. *What am I doing? Just apologize, Laney! You can't run forever.*

His voice interrupted her thoughts. "The moment I saw you, Laney, I knew my life would never be the same. But what I didn't realize is that you would change *everything*. I will never be the man I was before you again. He is gone from me forever, and a better, stronger, more grateful man stands in his place. And I'll choose you every day for the rest of my life if you'll let me love you again."

The thought of once again sharing her world with him tugged inside her. "I don't know," Laney whispered. Her heartbeat quickened, and her breathing became something she had to focus on to keep steady. She swallowed her sobs as she forced herself to regain composure. "This is something I have been hoping would happen since I left your house that day. Actually, no. That's not true. I haven't dreamt that you'd come back and grovel. I've dreamt that I would have the courage to tell you that I'm sorry for running." Her voice was tight in her throat, and she strained to get her words out. "The idea that you could still love me despite my track record of taking off when things get dicey is all I can think about. And as much as I want to be wrapped in your arms where I feel safe again, I'm scared to death, Blake." She clung desperately to each breath fighting its way out of her and wiped the tears that escaped down her cheek with the tips of her fingers. "It's not about whether I still love you because as hard as I've tried to stop loving you, I can't seem to."

The corners of Blake's lips tugged upward.

Seeing his smile, she pointed a finger at him. "But just because I love you, it doesn't necessarily mean I *want* to," she said, then paused, trying to wrap her head around the emotions swirling within her. She turned the blast of cold air on her face. The car appeared to shrink around her, and Blake's blue eyes made her brain fog over. "I just—I just need to process all this." She struggled to push down the pain that exploded to the surface. "Plus, I can't ask you to give up your dreams for me. That's not fair to you." Her eyes lowered to Blake's hand sliding into hers. Her quick, shallow breaths began to deepen and slow, and her lungs finally took a full breath.

His touch soothed her, sending a burst of warmth through her broken world and collecting the pieces of her tattered heart. After standing under the shadow of pain that had been cast over her for so long, she forgot how good it felt to be loved by him.

"Please don't run. I understand you need to think, so take your time and think things through. But please don't run away. If we're going to fix things, then let's fix them. I'll wait forever if I have to. Just promise me that you're open to the idea of us figuring this whole thing out together. Please come back to me. Don't condemn me to an empty shell of a life when I know what we can have together," he implored. His voice betrayed his tough exterior, reducing him to a broken man pleading for the woman he loved to let him love her again.

Looking into his eyes, Laney could see that he meant what he was saying. Now, if only she could convince herself to plant her feet firmly when she wanted to bolt—and allow him to have her heart.

Blake leaned in and wiped a tear falling down her face before following it with a light kiss on her forehead. He lingered close to her face, and not only did she let him, but she welcomed his nearness. Her pulse quickened, and a kaleidoscope of butterflies burst through her body. His lips on her skin felt better than she ever remembered, and right then and there, Laney wanted to throw open her arms and let him back in.

"Okay, I'll think about it. But right now, I have to go. I'm still on the clock." Her lame excuse not to face her fears fell flat. "Besides, I can't think clearly with you so close, and smelling so nice. Seriously, haven't you been hanging around at a construction site? Why don't you smell like sawdust and sweat instead of…" she trailed off.

A small ray of hope broke through the darkness inside him, knowing he still had an effect on her. He smiled and searched her eyes for the words her pretty lips weren't saying, but she looked away before he could see her cards.

Blake hesitated as he opened the door. "I don't want this to be the last time I ever see you," he whispered in desperation, his teary blue eyes begging for another chance.

I'll stay. Please make me stay. Deep down, she longed to tell him that. Yet she retreated like a coward and allowed her fear to rule over her heart.

She hesitated for a moment as she reached for the gear shift, and as he got out, she forced herself to put the car in drive. A sob caught itself in her throat, and she fought through gritted teeth to breathe past it. Before she could drive off, Blake leaned on the door frame with one arm.

"You know, I've come to realize that I could be in a room full of people, but no one sees me the way you do. I felt like a ghost in this world for so long until you walked into my life. Thank you for seeing the real me when no one else did. I love you, Laney, and I always will—because you saw me when I felt invisible." His eyes overflowed with both tears and gratitude as he forced a weak smile and shut the door softly.

Her tires screeched in protest as she pulled away from the one man she never wanted to be apart from again. She opened the floodgates and let herself weep as Blake faded further and further away in her rearview mirror. Laney couldn't help but look back at him. His shoulders were slumped, his eyes downcast. He was just as broken as she was, yet she poured a handful of salt into his wounds.

Chapter 30

The weather that night seemed to match Laney's mood. Dark, angry clouds formed in the skies above, and howling winds pushed them through the sky. The weatherman on the news warned everyone west of Salt Lake City that a late summer storm was headed their way, advising them to take shelter as soon as possible.

Giant gusts of wind whipped through the tall trees in her yard, ripping leaves from their delicate branches. Heavy rain pounded on the windows of her little cottage, making it hard to concentrate on anything but the noise. Laney sat on the couch with Murphy and listened to the wailings of Mother Nature outside. The lights flickered a few times, prompting her to light a candle and find a flashlight—just in case. Murphy seemed to share the same anxieties Laney did, only his were caused by the torrential weather outside, and hers were caused by the howling weather inside. Her heart stood tiny yet strong in the midst of the pounding pain that beat upon its vulnerable windows. But she wondered how much longer she could withstand the storm.

As she climbed into bed, Murphy purred and kneaded his paws on the blanket by her feet. His presence comforted her, and his rhythmic purrs lowered her blood pressure as the storm raged outside. Laney was grateful for the rescue cat that rescued her more than she did him. His tiny furry body warmed her from the outside-in as she drifted off to sleep.

Blake put a vinyl on his record player and stood at the window overlooking the Salt Lake Valley. He watched the storm clouds roll over the mountains to the West as the sounds of Journey played throughout the dim room. Lightning flashed through the billows of darkness, which would normally be fascinating to watch, but tonight, Blake worried instead. Lines of concern formed on his brow for the woman weathering the storm alone in a tiny house, so far away from him. He wondered if she was safe, if she had power, if she was sleeping soundly, or if she lay awake, thinking about him too. He hoped she longed for him the way he longed for her. Although, even if she did, she'd probably push those feelings down the same way she did to the cab driver who tried to bully her the day they met. Blake laughed at the image of a surprisingly fierce woman forcing that burly man to his knees. With just one hand, she could completely conquer anyone, no matter how tough they seemed. Blake knew he would never be free of her grasp on him, nor did he want to be.

Watching her drive away again made him more determined to win her back. This time, instead of sulking in sorrow, he rolled up his sleeves and decided to work harder to prove that what they had was worth fighting for. He knew that if she didn't take him back, it wouldn't be for his lack of trying. He'd exhaust every avenue possible before he let Laney slip through his fingers again.

The next day, news reports focused on the disaster that last night's storm had left in its wake, so Blake scrolled through photos and videos of broken windows and uprooted trees. One video showed a reporter wandering through the towns that were hit the hardest, interviewing people affected by the storm. The camera panned past some homes as the reporter spoke of the devastation. To Blake's shock, in the background, he saw his beautiful, relentless Laney sifting through the limbs of a fallen tree that had landed on her house. The wind blew stray hairs loose from her ponytail as she walked around in bright yellow rubber boots. She worked alone with a saw and a wheelbarrow picking up branches and stacking them into a pile.

Blake hastily threw on his clothes, grabbed his keys, and hopped into his Bronco. He sped down the highway, letting his heart lead the way to his damsel in distress.

As he exited the freeway in Laney's town, he was stunned at the amount of damage that covered the streets. He drove carefully through broken tree limbs and crooked power poles as he inched along the gravel roads.

The sudden roar of an engine in the quiet morning caused Laney to stand up and turn toward the sound. Blake's bright red Bronco pulled into her driveway, and she brushed her hair away from her face with the back of her dirty gloved hand. She had already been at it for a few hours, and she wondered how much longer she could hold out before she had to call her dad and brothers for help. Heaven knew they were all dealing with their own mess from the storm, so in usual Laney fashion, she told them she was fine. Now she stood in shock as Blake killed the engine and hopped out.

"I worried about you all night," Blake said, rushing across the lawn. "And it looks like it was for a good reason." He grabbed the branches hanging low across the eaves of her house and shook his head. "Are you okay?"

"I'm fine." She lifted her chin slightly and bit her lower lip. "Although my roof has seen better days."

"I came to help if you'll let me." His bright eyes searched hers for permission.

Laney's stubborn shoulders shrunk under the weight of the task at hand, and she dropped her pride in the pile with the branches. "That would actually be really nice," she muttered with a heavy sigh, tucking the rebellious strands of hair behind her ear and leaving a dirt smudge behind. "I'm not sure how much more of this I can do by hand, so I'll probably need to borrow my dad's chainsaw when he's done with it." She frowned.

"I stopped and grabbed one on my way over," Blake said as he jogged to the back of his Bronco. He pulled the chainsaw out of a long, black case and poured a bottle of fuel in it. The whir of the chainsaw was music to Laney's exhausted ears as the work became easier and faster.

Blake cut the branches away, and she hauled them off to the woodpile at the far end of the yard, next to the shed. She hated admitting she needed help, but she was so grateful for the extra pair of hands that her pride softened toward him a bit.

"Come winter, I'll be grateful for all this extra wood for the fireplace," she said with a grin, eyeing the work they had accomplished. "But the way I came about getting it is not so awesome. I'm just glad I'm not alone in this. Thank you for coming to help me." She forced a smile to hide her struggle.

"You'll never be alone again," Blake replied softly, stepping closer to her. He pulled off one glove, and with his thumb, gently wiped the smudge from her cheek. "I meant what I said. I'll wait forever, and I'll be here forever."

Despite everything that had happened, Laney allowed him to sneak through the holes in the fence around her heart and disable her alarms again. She pulled the fingers on her work gloves and dropped them at her feet. Her heart pounded in her chest, not from the strenuous work but from a yearning deep down to wrap her arms around him. To feel his strong chest against her, to feel his heartbeat under her fingertips, and to have the comfort she was deprived of from his body again. She hesitated for a moment, then raised her hands to Blake's chest and ran them around his muscular body to his back. As she stepped closer into his warm and safe arms, Blake dropped the chainsaw and enveloped her. The exhaustion, heartbreak, and stress erupted to the surface, and she couldn't hold the tears back even if she tried. She crumbled as he let her cry, where she always felt calm and protected and at home.

He tucked his face into her hair and breathed her in, knowing he may not get the chance again. Something poked his face, and he laughed as he pulled a twig from her hastily done hair.

"What's so funny?" Laney questioned, pulling back slightly.

"No, don't pull away yet," he pleaded, unsuccessfully, as she loosened her hold on him and stepped backward. The empty space between his arms immediately felt colder in her absence. "It was a giant twig in your ponytail." He held up the stick to show her, then tossed it aside.

"Wow! I wonder what else I'm hiding in there." She said with a laugh as she combed her hair with her fingers.

Her eyes were red from crying, her hair was a crazy mess, and she tromped around in those giant, yellow rubber boots when she worked. Yet she was the most beautiful creature on the whole planet. Blake suddenly realized he was staring too long, so he shifted his eyes upward to the roof. The fallen tree had been completely cleared away, revealing the damage underneath.

"We've still got a bit more repairs to do to your roof and gutters before autumn comes," He rubbed the back of his neck as he mentally assessed the damage. "But it's nothing we can't handle together," Blake added with a wink in Laney's direction.

"Are you hungry?" Laney asked, changing the subject. "I owe you at least lunch for all you did to help me today." She picked her work gloves up off the grass and smiled over her shoulder at him as she headed into the house.

Later that day, when Blake climbed into his Bronco, Laney stood there and watched him with her heart in her hands.

"I don't know how you knew I needed you today, but thank you," she murmured, speaking quietly. "I'm trying really hard to let myself open up, and your kindness when I was too stubborn to ask for help meant more than you'll ever know."

Before he backed out of the driveway, he watched her wipe her cheeks with the sleeve of her shirt.

"I'm always here when you need me, Laney. I hope you know that," he said through the open passenger window as he put the gear in drive. "I'm not going anywhere." Then, he lifted his hand and waved, smiled, and drove away.

Chapter 31

A few weeks went by with only a few messages from Laney. Blake split his time between Utah and California, and tried to be patient and give her the space she needed. She'd send the occasional message just to say, "Hi," but she held her cards close to her chest and took a long time to make her next move. She wanted to be completely sure that allowing Blake back into her life was what was best for the both of them. Although deep down she knew she wanted him back, her doubts of being worth the sacrifice of his career lingered at the back of her mind. She tried to stay busy, but her mind was constantly preoccupied with the handsome hero who stole her heart more than once.

The doorbell rang early one morning just before she left for work. But by the time she opened the door, the delivery driver was already off in a cloud of dust down the road. A long, flat box lay on the doorstep with no return address. Curiosity got the best of her, and although she knew it would make her late for work, she ripped into it on the kitchen counter. On top of something wrapped in stiff, white tissue paper was a bright red envelope with her name on it. Inside was an invitation for Blake's restaurant grand opening and a handwritten note:

Dear Laney,

There isn't anyone else I'd love to see more than you at the grand opening. This is a big next step for me, and having you there to celebrate would mean everything to me. Please think about it. No pressure, but I'd love to see you there this weekend. Oh, and you forgot something at my house in L.A. I thought you might want it back. I miss you.

Love, Blake

The tissue paper crinkled as she opened it to find the black dress she had worn the night of the wrap party. All the happenings of that night came rushing back—both the good and the bad—and she held the dress tightly to her chest as she relived each one. The sting of Alexandra's words had dulled over time, and now it meant almost nothing. But that night on the beach with Blake made her ache just like it had happened yesterday. She couldn't help but wonder if the memories made with Blake would always have a painful undertone to them or if they, too, would heal over time.

Before rushing to work, Laney hung the dress up in her closet. The shoes from that night were hidden in the very back corner of her closet. They sat tucked far enough in to not to be a constant reminder of Blake, but still there because she couldn't bear to get rid of them. Cinderella kept her glass slipper as a memento after all, so she felt justified in keeping a memento of her fairytale romance with Hollywood royalty.

That day at work, her mind wandered. *Should I go? Should I not? What would happen if I went? Am I ready to let Blake back into my heart completely? Am I ready to commit without fear?*

"Laney? Are you in there?" Trish called, waving a patient chart in front of her eyes to snap her back into reality.

Laney shook her head and refocused her attention. She was grateful that this day was almost over because she needed to mull over some things without distraction.

"Yes, sorry." She blushed. "I've got so much on my mind that focusing on insurance pre-authorizations and chart filing is killing me!" Laney sighed as she shuffled through her stack of paperwork.

"Let me guess. Captain Hottie is back in the picture?" Trish teased.

"Well, he wants to be. And I'm pretty sure I want him to be. But I'm so unsure of what to do because I don't want to get hurt again, you know? Am I a complete fool for wanting to take him back?" She buried her head in her hands on her desk.

"Absolutely not, girl! He's Blake Logan! You'd be a fool to let him go!" Trish exclaimed. "Now hand me the rest of your charts, and I'll finish up for you. You've got bigger fish to fry. Go home early." She took the stack away from Laney and moved it to her computer.

"Thank you," Laney responded gratefully as she grabbed her purse and slung it over her shoulder. "You're the best! See you later," Laney called over her shoulder as she clocked out down the hallway.

"See you Monday! I can't wait to hear the details!" Trish yelled after her.

When she got into her car, Laney messaged Angela.

Laney: Ange, I need some girl talk tonight! Can you come over in a bit so I can bounce some ideas off you? I have ice cream.

Laney was a ball of nerves the whole time Angela did her makeup and hair for the grand opening the next night.

"Girl, you have got to calm down! I'm going to smudge your eyeliner if you keep fidgeting like that!" Angela warned, holding a long, black eye pencil in one hand and a cotton swab in the other.

"I'm so nervous!" Laney protested. "Me showing up tonight is basically the equivalent of me standing up on a mountaintop and waving the proverbial white flag. I've held my stubborn position for so long that I'm nervous about stepping down. Am I ready for this? What if he decides this isn't for him after all, and three months from now, he goes back to his old life in L.A.?"

Angela shook her head. "You sound ridiculous, Lane. He gave up almost everything to come here and be with you. I'd say it's about time you threw him a bone. He has gone above and beyond to show you he loves you, don't you think?"

"Yeah, I suppose so. I'm just so scared."

"I know you are, but give him a chance. You know it was amazing when things were good. Let them be good again. You both deserve it. Let yourself be happy, Lane." Angela stopped applying her makeup and looked her straight in the eye. "You hear me? Get out of your own way."

"I hear you," Laney said defiantly and rolled her eyes. "You're so bossy," she joked. "But if this all goes south, I'm blaming you."

"Haha, it won't. Now get your cute butt in your car and go get your knight in shining armor."

With a nervous sigh, Laney spun around on the barstool and looked at herself in the mirror. She took a slow, deep breath and exhaled. "Wish me luck!" she said as she grabbed her clutch and keys with shaking fingers.

"You don't need it," Angela replied, cleaning up the makeover mess on her counter.

The drive into town was filled with self-doubt and thoughts of turning around. Her mind reeled, and Laney was grateful for the task of driving because it was the only thing that kept her thoughts relatively focused.

She pulled into the parking lot and the opening had already begun. After hitting every red light and traffic jam in Salt Lake Valley, she thought she'd miss the whole thing.

Live music pounded from inside the restaurant as she rushed through the parking lot. Flashbacks of the wrap party fought their way to the forefront of her mind, and pushing them back took too much energy. A man in a suit stood at the door with a clipboard in his hand and a serious look on his face. This was apparently a bigger deal than she realized.

"Name?" he asked dryly and looked up from his clipboard.

"Delaney Campbell," Laney said nervously, glancing down at the paper in front of him. Written next to her name were the letters "VIP."

"Welcome to The Firehouse, Miss Campbell. Right this way," he greeted, motioning to another door.

Further down the sidewalk was a door guarded by another suit with glasses. This guy gave her a special wristband and opened the door for her, the music overflowing into the open air as she stepped inside. The whole restaurant was decorated to look like a fire station, complete with a fire pole, surrounded by a brass railing that led down to a VIP lounge. Brass trim and accents reflected different shades of red in the dimly lit dining room, and a stage sat in one corner where a band played bluesy country songs. A wall filled with glass bottles of fancy liquor sat behind the bar, and several bartenders stood lined up, mixing drinks for the patrons. Above the shelves behind the bar hung Blake's dad's fire helmet. The white leather was smudged and faded from years of work and weathered from each rescue he had done. But it hung as the focal point of the restaurant, which was the perfect homage to James. Laney felt a lump rise in her throat as she thought about how much this place meant to Blake. She was busy searching the room for a familiar face when she suddenly felt a tap on the shoulder.

"Delaney," a voice sounded.

Laney turned to see Alexandra Chase standing behind her. Her hair was sleek and pulled up, and her makeup was perfect, as always—but there was something different about her. An air of humility showed in her eyes, and she looked happy.

"Oh. Hi, Alexandra. I didn't realize you'd be here." Laney stiffened and forced a smile as her nerves rose higher inside her.

"I wanted to tell you that I'm sorry for how I treated you. I was wrong, and what you said to me at the airport struck a chord. Thank you for helping me see that I had more in me than that."

"I could say the same about you," Laney replied.

Alexandra cocked a brow in confusion. "I'm not sure I understand."

"I never realized how much Blake meant to me until I was put in front of the firing squad. But now I know," Laney explained.

Alexandra grinned and offered her hand to Laney. "Truce?"

"I'd dare to even say friends." Laney smiled in return and shook Alexandra's hand.

"Sounds good to me. I'll see you around," Alexandra said, her grateful eyes blinking back tears as she stepped away and disappeared into the crowd.

Suddenly, a soft pair of motherly arms wrapped around Laney's shoulders. "Laney, it is so good to see you again," Diane said as she squeezed Laney tightly. "I know it will mean a lot to Blake to have you here. Go hang out down in the VIP lounge, honey. It's quieter down there." She put a hand on Laney's back and guided her to a stairway. "I'll be down in a minute, I've got to help someone in the kitchen."

"I'm glad there's another way down besides the pole," Laney said with an awkward laugh as she tucked her hair behind her ear. She gripped the railing as her wobbly legs took each stair.

The sounds of upstairs faded as Laney entered the VIP lounge. It was full of fancy celebrities and friends of Blake, and Laney watched as he moved from one group to another. He looked relaxed, listened intently, laughed, and engaged in genuine conversation. His demeanor was completely different from that night at the wrap party, and he carried an air of class and refinement that Laney hadn't seen around the celebrity crowd before. He left the conversation to greet a new set of guests, and after they dispersed toward the bar, his eyes wandered the room in search of her. As his eyes met hers from across the room, everything slowed. The crowded room fell away, and silence overpowered the noise and settled in her ears. Her pulse quickened, and the familiar butterflies returned as he connected with her from across the room. Their eye contact held steady as he moved toward her, and her mind raced with everything she wanted to say.

"You came," Blake whispered, his shaking voice betraying his nerves.

"Sorry I'm late," she replied. "Traffic was awful."

"You're right on time." He smiled as relief washed over him. "I was afraid you weren't going to come."

"I wouldn't miss such a big night for you," she said, touching his arm. "That, and the dress was a good selling point." She chuckled and fidgeted with her dress, smoothing the fabric around her hips.

He laughed and brushed a curl from her forehead. "You look beautiful," he complimented, his eyes sparkling as he memorized her face for the millionth time.

"Thank you. I know you have a lot of people you need to visit with, so if you have to go, I understand."

"That can wait. I've been visiting all night long. Come with me," he said, grabbing her hand and leading her up to his office at the back of the kitchen.

The sounds of the crowd faded behind the swinging door, and the bustle of the staff quieted as he pulled his office door closed.

"Sorry, I didn't think about cleaning up in here first." He blushed as he shuffled papers on his dark mahogany desk and fastened them together with a paperclip. Then, he moved some boxes from a small countertop along one wall to the floor and leaned back against the cold quartz.

"Oh, don't even worry about it," she said, setting her clutch next to him on the counter before leaning on one elbow. "Things must've been crazy with all the prep for tonight."

"Yeah, it's been pretty stressful," he replied with a sigh. "But totally worth it. Anyway, I didn't bring you back here to see my hot mess of an office. I made you something, and I had to hide it back here so it wouldn't accidentally get used tonight." He grinned like an excited boy as he pulled a cherry pie from the mini-fridge near his desk.

"Oh man, I'm already salivating!" she exclaimed, eyeing the pie.

"Whipped cream or à la mode?" He asked as he plated them both a slice.

"Hmmm, that's a tough one. But let's throw it back to my first time and go with whipped cream," she said. She grabbed each of them a plastic fork from a jar on the counter as he added a tower of whipped cream to both slices.

The first bite crumbled in Laney's mouth, and the tart cherries tickled her tastebuds. Blake paused, and watched her as she closed her eyes and savored every bite. Her pretty mouth grinned with each forkful until her plate only had crumbs left.

"You've still got it, Logan," she praised.

"I try," he replied bashfully, clinking his fork in cheers with hers.

She wiggled her feet uncomfortably in her shoes and adjusted from one foot to another. "These shoes are gorgeous, but they definitely aren't my slippers." She glanced down at them and laughed dryly.

"Give them a rest for a minute then," he replied as he set their plates aside and lifted her up onto the counter.

Her shoes hit the floor one at a time as his closeness paused time. His hands burned on her waist, lingering in their familiar place longer than they were supposed to. Her breath hitched, and her hands stayed on his arms, unsure whether she should let go or hang on for dear life. Their faces slowly brushed together, his subtle cologne filling her senses and igniting her inside. His bright blue eyes pierced hers, and a thousand words were spoken with nothing being said. His chest rose and fell with the quickening of his heart, and she was grateful that at least she was not alone in the complicated feelings resting between them. His focus moved from her honey-brown eyes to her soft pink lips, and her chin raised slightly to invite him in. His fingers moved from her hips to her face and lightly caressed her jaw, leaving a warmth in their wake. He leaned in to close the gap between their mouths but stopped just before his lips touched hers.

"Do you trust me?" he whispered, causing her to open her eyes.

"I want to," she replied breathlessly.

His cheek brushed hers as he stayed in her space. "Then let's work on that before we do any more of this," he said low in her ear, sending chills down her right side. "I want to know that if I'm giving my whole heart to you, you'll be able to trust me enough to do the same. And the next time I kiss you, I want there to be no doubt whatsoever in your mind that I will never hurt you again."

Her heart pounded in her chest as he pulled away, and the fog that covered her logic lifted. No words came, so she nodded in understanding. Her mind raced as she slid back down to the floor and slipped her feet into her heels.

"We should get back to the party," she muttered, running her fingers through her hair.

"Yeah," he replied with a sigh, "before I change my mind and kiss you like I want to." He winked, sending a wave of fire through her.

After the last guest left, Blake pulled her onto the empty floor.

"Dance with me," he requested.

"But there's no music," Laney said, laughing awkwardly as the staff cleaned up around them.

Blake just smiled, nodded toward the piano in the corner, and it began to play an old favorite.

After a few beats, a voice broke into the melody and sang the words that made her believe in true love again.

Laney turned toward the familiar voice over her shoulder to see Austin Grant serenading them from the piano. With a gasp, she whipped her head back and stared at Blake in disbelief.

"Are you kidding me right now?" She laughed in astonishment. "This can't be real."

Blake's eyes sparkled with satisfaction. "It's nice to have connections sometimes."

Laney kicked off her heels, and he pulled her in tighter as her bare feet traversed the floor along with his. It felt amazing to be in his arms again, yet she couldn't help the self-doubt that still hung in the back of her mind like a loitering teenager.

The last of the beautiful notes sounded through the night air, and Austin stood up to leave.

"I'm going to say goodbye to Austin real quick," Blake said as he stepped away. "Would you like to meet him?"

"I'd love to," she said with a nod as he grabbed her hand and led her across the floor.

"Austin, thanks for staying for an encore." Blake shook his hand. "This is Laney, the girl I've been telling you about."

Laney extended her hand and smiled shyly, her nerves jumping all over the place.

"Your reputation precedes you, Laney. Thanks for giving this fool a third chance. He was pretty torn up there for a while," Austin said, taking a jab at Blake.

Laney chuckled and tried her best to hide the emotions rising to the surface as the past reared its ugly head. Despite her efforts, the horrible voice inside her that made her doubt everything got louder and louder as the conversation continued. By the time Austin turned to leave, clouds had settled over the moment.

Austin grabbed his guitar case and called out over his shoulder as he left the restaurant.

"Congrats on the chasing your dreams, Blake! See you when I see you, man! And Laney, it was a pleasure!"

Then, the door shut behind him, and the only noise left was the sound of clinking glasses and the staff clearing tables.

Laney stiffened and avoided eye contact.

"You okay?" Blake asked her as he led her out to the gas fireplace on the screen porch.

"Come talk to me out here where it's quieter."

"I'm just confused," Laney squeaked, trying not to cry. "Things are so good, then I'm reminded about the past again, and all the pain comes rushing back so fast. I don't know when it'll ever go away." The flames from the fireplace blurred behind her tears. "I want to open up to you, I do. But there's still that doubt at the back of my mind..." she trailed off.

Blake felt the frustration building like a broken pressure valve.

"Have I not shown you that I'm in this for the long haul? This is me trying, Laney. What else do you want me to do to prove to you how much I love you?" His eyes flashed with frustration. "I don't know what else I can do to make you trust me. What do you want from me? What do you want, Laney?"

"You! I want you!" she erupted, her tears overflowing her eyes. "I've wanted you since the moment you climbed into my car. I've wanted you and craved you and needed you more than I've needed anyone in my whole life. And it scares me to death because I hate needing anyone. But as much as I don't *want* to need you, I do. I can't help it. I've never felt for anyone what I feel for you. Then I lost you, not once, but twice. And it stung more deeply and more painfully than I had ever experienced before…"

Blake interrupted. "—Then stop running, Laney! Just stop! The first time, I deserved to have you run out on me because I was a coward. But after all the drama with Alexandra, you gave up too quickly. We were supposed to stand back-to-back and take on the world together, but then you left me to do it alone. And yet I still trust you enough to move here and fight for us because I believe what we have comes only once in a lifetime. If you want this, stay and fight! Quit running away when things get hard. If you ever cared about me at all, stand and fight, dammit!"

Her voice dropped to a whisper when she finally replied, "You're right." Her eyes fell to her wringing hands. "You're right about everything. I left you standing completely alone when you needed me most, and I walked away with barely an explanation and hardly a fight." Her tears collected on her eyelashes as they fell, causing her mascara to run. She took a deep breath and dared to look up at him. "I'm a coward too. I sabotaged the best thing that has ever happened to me because I was so scared you'd walk away, Blake. I knew I wouldn't survive losing you again, so I bit the bullet and left you first. You'll never know how sorry I am for that." Her breaths were shallow and quick, and she struggled to get words out and air in. "I'm so afraid of getting hurt. What if we hurt each other again?" She tried unsuccessfully to get a hold of her breathing. Her heart took off like a runaway horse, and no matter how hard she tried, she couldn't slow it down. There was a pleading vulnerability in her voice that he'd never heard before, and a flash of fear clouded her whiskey-colored eyes.

"But what if we don't?" he whispered back. He stepped closer, filling her personal space with his wonderful-smelling body. He was so strong in that moment, like he knew he had the upper hand on her. But instead of taking her forcefully into his arms and kissing her hard like in old romance movies, his hand gently moved to her face, wiping the tear tracks from her cheekbones to her neck.

"I know you don't need saving, Laney. I know how tough and independent and fierce you are, and I know you can take care of yourself. I'm just asking if you'll trust me enough to let me have a turn once in a while. You're everything I've ever wanted, and I know you probably don't need me as much as I need you, but I can't imagine leaning up against anyone else in this life but you. Life is hard. But without love, without you, it feels unconquerable. Being with you makes me feel like I can take on anything that comes my way. You can have the shield, the sword, and the glory. I just want you to lay down your armor and let me love you again." His blue eyes studied her face intently. "The first time I let you go, I was a fool. And the second time, I should've run after you. I knew we were making a mistake, and that'll always be my biggest regret because I lost so much when I lost you twice."

A tear slipped down her face as she closed her eyes and tipped her head onto his hand. It felt good to be needed and to feel protected and safe. She didn't have to do this all on her own.

He was everything she had ever wanted, and there he was, offering his beautifully torn heart to her.

Her hands traveled up his shoulders to his face. She ran her fingertips across his well-trimmed beard as she studied his features.

"How do I let go of this fear?" Her voice cracked as she spoke.

"You don't. You let me love you deep enough, for long enough, and it'll let go of you," he replied, tilting her chin toward him and lowering his lips onto hers.

She met his kiss with an urgency and a depth fueled by months of wanting him but not allowing herself to have him. A fire burned wildly between them, and at last, she let go of doubt and stepped out in the open, where both the sunlight and shadows existed. She was no longer afraid of the darkness and its unknowns. Instead, she focused solely on the light and the warmth it gave. Her scarred heart was his, as it always had been, and she could finally give it freely, without fear.

Chapter

32

Blake's Bronco roared down the dirt road as the late Autumn sun set behind him, a cloud of dust and leaves rising and falling in his wake. His fingers drummed on the steering wheel, venting his nerves on something tangible. The conversation he was about to have could make or break him, and the jar of frantic butterflies in his stomach knew it too. He took a deep breath before getting out of the car and walking the long sidewalk up to the house. It took all the courage he had to raise his shaking hand and hit the doorbell. Then, he waited for what felt like an eternity for someone to answer. Finally, the front door swung open, and Laney's dad greeted him warmly.

"Blake, what a surprise! Come on in. What brings you by tonight? Laney isn't here. She's still out shopping with her mom," Laney's dad said as he reached out to shake Blake's clammy hand.

"I was kind of banking on that, sir." He gripped Robert's hand tightly to hide the apprehension he felt. "I was hoping we could have a talk, just the two of us," Blake said with a cracked voice. He had finally found a woman he loved enough to ask the scariest question he'd ever ask a father, and he drew a blank when clarity of thought mattered most. His nerves flooded his insides as they walked through the house to the kitchen.

"I was out back grilling up some dinner. I can throw another steak on there if you'd like. You want one?" Robert asked over his shoulder.

"No, sir, I'm good. Thank you."

Blake followed Robert, and they sat together on the back patio in the crisp night air while the savory smell of steak grew stronger as it sizzled. Blake took a deep breath to steady his nerves, and before he lost his courage, he blurted out, "Sir, I want to ask Laney to marry me, but I need your blessing before I do."

Robert paused mid-steak-flip and turned to look at Blake. "Son, I don't know if Laney ever told you this, but you're not the first man to ask me that question. Did you know that?" Blake shook his head, as shock filled him.

"A few years ago, the wedding was all planned. Tuxes were rented, dresses were fitted, and flowers were delivered. The church was full of people, but she stood alone in the doorway of the chapel with tears in her eyes because her groom had left her at the altar. He wrote a note on a napkin and took off. He didn't even have the decency to tell my little girl to her face that he wasn't man enough for her." Robert wiped a stray tear. "I had never experienced pain like I did that day when she cried in my arms. So I don't take that question lightly. I made that mistake the first time, and it hurt my daughter. I told myself that the next time I gave my blessing would be the last time I gave it. Are you sure you're ready for that, son?"

"Absolutely," Blake spoke softly. The reality of the moment overwhelmed his thoughts, and he couldn't imagine how her face must've looked when she discovered her groom had abandoned her. "Losing her once made me realize how much I cared about her. And losing her twice made me realize I was an idiot for letting her go in the first place. I would never be foolish enough to let it happen again."

Laney's dad held eye contact with him as he slowly closed the grill and sat beside Blake.

"My Laney is frustratingly stubborn. She spooks easily, she holds grudges too long, and she's slow to forgive at times. But you'll never find another woman who loves the way she does. When she lets you in and gives her golden heart to you, she does it completely. Loving a strong woman like Laney takes a special kind of man, and she's not vulnerable with very many of us. But once you're in, you're in for good. Can you handle that responsibility?"

The weight of Robert's question rested heavily on Blake's shoulders.

His voice cracked as he spoke. "I know I can, sir. Because *not* loving her is far more difficult to live with than anything else I've ever experienced with her. She's everything to me, and I promise to give her my whole heart. I'll never be the same man I was before I met her because she shined her light into the darkest parts of my world and made everything come alive again. And I'll do everything in my power to make sure she never goes another day without knowing how loved she is."

Robert's eyes welled up as he listened to Blake. "Well then, son, I'll give you my blessing, but never forget the gravity of that, got it?"

Blake nodded solemnly. "Thank you. This means more than you'll ever know, sir."

"I've never seen her happier than she is when she's with you. And I have to respect anyone who can get a strong woman like Laney to let them in after what she's been through. Welcome to the family, son." Robert's fatherly arms wrapped around Blake and squeezed him tight.

Blake didn't realize how much he missed being called "son," and his eyes filled with gratitude.

"Thank you, sir. I won't let her down," he said, shaking Robert's hand as he stood to leave.

"You're sure welcome. And call me Robert. We're practically family now." He smiled over his shoulder as he walked Blake to the door. "Now, the hard part isn't convincing me to let you, but convincing *her* to marry you," Laney's dad joked. "Good luck, son," he said as he shut the front door behind Blake.

Blake's elation at gaining Robert's blessing was overshadowed by the ache he felt, knowing she had been hurt so deeply before him. So much made sense now. The way she kept her guard up, how easily she was able to discount his actions and feelings, and how she was able to walk away without hesitation. His mind raced as he drove home in silence, analyzing every confusing incident with her that suddenly became so clear. The woman whose actions baffled him finally made sense. And he would use this new understanding to handle her delicate heart with gentler hands.

Chapter

33

The miles stretched on forever after an exhausting and long day. Laney's hospital badge clicked against the rearview mirror as she put more and more miles between her and work, and she sighed as she pulled her ponytail loose and rubbed her tired scalp. Thoughts of her PJs and a date with her DVR drove her on through the Salt Lake Valley until, at last, she pulled down the snowy lane toward her tiny house. As her headlights flashed onto her freshly shoveled driveway, the red silhouette of Blake's Bronco stood in the dark. She smiled to herself as she opened the garage, parked her car, and killed the engine.

The smell of tangy pasta sauce hit her first, tickling her senses with the perfect blend of garlic and tomatoes, followed by the sounds of Journey playing on the record player.

"Mmmmm…" she purred as she hung her keys and purse on their hooks and rounded the corner.

Blake stood at the stove, wearing the coal-black apron Laney bought for him to use at her house, and stirring the sauce for one of her favorite recipes. Laney leaned against the counter and watched him from behind, trying to wipe the grin from her face, although her efforts were meager at best.

"Hey, how was your day?" Blake asked, turning around with a wooden spoon pointed at her to taste.

"Much better now," she murmured with a sigh as the sauce slid down her throat. "You have that down to an art, you know. There's no one who can make chicken parmesan like you."

"Thanks." He turned and peeked into the oven. "You have perfect timing. Everything is ready."

He plated their dinners while she poured the wine and downed her first glass.

"Your day was that bad, huh?"

"Oh man, it was. You know, I love my job, but some days it takes more than one glass of wine to shake off the weight of it," she replied with a groan. "But at least I don't have to cook. Can I keep you on reserve in my pantry and have you do this every night?" she asked as she followed him to the table.

"Sounds good to me. But just so you know, a personal chef who is also a bestselling author of my caliber doesn't come cheap." He grinned over his fork.

"I'll do whatever it takes," she said as she took another melty bite.

"Duly noted. So what made work so stressful today?"

"Well, unfortunately, we've been extra busy lately, which is never a good thing in my field. More bad news than good…" she trailed off.

Blake recalled the moment Danielle told him over the phone that Noah had cancer. The sting of that memory barely dulled over time, and he understood what she meant.

"But enough about me. I need something else to distract me. How's the restaurant?"

"Well, I finally hired a full-time general manager, and she's awesome!"

Laney pictured some leggy brunette working side by side with Blake, and a pang of unfamiliar jealousy clouded her mind. She cleared her throat.

"She?"

"Yeah. She's the wife of one of my dad's old rookies who just moved to Salt Lake City. Their last child moved away to college in September, and she was going stir-crazy in her empty nest. She used to run the fundraisers for the firehouse, and her organizational skills are just the icing on the cake. Her first night working, she had every shirt tucked in and everyone toeing the line. She runs a tight ship, but she's like the cool mom everyone loves."

Laney involuntarily sighed with relief.

"That's great! I'm glad you have someone to help bear your burdens. I can't wait to meet her."

"And I can't wait to spend less time running the place. I finally found someone to do the books as well. It'll be a huge load lifted once everyone gets caught up to speed," he said, stretching his back and shoulders. "Now, I might actually get to see you more often than I did when I lived in L.A." He took a bite of chicken, chewed slowly, and swallowed. "Also, Joe sent me a new script, and it's awesome. If I agree to do the movie, we'll start filming after the new year."

"That's great!" she replied. "Where will you shoot?"

"Greece," he said with a huge grin. "Please say you'll come out and see me on location while I'm there. It's such a beautiful country."

"That sounds amazing. I've always wanted to see Greece." She took another cheesy bite. "I'm glad things are working out between you and Joe."

"Me too. He really is good at what he does. We just needed to come to a better understanding, that's all."

When they were both done eating, he stood, took their empty plates, and headed to the sink. And when she sidled up next to him to help, he pointed her to the couch.

"Go, sit. Kick your feet up, and let me spoil you."

"But you cooked. It's only fair that I'm on cleanup duty," Laney protested.

"Not tonight, it's not. If you want to help me, turn on a movie for us, and I'll watch from the kitchen until I'm done. Now go get in your comfy pants and rest."

Her mouth opened in another protest.

"Not a negotiation, Campbell," he stated, trying to sound firm but unable to hide the teasing tone in his voice.

"Oooh, you're gonna use the last name, huh? You must mean business then." She kissed his shoulder blades as she passed behind him and walked down the hallway. "Fine, you win this time! But don't let it go to your head, Logan!"

He grinned into the suds, and his chest warmed. This was what life was supposed to be like. Playful banter, the love of an amazing woman, and food that feeds the soul on top of it all. Life was good.

Laney stretched her neck at her desk and checked the clock above her desk. Barely noon. This was going to be another long day.

"Laney, dear," the receptionist called from down the hallway. "There's someone here to see you."

Laney stood and peeked around the corner to see a woman hauling a folded table and a large bag toward an empty conference room. Curiosity got the best of Laney, and she followed the woman down the hallway.

"Hello, Miss Campbell. I'm Virginia, your masseuse. Mr. Logan hired me for the afternoon to give massages to you and your coworkers," the woman said as she set up a fancy massage chair. She set up a portable speaker with soothing music, and dimmed the lights in the room. "If you're available now, I can do your shoulders, neck, and back."

"Wow." Laney's mouth slacked open. "That would be really great, actually. My lunch starts in five minutes. Let me clock out and lock my computer. I'll be right back," Laney said before disappearing down the hall.

"Trish!" Laney called out. "Guess what? Blake hired a masseuse to massage us on our breaks today."

"No way. I've had a knot the size of Texas in my back for a week now," Trish said with a groan, rubbing her shoulder blade.

"I'm going to go now, and you can go during your lunch after me. Sound good?"

"Sounds awesome!" Trish replied excitedly.

Laney's face melted into the headrest hole as strong hands forced her tension away, and when her half-hour was over, she stood up a new woman.

"This was just what I needed, thank you." Laney sighed and pulled her hair out of the ponytail it was in. Before returning to work, she grabbed her wallet from the table by the door to tip the masseuse.

"Oh no, Miss. Mr. Logan has already taken care of the gratuity," the masseuse said softly, not breaking the calm in the room. "If anyone else would like a massage, I'm here until 3 p.m."

"Perfect! I'll send the next person in," Laney said over her shoulder as she left the dim room and stepped out into the bright hallway. Her eyes squinted under the strain of the fluorescent bulbs while she rolled her shoulders and sighed. "Back to reality."

Trish rounded the corner after her session half an hour later.

"If you don't marry that man, can I?" Trish teased, stretching her happy, relaxed muscles.

"Whoa, there. Let's not put the cart before the horse," Laney said, shaking her head.

"Oh, the only horse I have in this scenario is horse-drawn carriage with you and Blake in the front seats, and tin cans clinking from the back under a Just Married sign," Trish said, bubbling with laughter.

"Wow, you have quite the imagination, Trish." Laney laughed along. "But seriously. Rushing things is what burned me the first time. I want to be sure this is really right for both of us before I let myself open up again. So no horse-drawn carriages yet."

"Well, suit yourself. But I'd be running full-bore to make that gorgeous man mine." She wiggled a ring finger. Trish smirked at Laney over her shoulder before disappearing behind an exam room door.

Laney grabbed her phone and typed up a quick message to Blake.

Laney: Your masseuse is a dream come true! Everyone in the office wants to marry you now. Well, except Dr. Hansen. Although, he did say something about adopting you...Thanks so much!

Her phone chimed, from an incoming message from Blake.

Blake: You're sure welcome! I'm glad you enjoyed it. Dinner at the restaurant tonight?"

With a beaming grin, she replied.

Laney: I'd love to. And I have something for you, btw. I'll come straight over from work. I added a change of clothes in my emergency bag for this very reason!

Blake: I'd expect nothing less. See you soon.

Laney pulled into the snowy parking lot just as the dinner rush began. She stepped through the door—gripping a large gift bag in her shaking hands—and focused her thoughts on the newly decorated restaurant instead of her nerves. Christmas garlands draped across the counters and bar, and a lean tree decorated in red and gold stood like a giant toy soldier near the stage. Sparkling lights hung from one end of the ceiling to another, creating the perfect ambiance for the holidays.

The restaurant bustled with the usual weekend crowds, and a live band performed on the stage in the corner. She surveyed the room—the brass reflecting the mood lighting and the intimate tables had crisp red linens and starched napkins. The waiters and staff wore white shirts and black vests, and because of Darla—Blake's new general manager—they were the epitome of perfection.

"Hi," Blake whispered in her ear as he snuck up behind her, placing his warm hand on the small of her back. "We'll be dining at the VIP table tonight."

He led her up a spiral staircase above the bar, where one cozy table sat bathed in candlelight. The music floating from below could still be enjoyed, but even more so from their tiny corner of the world, away from prying eyes.

"I figured this spot could be used for more than just storage. Do you like it?" he asked as he pulled out her chair.

"It's beautiful!"

"It's yours any time you want it. Darla has everything under control tonight, so you've got my undivided attention."

After the waiter had left with their order, Laney took Blake's hand from across the table.

"Blake, are you happy?" Laney asked.

Surprised by her question, he let out a burst of laughter.

"Of course I am! Why would you wonder that?"

"Because the life you used to live was full of glitz and glamour, and it never got dull. But this life…" she trailed off nervously.

"Is more than I could have ever asked for," he said, completing her sentence. "You want the truth?"

Her stomach tied itself in knots at his question. The truth may be a hard pill to swallow, or it could make her heart soar. It was a risky game to play, so she hesitated to answer.

"The truth is, I never knew how much I was missing. I thought I had it all: money, fame, a fancy life. But the truth is, Laney, you slammed into me on the lonely path I was on and knocked me completely off course. I never in a million years dreamed that life could be so good. Yet, here I am, sitting across from the most amazing woman I have ever met, eating in a restaurant I opened in honor of my dad. Happy doesn't even begin to describe it." His eyes sparkled at her in the candlelight, and she swallowed hard against the lump rising in her throat before saying anything.

"I have something for you," she said as she gathered her courage and reached under the table for the gift bag.

"What's this for?" he asked, pulling the tissue paper out. He laughed as he pulled out a worn-out pair of Laney's sneakers. "Okay, now I'm confused."

"They're my running shoes. They're yours now. I'm done running," she said softly, her eyes glistening with tears in the candlelight. "I never dreamed it could be this good either. And when things were going well, I somehow convinced myself that I was undeserving of it or that it was too good to last. You make me feel unarmed and out in the open, and that used to scare me. But it doesn't anymore. It makes me excited and grateful and so glad that you got into my car that day. I don't know what I'd do without you in my life, and I hope I never have to again."

He stood from his seat and pulled her up into a tight, Blake-scented hug.

"This is the best gift ever, thank you," he replied, beaming from ear to ear. "I'm so glad we're finally on the same page."

Blake's eyelids hung heavily as he pulled into Laney's driveway. It had been another long day at the restaurant, where he spent most of his time catching the new chefs up to speed. Running the kitchen and keeping the books for so long by himself had taken its toll. And he was still trying to catch up on rest, now that he could hand-off some of his responsibilities. Blake killed the engine, took a long, deep breath, and let his head fall back against the headrest as he shook off the day. Letting out a bone-weary sigh, he dragged his lead-like limbs toward her front door, barely getting one heavy foot in front of the other.

Laney's Christmas tree cast a soft golden hue through the picture window and onto the snow lining her front walk, making the icicles hanging from the roof sparkle in the lights. Her house looked like a vintage Courier and Ives painting from the street, and it beckoned him to come in from the cold. The jolly music of a Johnny Mathis Christmas record reverberated quietly in the winter air around him. Murphy was sitting in his spot on the window-sill, where he could spy on the neighbors, but he jumped down toward the door when he saw Blake arrive.

Laney heard the front door open, and she looked up from the Christmas train set she was assembling on the floor. Murphy greeted Blake with his usual figure-eight dance around his legs while Blake removed his snowy boots at the front door. The smell of apple cinnamon filled his nose as he stepped into the warmth around him, and instantly, his shoulders relaxed. Laney climbed to her wool-stockinged feet with a look of happy surprise on her face.

"Hi! I didn't know you were stopping by tonight, or I would've been a bit more prepared." She glanced over the mess of decorations and boxes covering the front room as she slipped her arms around his shoulders.

"I was in the neighborhood," he lied through his grin.

"Sure you were, way out here in the middle of nowhere." Laney laughed, rolling her eyes playfully at him.

"I know we have plans for tomorrow, but I couldn't wait that long," Blake told her. He sighed, letting the stress from his long day drop to his feet as he sunk into her arms.

"Busy night at the restaurant?" Laney asked.

"Yeah. I just need a place to untangle my mind. I'm glad the restaurant is successful, but I didn't think it would get so busy this quickly. I'm so glad I hired a GM to help me run the place. There's no way I could do all of it without help. I can't imagine doing all these late nights by myself. I'd never get to sleep."

"Agreed." Laney nestled into his chest. "I feel like I saw you more when you lived two states away," she teased. "Come, sit down." She gestured at the sofa. "I'll make some hot chocolate."

Blake dropped like a lead balloon onto the cushions and put his feet up on the ottoman in front of him. Resting his bones was a rare occurrence lately, and it felt so good to slough off his day and soak up some of Laney's calmness. His breaths deepened as his tired body melted further and further into relaxation.

Laney returned shortly with two steaming mugs in her hands to find him fast asleep with Murphy on his lap. *I knew he was a cat person.* She giggled to herself as she placed the mugs on the coffee table and covered his shoulders and arms with a fuzzy gray blanket.

"Hmmmm," Blake purred contently in his sleep as his comfort increased. And just like that, she kept his chaotic world at bay.

Laney curled up next to him and rested her head on his broad shoulder that had been carrying the responsibilities of several people. She sat in the soft glow of the Christmas lights, sipping her hot cocoa and listening to him breathe. The low tune of "Silver Bells" drifted in the air, filling her with gratitude for the beings next to her that stuffed her heart with love and her home with joy. This Christmas was by far different from the last one. And although the past few years had been hard, she was grateful for the journey that led her to this point in her life.

Blake slept beside her, his face weathered by the stress of hard work. For so long, he had been the first to arrive at the restaurant and the last to leave, which meant a lot less time for Laney than he hoped for. She would drive evening Lyft shifts toward Salt Lake City so she could stop in for late-night dinners with him. But even then, he had to leave the table a few times to tend to the staff. Her mind reflected back at those candlelit nights spent overlooking the glowing city below, with live music playing in the background. She was so proud of his successes that she didn't mind the late nights, but she worried about the toll they were taking on him.

The chimes of the clock on the wall pulled her from her reverie, reminding her how late it was getting. She slipped from the couch and left

Blake under the blanket to sleep. In the entryway, she stopped and turned around, memorizing the glow of the tree on the face of the man who stole her heart. Murphy glanced up at her, his tail tapping the couch slowly. He seemed to weigh the pros and cons of staying put or following Laney. But ultimately decided he was content where he was at with Blake, so he nestled back into the ball he was shaped into.

"I don't blame you for wanting to stay with him," Laney whispered to Murphy. "Smart cat." She smiled as she locked the front door and disappeared down the hallway into the darkness.

The morning sunlight peeked through the icicle-framed window and gently nudged Blake awake. It was still hours before he would need to show up at the restaurant, but his brain was alert, making falling back to sleep impossible. He folded the fuzzy blanket that Laney had covered him with, and he laughed as Murphy opened one eye to look at him. They both knew it was too early to be up on a Saturday morning, but only one of them was foolish enough to succumb to it.

Blake tiptoed down the hallway to Laney's room, where she lay passed out cold in yesterday's clothes on top of her bedspread like a doll cast aside by a distracted child. He chuckled at her disheveled state and kissed her forehead as he tucked his blanket around her. On her nightstand was a notepad filled with a checked-off to-do list. Blake tore off a piece of paper from the bottom of the pad and wrote:

Ornament exchange tonight at my house. See you at five.
Thanks for the good night's sleep. I needed it.

Love, Blake

Then, he rested it on the pillow next to her head and slipped out the front door into the brisk winter air.

Laney's heels clicked as she climbed the cement steps to Blake's front door. The scent of fresh pine filled the air surrounding his new home on the east side of Salt Lake City. And she stopped for a moment on the porch to watch the sun kiss the mountains to the west goodnight. Her breath formed clouds in front of her face and floated up to join the wispy pink clouds hanging lazily in the orange sky. She rapped her knuckles in rapid succession on the front door and stepped back to wait, clutching a small red gift bag in her cold hands.

Blake cracked the door just enough for him to slip out onto the porch. His face brimmed with excitement as he greeted her with a kiss.

"I've been counting down the minutes today." He beamed eagerly at her. "But you can't come in without this," he told her as he held up a blindfold and tied it around her head.

"Wait, what? What's going on here?" Laney laughed as he spun her back around and took her hand.

With her sight inhibited, her other senses heightened—the sound of the door opening, the contrast of Blake's warm hand nestled into her frozen one, and the smell of cherry pie as they stepped into the house. Laney paused as Blake took her coat and hung it in the hallway closet.

"Is that pie I smell? What have you got up your sleeve, Logan?" She giggled under the blindfold.

"You'll see, come this way," he said as he led her down the hallway to the great room. "Wait here," he added as he brought her to a stop. His footsteps faded as he walked away. Laney could hear the record player start playing from the corner of the room, and Louis Armstrong's voice crooned through the speakers surrounding her.

Laney's face filled with joy as her favorite song began to play. Blake stood across the room from her, watching her sparkle in the tree light—the most beautiful woman he had ever seen.

"You'd better get this blindfold off, or my tears are going to smear my mascara," Laney warned with a laugh, wiping them from her cheeks.

"Okay, you can take it off," Blake said, a smile in his voice.

Laney lifted the fabric from her eyes and gasped as she took in the room. Candles lit up every surface, casting dancing shadows on the walls, and in the center of the room stood a fragrant evergreen covered in twinkling golden lights. A star stood high near the ceiling, and silver and gold ribbon wrapped the tree from top to bottom. Laney stepped closer to the glow, and her smile faded into confusion. On Blake's big, beautiful tree, there was only one ornament—the tree house Laney had given him last year. It sat lonely, right in the middle at eye level. Laney reached up and read the message she had written on the bottom as a whole flood of memories washed over her from a year ago.

Blake slipped his arms around her waist and kissed her head.

"You only have one ornament, silly," Laney teased.

In response, Blake held up a tiny box in front of her. "Yeah, it's my version of a Charlie Brown tree," he joked. "Only the branches are a bit fuller."

"Open your ornament first. Your tree looks so sad with only one." She handed the small red bag to Blake and laughed.

Beneath the tissue paper was a tiny, white leather fireman's helmet, a miniature replica of Blake's father's that hung in the restaurant. It had every scratch, dent, and worn spot that James's had, down to the tiniest of details. The old ladder company number was delicately painted in the middle of the shield, encircled by "Logan" at the bottom and "Fire Chief" at the top. Blake's eyes filled with tears as he caressed the tiny tribute to his hero.

"This is so fitting, thank you," he gushed, enveloping her in his arms.

Blake smiled proudly as he hung it on his tree next to the tree house from the year before.

"It's perfect!" He beamed.

"Okay, now it's your turn." He swallowed hard as Laney tore open the delicately wrapped paper.

Inside the box was a giant ring that looked more likely to fit a wrist than a finger, with an oversized crystal gemstone at the top.

"I'm not sure I get this one," she said, puzzled then turned toward Blake to find him down on one knee.

Laney gasped, her hands flying to her mouth.

"Laney Campbell, you are the most amazing woman I have ever met." Blake's voice cracked, and his hands shook as he opened a tiny black box, revealing a sparkling ring inside. "I have tried like a fool to live without you twice, and it simply cannot be done. You came into my life at a time when I didn't even realize how much I needed you, and you showed me a love I never knew I was missing. You have completely turned my world upside down, and I can't imagine my life without you. This tree only has two ornaments on it because I decided it needed a story too. One that I want you to write together with me. Will you please do me the honor of being my wife and helping me fill our Christmas trees with memories for the next ninety-five years?"

Laney blinked at the tears filling her eyes, setting them free to run down her cheeks. She had dreamed about this moment for so long, and here she was, in the glow of the Christmas lights, with the man of her dreams asking her to be his forever. She caught her breath and looked into Blake's beautiful blue eyes.

"I can't think of a greater adventure than to ride life's waves with you." She smiled as another tear ran down her face. "You are everything I've ever wanted, and I'd love to grow old with you. I love you with my whole heart."

"So, is that a yes?"

Her eyes sparkled with unrestrained joy as she slipped the ring on her left ring finger, and replied, "I'm game if you are."

"Cut!" The director yelled, stopping the scene. "Let's take a lunch and we'll reconvene at one o'clock!"

Blake climbed down from the platform he stood on and searched the crowd.

"Daddy! Daddy!" a tiny two-year-old with her mother's golden hair came running out of a sea of people. She latched onto Blake's leg, looked into the depths of his soul with her beautiful brown eyes and said, "Did you get the bad guys this time?"

"I sure did, Bridget!" he replied, tossing her up onto his shoulders. "Where's your mama?"

Bridget pointed a pudgy finger over the heads of the movie crew. "There. She's slow 'cause of baby James."

Laney waddled through the group of extras dressed like aliens and smiled. "She's way faster than I am at this point." She exhaled slowly and rubbed her pregnant belly.

Blake kissed Laney on the top of her head and let out a sigh of contentment. "Wanna go to my trailer for lunch, or eat with the cast and crew like last time?"

"Well, this lil' lady needs a nap, and so does her mama. So I vote for a quiet lunch, just the three of us. Then while daddy runs off to finish saving the world, we can sleep." She grabbed Bridget's little shoe hanging down and wiggled it.

"Sounds good. I'll have it brought over." Blake said, sliding Bridget down to the ground. "Meet you there?"

Laney took Bridget's hand and nodded.

As Laney and Bridget crossed the set, Blake watched them in awe. It seemed like yesterday that he saw Laney take down a disrespectful cabbie. And now here they were figuring out how to balance love, careers, marriage, and parenthood. He thought of all the things that could've kept them apart, and how the forces that kept them together were so much stronger than any obstacle they faced. He was grateful that even during the frustrating times, imperfect fights, and the everyday battles, that he chose to lean up against her. And that she chose to lean up against him as well. His eyes stung with tears and he blinked hard to hold them at bay.

"Hey Laney!" He called out across the crowd.

She scooped Bridget up into her arms and turned toward him.

"We made it," he said proudly.

Laney grinned and pondered at the beautiful life they had. "Yeah, we sure did."

The End

Thank you for taking the time to read my novel.

I hope you enjoyed reading it as much as I enjoyed writing it. My favorite thing is a great escape into a good happily ever after, and I hope your book-cation was just what you needed to recharge!

I value your opinion as much as other potential readers do. Please find me on Amazon and Goodreads to leave a review.

Also, I'd love to connect on social media.

Instagram.com/AuthorNoelleDavenport

Facebook.com/AuthorNoelleDavenport

Looking for a little more romance? Get a FREE novella ebook and the latest book releases at **NoelleDavenportBooks.com**.

www.ingramcontent.com/pod-product-compliance
Lightning Source LLC
Chambersburg PA
CBHW051524260626
47170CB00003B/775